The Minotaur

Takes

a

Cigarette

Break

John F. Blair,
Publisher

Winston-Salem,
North Carolina

The Minotaur

Takes

a

Cigarette

Break

Steven Sherrill

*The paper in this book meets the
guidelines for permanence and
durability of the Committee on
Production Guidelines for
Book Longevity of the
Council on Library Resources.*

DESIGN BY DEBRA LONG HAMPTON

Library of Congress Cataloging-in-Publication Data

Sherrill, Steven, 1961–

    The minotaur takes a cigarette break/Steven Sherrill.

        p.   cm.

    ISBN 0-89587-197-1 (alk. paper)

        1. Minotaur (Greek mythology)—Fiction.   2. Cooks—Southern
States—Fiction.   3. Southern States—Fiction.   I. Title.

PS3569.H4349   M56   2000

813'.54—dc21   99-059651

To my parents, Jim and Doris,
to my wife, Barbara,
and to Maude,
who daily teaches me
what is important in life

PROLOGUE

The Minotaur dreams of bargains struck, dreams—
Brave young Theseus, golden boy, butcher extraordinaire.
Theseus deep in the Labyrinth comes face to face—
Umbilicated hero, bound by fate, bound by love, bound
by the filament of mislaid want. Comes face to face
in the chambered pit—hewn out of darkness,
the chisel and rasp, tools of deceit. Crafted
from the planks and bones of mendacity. Theseus
comes face to face with the asthmatic huff
and the pernicious snort of desire, rendered pure.
The by-product, hobbled from shame and hidden
away—until Theseus—Theseus comes face to face
with the Minotaur. Theseus barters for his life.
In the Labyrinth all deals are shady. Skullduggery
holds sway. From the front door ashen Theseus
puts on a good face, touts his victory—the Monster
to market—while from the back the Minotaur skulks
into a tepid eternity; high, the costs of living.

CHAPTER 1

*T*he *Minotaur sits* on an empty pickle bucket blowing smoke through bullish nostrils. He sits near the dumpster on the dock of the kitchen at Grub's Rib smoking and watching JoeJoe, the dishwasher, dance on the thin strip of crumbling asphalt that begins three steps down at the base of the dock, runs the length of the building's backside and stops abruptly at the overgrown bank, thick with jimson weed, honeysuckle and scraggly pine, leading down to the interstate. It's hot, and through the haze and the treetops the Minotaur can just make out a piece of the billboard advertising the restaurant: *Next Exit.* The Minotaur doesn't like to smoke but smokes anyway, smokes menthols because he likes them even less, while JoeJoe dances to the static-y music thumping out of the boom box at his feet, the music fighting with the sounds of the exhaust fan over their heads and the incessant traffic on the highway below. It's hot. As hot outside as in the kitchen. JoeJoe's black face and arms jut from the stained white uniform, jerking and twisting in furious rhythms; his chocolate skin has a sheen of sweat. The steps, the loading dock, the dumpster gaping open like a dumb metal mouth, the pavement itself, even the weeds and bushes have a permanent layer of grease, of animal fat spilled or blown through the exhaust year after year. Everything stinks. Everything is slick and hard to hold. But it's like the heat—people get used to it.

"Order up," the Minotaur hears from the tinny little speaker hanging just inside the kitchen door.

It's Adrienne; she's the only one who whines like that. The Minotaur picks at a dried gravy stain on his apron, thinks for a minute about Adrienne. *Titties*, he thinks. He thinks it because everyone else says it. Big titties bouncing inside the ruffled tuxedo shirt that is her uniform, and a big nose, both of which stir his soup. But these kinds of thoughts never lead anywhere and are ultimately painful to him, so he doesn't linger on them. Besides, she always seems mad at him.

The Minotaur is a line cook; he works the dinner shift, in at three and out at midnight after cleanup, later on the weekends. He works the hot line: the steam table, the FryDaddy and the convection ovens. Most of the appetizers and a few of the entrees come from his station. When it's slow he helps with salads and desserts as well. On busy nights there are two others on the line: Cecie on salads and a lean quiet man named Hernando who works the sauté station and cuts the prime rib on Friday and Saturday nights.

"Order up!"

She is impatient. Grub has those damn speakers wired all over the back of the house, even in the cramped airless bathroom designated for the kitchen workers, so Adrienne knows the Minotaur can hear her. As much as he is unable to fathom the span of his earthly existence, time, in its smaller and more manageable increments, is important to the Minotaur. Normally he's very prompt, even with the waiters and waitresses he doesn't like, but this hasn't been a good day. Half an hour earlier he had been making crepes, two at a time. It was a methodical task, one that he enjoyed. Oil the shallow pans with a little clarified butter. When it's hot ladle in just enough batter to cover the bottom. Over a medium flame the thin pancakes turn a beautiful golden brown in less than a minute. Crepes imperial, two rolled crepes filled with a thick seafood-and-mushroom mix, doused with hollandaise sauce. It's one of the most popular items on the menu.

The Minotaur's vision is troublesome. Clarity is not the issue; even after all these years what he sees, what lies within his field of vision, he sees sharply. The problem is the bridge of his nose, a black bony expanse lying between wide-set eyes. It creates a blind spot for which the Minotaur compensates by cocking his head a little to one side or the other, depending on what he is looking at. Up close a thing, a person, right before his eyes becomes all but invisible. Half an hour ago he was ladling crepe batter into a pan, turning the pan with his wrist to coat the polished surface, when one of the waiters asked him for a match. As he turned to speak to the waiter, he misjudged. The crepe pan banged against the container of drawn butter, knocking it over. The golden liquid spread quickly over the worktable. Some fell in a threadlike stream first down the thigh of the Minotaur's salt-and-pepper work pants, then across the scuffed tops of his steel-toed shoes, before finally pooling on the floor beneath a thick honeycomb rubber mat. Most of the spilled butter, however, took a more dangerous turn, washing across the stainless-steel tabletop and into the crusted burning eye of the stove, where it ignited. Fires are not uncommon in the kitchen. In fact, controlled fires are often necessary to burn away the alcohol in a pan, leaving behind only the sweet essence of a brandy or a Marsala. In the dining room, fires are an expected part of the pageantry of some entrees and desserts. But the Minotaur's fire was neither planned nor controlled. The flames leapt instantly, wildly toward the exhaust vents overhead. The hot orange tongues danced in the wide black eyes of the Minotaur, who stood paralyzed, clutching the crepe pan in his fist.

The Minotaur's vision is troublesome. He watched from the periphery as Cecie, quick-thinking Cecie, came from behind the reach-in coolers, where the bins are stored under a low worktable, with a heavy scoop full of salt. Cecie doused the flame in one pass.

"What a fuckup," somebody said.

"Go have a smoke," Hernando said, starting to clean up the mess. They look out for each other; it's one of the things the Minotaur likes about the kitchen.

The Minotaur sits on the back dock and smokes. Filter pinched between black lips, he draws deeply on the cigarette, pulling the orange tip nearly into his mouth. Then he flicks the butt away. He can almost hear it sizzle in the oily air.

"Come on, M! It's getting busy." It's Adrienne; she's standing just behind the screen door. The Minotaur can see her breasts, parted by the fabric ruffle, pressed against the screen door. Her face, farther back, less clear, seen through the metal mesh, looks mechanical—hard and bloodless.

"Unnnhh," the Minotaur says to no one.

"I know what you mean," JoeJoe answers, sitting on the steps as the Minotaur stands, knots his stained apron around too-thin almost womanly hips, straightens the altered collar of his chef's coat, then goes inside.

Cecie is just inside the back door cutting radishes at a high stainless-steel table. At barely five feet she has to stand on an upturned case of powdered Au Jus to see over the mountain of cut broccoli, cherry tomatoes, yellow squash, peppers, cheeses, cans of sardines and everything else. Looking close it's not hard to see all the little scars on her fingers and hands, like tiny shooting stars burning white in the black night of her skin. The Minotaur stands close behind her, his hot bull breath spilling over her shoulder. Cecie knows what he wants. Without looking she plucks one silvery sardine from an open can and reaches back. The Minotaur takes it from her fingers with his mouth. She wipes the ample saliva on the leg of her uniform. He looks to make sure some of the waiters are watching, then pinches her skinny little ass. Cecie feigns offense. She makes like she wants to stab him with the chef's knife, the blade nearly as long as her forearm. Then she winks and goes back to cutting radishes. Cecie keeps telling him she'd like to take him home some night, husband or no. The Minotaur waits hopefully. Husband or no.

On the line the tickets are stacked three deep. Hernando

works four sauté pans at once. From his back pocket he pulls a pair of tongs, turns a sizzling chicken breast in one of the pans, then claps the tongs twice at the Minotaur's crotch, as if he's going to pinch his balls. Hernando points with the tongs at the two stuffed flounder orders on the first ticket. The Minotaur goes to work.

For the first few months he worked here it always surprised the Minotaur that people would come to eat at a place called Grub's Rib. But come they do, despite the distance from the city and despite the defunct Holiday Inn across the street; they come and line up at the door most nights. Weekends, when prime rib is the special, it's almost impossible to get in without a res-ervation, and even then David, the host—some of the waiters call him the hostess—gets so frazzled that it may take an hour to get a table. Most people think it worth the wait. Grub is the king of the T-bone and the rib roast, his reputation for tender meat pulling people in night after night. They line up, stomachs groaning; they pace anxiously and make small talk outside the imitation oak doors until the five-thirty opening. David says he can feel their eagerness—desperation, he calls it—seeping through the doors even before he turns the key. Desperate or not, every time those doors open, a hungry crowd spills into Grub's Rib: three narrow windowless rooms, a step up, two steps down, red carpet, mirrors, gold tatting, faux medieval trap-pings hanging from the walls. A few hours later they trickle out, liquor on their breath, grease on their chins, sated.

This hot night passes quickly, without further catastrophe. The Minotaur doesn't mind the heat, finds it vaguely comfort-ing, and the oil in the air makes the skin of his head and neck soft, less likely to crack open and bleed. The Minotaur doesn't mind the cleanup either. There is a sense of teamwork and order into which he is drawn. Each person breaks down their own station, wrapping what can be saved for the next day, discarding the rest. Everything is cleaned with diluted bleach. Cecie helps JoeJoe with the pots and pans. Hernando does the prep list and ordering. The Minotaur takes care of the walk-in, cleaning and organizing the disarray of the evening. Cecie sweeps the floors and most often has to be reminded to get under the ovens. Cecie sweeps while the Minotaur and JoeJoe heave the overflowing trash cans up and into the dumpster. Hernando hoses down the tile floor, and everyone squeegees it dry. The Minotaur likes the banter, JoeJoe's incessant monologue about girlfriends and getting high, because he is not free with his own speech. He likes Cecie's flirting. He also likes Hernando's silence, reading confidence into it.

While the kitchen crew cleans, the waiters do their side work.

"Here you go, guys," Timothy, one of the waiters, says, lining up three beers across the shelf above the heat lamps. "Thanks for your help."

Later a new waitress named Kelly brings three more. She's so quiet, lost in the din of the cleanup, that it takes her a few minutes to get their attention.

"Thank you," the Minotaur says in his nasally thick-tongued way, but Kelly is already out in the wait station wrapping desserts. The Minotaur has little tolerance for alcohol. Always has. He gives his second beer to JoeJoe.

It's inventory night. After the shift is over, after the kitchen has been cleaned and JoeJoe and Cecie have left, Hernando is in the stockroom checking off items on a broken clipboard. The Minotaur does a final walk down the line to make sure all the cooking equipment is turned off.

"Unnnnhh," he says to Hernando, who will be in the kitchen for at least another hour.

"*Hasta*. See you tomorrow, M."

The empty dining rooms are quiet. The scents of cooked meat, cigar smoke and cloying perfume hang in the air, made almost visible in the pale light from the torch-shaped sconces along the walls. In the back, in the room near the service bar, some of the wait staff sit in a deep booth figuring their tips. The Minotaur can hear their fingernails click against the calculator buttons. He makes himself a glass of ice water and stands by the bar listening to them talk. The conversation soon turns to going out, going together to a bar or maybe to the Pancake House for a late-night breakfast. The Minotaur steps closer, but just a little, enough so that if one of them happens to look up he'll be in their line of sight. The Minotaur leans stiffly against the bar. Head down, he toes the worn carpet. They decide on the Pancake House without ever looking up. They'll take two cars.

"Unnh," the Minotaur says softly, and leaves Grub's Rib for the night.

In the empty parking lot a milk-white moon, only a little cooler than the sun, rises over the city and finds the Minotaur alone. It casts just the hint of a shadow against the pavement. In shadow the Minotaur is large and powerful. In shadow the Minotaur looms over the expanse of asphalt and stretches nearly to the door of the deserted hotel. The quiet is disrupted by the deceleration of a truck as it pulls off the highway somewhere out of sight.

The Minotaur unlocks the passenger door of his car. It's a Vega hatchback, 1975 model. He drives a fifteen-year-old car precisely because he has to maintain it, taking a small subconscious pride in making it run year after year. He unlocks the passenger door because the driver's side lock is broken. The Vega is too small and the Minotaur's head and upper body too cumbersome for him to climb over the gearshift and the hump rising between the bucket seats, so he fingers the lock from inside and steps around. When he puts the key in the ignition and turns the switch there is a single audible click and nothing more. Again he turns the key, and again just one click. It's the solenoid. The Minotaur snorts once through deep nostrils and goes to the back of his car, where he keeps his tools. The box is clean and the tools well ordered. Order and place are important to the Minotaur. He takes a short, thick, cold chisel from the bottom of the toolbox, opens the Vega's hood and raps the solenoid switch twice with the heavy tool. The car starts with the first turn of the key. No hesitation. Tomorrow he will go to the salvage yard and the auto parts store for a used door lock and a new solenoid.

In the rearview mirror, as he pulls out of the parking lot, the Minotaur sees the waiters and waitresses coming out. He watches David lock the door. He watches them as they take off their short aprons, their bow ties, watches them pocket their wine tools, count their money, laugh. The Minotaur cocks his head to see the road before him, opens the window and sucks in the stifling night air.

CHAPTER 2

*T*he *Minotaur wakes* without an alarm clock and always has; he wakes in the dead center of his narrow bed. He lives in a mobile home haphazardly furnished by the long-dead wife of his landlord, one dilapidated trailer among five laid out end to end, horseshoe fashion, around a small plot of crab grass, mimosas and dogwoods, also left over from the wife. Lucky-U Mobile Estates lies on the outskirts of the city, beyond most zoning laws, which are lax anyway. Sweeny, the landlord, lives in a brick house at the head of the washed-out gravel drive. During the evenings, on a small deck listing to one side at his back door, he frequently sits in his underwear, one pale bony leg draped over the other, drinking beer from a can, belching and overlooking his domain.

The trailer is old and cramped, not designed for the likes of the Minotaur. He lies in the center of his bed vaguely remembering a time of more space, a time even before beds. But those memories are fleeting, nebulous. They fill him by turns with melancholy and a vague terror. Summer heat, undaunted by night, overpowers the oscillating fan on his chest of drawers. The air is so humid it's almost visible; the topsail of the boat in the framed photograph on his wall seems to flutter. The sheets and the Minotaur's pajama pants are damp from sweat. A baby-blue chenille bedspread lies bunched on the floor, kicked away during sleep. A dog barks outside his window.

"Buddy! Shut up!" Sweeny yells from somewhere inside his house. Buddy, a wheezing piebald English bulldog, does in fact stop barking. Without looking the Minotaur knows Buddy is pacing back and forth on the concrete floor of his narrow chain-link run. Without doubt he knows that Buddy will start barking again in a few minutes. The dog run is small. The low wooden shelf offers little shade from the sun. Buddy's only distraction is half of a chewed basketball. The Minotaur understands completely Buddy's need to bark.

"Unnnhh," the Minotaur grunts as he rises. In the galleylike kitchen of the trailer he puts the *briki*—the small brass pot that is his oldest possession—on to boil. Greek coffee is his one extravagance. Dark as pitch and oily, with lots of sugar. The Minotaur once knew people who read fortunes from the coffee grounds, who would flip an empty cup upside down, spin it three times and from the lay of the dark bitter grounds make predictions.

He has errands today: the solenoid switch and the lock for

his car door. Errands give the Minotaur purpose. Sitting at the kitchen table, sipping hot coffee from a chipped but favorite demitasse, he plans his day. He has errands, but he cannot predict their outcome. First a shower, then he'll drive out to the salvage yard to find a lock for his door. They know him at the salvage yard; he's a familiar face who will be allowed to wander among the rows and rows of junked cars, to wander freely with his tools looking for a Vega with an intact driver's side door. On the way home he'll stop at the parts store for a new solenoid. They're fairly inexpensive. After installing both the lock and the solenoid, assuming all goes well, he should have time for another shower before work, time to apply the various salves that keep his skin, particularly the transitional skin, in good condition. Maybe there will be time to sand and polish his horns. The Minotaur always plans his day.

As the Minotaur walks to his car Buddy charges the fence, snorting, slobbering and barking maniacally. The Minotaur is no longer afraid of Buddy, and he knows the dog means no real harm. But they have an unspoken understanding. Each of them has a history; each clings to an image, however diminished, of himself and his place in the world.

Before turning the key in the Vega's ignition the Minotaur gets his tool ready. Like the night before there is one solid click and nothing else.

As the Minotaur opens the hood Sweeny comes out his back door with a tin pie plate full of table scraps for the dog. "That damn solenoid again?" Sweeny asks, stopping to poke his balding head under the hood and scowl at the dirty four-cylinder engine.

"Mmnuh," the Minotaur answers, meaning *Yes* and *Good morning*.

"You ought to get yourself a real vehicle," Sweeny says, then winks at the Minotaur and points with his thumb toward the front yard, where, as always, there are several cars and pickups parked at an angle along the road with hand-painted *For Sale* signs propped in their windows. Most of the cars Sweeny gets cheap from people down on their luck or ignorant of their vehicle's value. He then makes the necessary repairs or improvements and sells at a nice profit. The Minotaur admires Sweeny's entrepreneurship, his business savvy. In fact it was Sweeny's front-yard car lot that led the Minotaur to a mobile home in his backyard.

The Minotaur is a nomad in the largest sense of the word. He finds it necessary, given the transient nature of everything around him, to relocate on occasion. He does not move with the seasons. Nor does he follow herds or rivers or constellations. His moves are with the centuries, more or less. Often, while driving, he takes time to think, to ruminate on the conditions of his life. As it happened some year and a half ago, the Minotaur was driving his Vega filled to overflowing with his essential possessions—his tools, a canvas roll for his knives, his uniforms, a few clothes, various grooming items, other sundry articles—driving through the southern United States chewing on the notion that, despite constant attention to frugality, he owned too much stuff. While pondering his two options—to abandon the least essential box of goods and further trim his already spare inventory or to succumb and in some way increase his storage space—the countryside passed him by. The Minotaur habitually avoids the interstate highway system. Time is important to him but has to be kept in perspective. He feels that the few minutes saved by using the interstates are irrelevant and come at the cost of impersonality, of sameness, of lifelessness. He was driving, then, through the rain on the back roads of North Carolina's Piedmont region, on curvy irregular tarmac threads that seemed to drift and wind according to no plan among stands of pine and oak trees, along and across creeks and shallow rivers, sometimes over, sometimes around rolling hills that often dissolved into low-hanging, heavy, gray clouds. There was an old and tired quality to the landscape that brought comfort to the Minotaur.

The cresting of one such hill coincided with a break in the clouds. The Minotaur's take on the symbolic has changed over the years. He has become less demanding and more open-minded of what life presents him. The road fell away before him, stretched out between a newly plowed field and what he at first thought was the parking lot of a small store. Upon getting closer he saw that it was not a store or a parking lot but three cars, a couple of pickup trucks and a riding mower lined up for sale on the front lawn of a brick house. The Minotaur passed slowly. There, glinting wetly in the momentary sun, a dull red station wagon caught his eye—some sort of Ford, Taurus probably. Nearly a year and a half ago the Minotaur turned his car around, pulled off the road, got out and stood in the damp crab grass to look over Sweeny's cars.

"She runs like a top," the man said as he walked up, scratching the entire time the little hollow centered beneath his lower lip, scratching with the dirty nail of his index finger. A sagging but lean man in slate-gray work pants and a T-shirt, he stopped long enough to clear his throat and spit on the grass.

"Unnhhh," the Minotaur answered, almost to himself.

"I'm asking three, but I'll let you have her for twenty-five hundred."

The Minotaur circled the station wagon slowly, stopping occasionally to think, hands in his pockets, mindlessly scratching at the ground with one toe.

"Name's Sweeny," the old man said, circling opposite the Minotaur, using the hem of his shirt to polish random spots on the car.

"Mmmm."

The Minotaur knelt behind the car and cocked his head to peer into the exhaust, looking for telltale signs of oil. Then, while down on one damp knee, he heard the dog, a rapid, raspy, strained bark coming closer and closer. The Minotaur stood up. Dogs make him nervous.

"Buddy! Here, boy!" Sweeny said, then contorted his lips and gave a piercing whistle.

Squat and broad, almost as wide across the chest as he was tall, the dog rounded the corner of the house at top speed. However, bowlegged and musclebound, more jowl than haunch, the bulldog at top speed was neither a graceful nor an impressive thing. The Minotaur took the opportunity to position himself on the other side of the car. Just to be safe he reached out for the door handle, ready.

"Uuunnnh," he said, and the tone was anxious.

Sweeny stood between the charging dog and the car behind which the Minotaur hid. Sweeny didn't seem anxious. To the contrary he seemed expectant. The old man whistled again and stomped the ground with a booted foot. The Minotaur, unsure of what the dog would do, tasted fear in the back of his throat, the taste of cut grass. He felt the muscles and sinews of his heavy neck grow taut. He lowed softly.

The dog came closer and closer, heading straight for Sweeny, the car and the Minotaur, and it was obvious to the Minotaur that the dog had something specific in mind. But much to the Minotaur's relieved surprise the bulldog did not veer around Sweeny at the last minute, did not, as the Minotaur feared, circle the Ford wagon with his teeth bared and the Minotaur in mind. Instead the dog charged directly at Sweeny, who stood—one foot planted forward, fists clenched, grinning—in its path.

"Get it, boy!" Sweeny said, and Buddy the bulldog leapt the short distance onto the man's extended leg—mounted his leg as if it were a bull bitch in heat and began to hump.

"Get it!" Sweeny said, as if it were the most natural thing in the world.

"Get it, Buddy! Get it! Get it, boy!" Sweeny said between fits of choking laughter, bouncing the leg up and down on the ball of his foot, Buddy clinging tightly, short forelimbs wrapped just beneath Sweeny's knee, eyes rolling about madly as he humped at the boot. The Minotaur watched. It was an unsettling show, but he'd seen worse.

After a minute or so Sweeny tired of the game. "Get off me!" he shouted. He kicked his leg out and sent Buddy sprawling with a yelp. The dog walked slowly and stiffly around the corner of the house without looking back.

It took several minutes for Sweeny to catch his breath

enough to speak. "He's a damn sight, ain't he?"

"Mmmuh," the Minotaur said, opening the driver's door of the Ford to look at the odometer.

"Them's all highway miles," Sweeny said. "You want to take her for a spin?"

The Minotaur did want to drive the car. He couldn't afford it, not even for twenty-five hundred, but he wanted to pretend for a little while that he could. He climbed into the driver's seat but kept the door open and one foot on the ground. The car smelled of stale tobacco and sour milk. Its faded dashboard was beginning to crack. On the floor a trampled pacifier lay with its rubber teat pointing upward. Scrawled on the underside of the passenger's visor, in purple crayon, was the word *poop*. And protruding from the heat vent over the AM radio was what looked like half of a cookie. *It would be a fine car*, the Minotaur thought. He closed his eyes and imagined driving it for years and years, getting to know it as intimately as he knew the Vega. When Sweeny jangled the keys inches from his ear the Minotaur startled. His head pitched back and the tip of his right horn pierced and dug into the headliner, ripping the fabric and the foam padding for several inches.

"Shit fire, boy. You're awful jumpy."

"Unnnhh!"

As with his possessions and actions there is a conscious economy to the Minotaur's speech. The mechanics of word making in his mouth do not differ so much from those of men. There are the larynx, the soft velum, the glottal structure. There are the folds of flesh that trap and manipulate the wind passing through his throat. More important, the codes of language exist in the Minotaur's mind. His thought, his subvocal speech, is complex. He wants to say, *I am tired of these horns and all that they mean.* Not brilliant, but certainly not the sentiment of a complete fool. The problems lie in articulation and enunciation. No matter how sweetly worded or wise the Minotaur's ideas may be, when he puts them to tongue, terrible things happen. In the clear field of his mind things are precise. But when filtered through the deep resonating chamber of his nostrils, pushed up the cavernous expanse of his throat and across the thick bovine tongue, his words come out tortured and mutilated—deep, nasal, almost whining. The Minotaur is painfully self-conscious of how he speaks. Over the years he's come to depend on contextual grunts, which suffice most of the time.

"Unnnhh," he said, eyeing the ripped headliner.

"Don't worry about it," Sweeny answered.

But the Minotaur was prone to worrying. For a long time he has suffered under the weight of his past life, the rumors and the all-too-true. He struggles now to live without trouble or conflict. Reputation has to be attended moment by moment.

Sweeny didn't seem to care about the torn headliner, but when the Minotaur opened the Vega's hatchback and took out his toolbox and from it a fabric repair kit, the old man was impressed. They talked—Sweeny mostly—while the Minotaur repaired the rip, and when the Minotaur made it clear that he was traveling, looking for a place to settle, Sweeny genuinely wanted to help.

The Minotaur spent the rest of that afternoon at Sweeny's. They walked from car to car. A wheel well here, rusting out, needed sanding and Bondo. The Dodge truck could use a carburetor kit, maybe points and plugs. There would be a steady flow of cars coming and going, and the repairs would be endless. Sweeny walked him to the back of his house, where Lucky-U Mobile Estates made up the perimeter of his property. Sweeny showed the Minotaur the two vacant trailers. One, a dull white rectangle of corrugated aluminum, sat on a brick foundation at the mouth of the drive. It was the cleanest of all the trailers. The second, at the back of the lot, perched on cinder blocks and facing the back of Sweeny's house, with a clear view of the dog run, was smaller and much older. It was painted a dull nautical green and had a cabin-esque bay window at one end and a squat, boxy, windowless appendage rising from the roof at the opposite end, which gave it a desperately boatlike appearance. From inside, through a smudged window, the Minotaur could see Sweeny's back door and deck. In the shadows beneath the plank floor Buddy lay panting.

A year and a half ago the Minotaur and Sweeny came to an agreement. He would do all the repairs on the cars that Sweeny picked up for resale. In exchange the Minotaur would live rent free in the boat-shaped trailer, and Sweeny would give him spending cash for groceries and whatever else he needed. If and when a job came along the Minotaur could cut back on some of the repair work and begin paying a rent that they both agreed was fair.

The Minotaur had to think about the arrangement. Hasty decisions get him into trouble, an eons-old pattern that renders every choice, every decision, troublesome. Not until the *bad* in any flawed decision comes to bear is the Minotaur able to see his error.

He left Sweeny's with his Vega full of possessions and drove around for most of the afternoon grunting quietly to himself before giving in to his elementary version of faith. Just before nightfall he crested that hill again. He was asleep in the narrow bed by ten o'clock, the few boxes holding all that he owned crowded with him in the bedroom.

Little has changed at Lucky-U Mobile Estates since then. The Minotaur is working now, at Grub's Rib across from a condemned Holiday Inn out on the highway, but he still fixes cars for Sweeny. He's yet to buy one.

The Vega starts after being thumped with the chisel. As he drives out, the Minotaur nods to Sweeny.

The day goes as planned. In the salvage yard he finds a junked Vega quickly, and aside from the wasps nesting in the open dash that he has to swat continually, he gets the lock out of the door with ease. Nor is there a problem with the solenoid. Under the watchful eyes of the piebald dog the Minotaur works on his Vega—the hood, the hatchback and both doors gaping, beneath the sweet pink flowers of the mimosa tree in the center of the trailer park. He even has time to bathe before work.

CHAPTER 3

*T*he *Minotaur meets* David the hostess coming through the wait station. It's barely six o'clock, and David already looks tired, like he's about to cry. Two of the busboys called in sick. Years ago David taught history, junior high then high school. He's still prone to slipping esoteric facts and utterly useless trivia into conversations. Occasionally rumors circulate, all variations of the same, as to why he stopped teaching. The Minotaur doesn't care; David is a kind man who treats him with respect. David carries a small round tray, its cork surface nearly covered by dirty glasses. Lipstick and grease stains smear the rims. The Minotaur hates it when people drop their cigarette butts in the melting ice. A wet rag hangs across David's forearm; the smell of ammonia stings the Minotaur's eyes.

Two waiters stand by the ice machine cutting lemons—Mike and Shane, but the Minotaur has trouble remembering which is which.

"I smell hist'ry," one of them says mincingly.

They both snicker.

David ignores them, but the Minotaur tastes bile in the back of his throat.

"Rolaids?" he asks David, heavy on the *R*. They share the symptoms of a nervous stomach, so the Minotaur knows that David has several large bottles in the office.

"Sure thing, sugar. I'll bring them back."

"Unnnhh," the Minotaur says as David goes through the swinging door into the dining room.

"Fag, fag, fag-a-la," one of the waiters singsongs, and the Minotaur can hear them laughing even as the door to the kitchen swings shut.

The strata of restaurant workers are complicated and overlapping. As with most things there are hierarchies. Management, of course, is the elite, operating at a remove. And the wait staff is superior to anyone in the kitchen. Within each group there are subgroups. Among the waiters and waitresses, a cliquish bunch by nature, there are unspoken divisions: the eager careerists, often thin and obsequious; the resigned, who, after years of eliminating other choices one by one through bad decisions or, worse, indecision, have nothing else to do; and the largest group, impudent and transitory, the college students. Piedmont Community College provides Grub's with a yearly crop of workers. Most have a mocking disdain for the job. The Minotaur often thinks, *I don't want to be like any of them.* But in his own clunky half-baked way the Minotaur also thinks, *If it weren't for my thick tongue, the bovine speech, if it weren't for my vision, oblique as it is, I could be one of them.*

JoeJoe is shucking oysters at the sink, lining them up neatly in a tub of crushed ice. JoeJoe wears a steel-mesh glove on his left hand to protect him from slips of the oyster knife. Almost everyone in the kitchen has a scar in one palm or the other.

"Hey, M, got a smoke?" JoeJoe asks.

The Minotaur nods in the direction of the dock. His prep work is done, and the orders are caught up for the moment. JoeJoe peels off the glove and follows him outside. JoeJoe pulls a blue plastic lighter from his pants pocket, holds it up to the sun and squints. He shakes it vigorously, then rolls his thumb across the strike wheel one, two, three, four, five, ten, fifteen or more times in quick succession before a low tentative flame allows him to light the cigarette. He shields the lighter with one hand and offers to light the Minotaur's cigarette as well. The smell of flint fills the Minotaur suddenly and inexplicably with nostalgia. He almost feels like crying. JoeJoe puts the lighter back into his pocket.

"How about that new one? Kelly? That her name?" JoeJoe asks, holding both hands in front of his chest, indicating breasts.

"Unnh," the Minotaur answers, noncommittal.

"I'm an ass man myself," JoeJoe says. "Convicted. But she's got one proud set."

"Mmm."

The Minotaur likes JoeJoe, a fluid ropy man who seems to be dancing even when he's washing dishes. Likes his unabashed youth. Likes the way he can just say these things. There was a time when the Minotaur acted and reacted in pure base instinct, and people feared him for it. But time has worn him down. Now, among cocky boys and arrogant men, he is reserved and hesitant, unsure. He has in fact noticed the new waitress, but not her breasts. JoeJoe and the Minotaur smoke and talk, about Kelly, about the other waitresses, until David comes out with the Rolaids, three chalk-white tablets in his upturned hand.

"Hernando needs you," David says. "And I want to ask you something later."

"Unnh," the Minotaur says, and follows David inside. Cecie is bent over a five-gallon bucket of mayonnaise, trying but unable to take off the lid. Her thin and high haunches press against the checked fabric of her taut uniform—a little lean for the Minotaur's taste but inviting nonetheless. Pretending to need something from over her head the Minotaur steps behind Cecie just close enough so that they touch, her skinny buttocks on his thighs. She's making bleu cheese dressing for the salad bar. *The Original Salad Bar*, it says on the billboards along the highway, *50 Items*. Next to the melt-in-your-mouth prime rib, it's Grub's most touted claim. They say it was the first in the area. Fifty items. The Minotaur isn't good with numbers. Even the simplest calculations get lost in the twists and turns of his thinking, but he's sure that fifty is an exaggeration.

"Hey, now!" Cecie says, butting him with her backside. "Don't start something you can't finish."

"Mmmnnh."

"Here, stud-boy. Get this lid off for me."

The Minotaur helps Cecie with the lid, then holds the bucket at an angle so she can spoon mayonnaise into a mixing bowl. With a long stainless-steel whip Cecie stirs the dressing to the right consistency. She dips her middle finger in to the second knuckle and offers it to the Minotaur's mouth. He takes her finger between black rubbery lips, holds it pinched gently in his wide and worn teeth, tasting the musty bleu cheese on his tongue.

"Unnh," he grunts.

"More salt?" Cecie asks.

"Order up," Kelly says.

Kelly. She has watched the whole thing; the Minotaur can tell by the look on her face.

"Un," the Minotaur says with Cecie's finger still in his mouth.

"I have a chicken divan," Kelly says, looking away. "And some appetizers."

The Minotaur feels the blood in his face and is thankful for thick black skin.

The night's business comes in waves: a rush here, a lull there. During the busy times they work in well-rehearsed routines, using only the most necessary words.

"Fire, table thirty-one."

"Can I get a setup for a shrimp cocktail?"

"Need a peach melba, one flan and a plain cheesecake."

Tonight, like busy nights during prom season and the holidays, Grub himself comes in to expedite. A roundish man with hooded eyes and a pronounced dewlap, a man with an obvious passion for food, he fills the role well. He takes the orders from the wait staff, calls them back in perfectly orchestrated sequence, loads the heavy trays for pick up. Grub has a thing about sending out cold food and often calls to the carpet the unfortunate waiter or waitress who is tardy in picking up a ready order. Everyone minds their p's and q's when Grub is in the kitchen.

For all of Grub's bluster and snorting the Minotaur knows him as a man with heart and compassion. When the Minotaur pulled up to the back of Grub's Rib not quite a year ago, for no better reason than the clear directions on the highway billboards, when he got out of his car dressed in uniform—the altered white chef's coat, the salt-and-pepper-checked pants, the thick-soled steel-toed shoes—when he rang the delivery bell at the back door clutching the canvas wrap that held his knives, sharpening steel, vegetable peeler, melon baller and other tools of his trade, it was Grub who answered the door.

"Work?" the Minotaur asked, struggling for clarity.

It was the day before Thanksgiving. Grub opened the door wearing a blood-spattered apron and holding a boning knife in his hand. He looked the Minotaur over. Without speaking he opened the screen door wider for the Minotaur to pass. Just inside was a long worktable, and on it were a cutting board and a case of whole turkeys, each snug inside a Kryovac plastic wrapping. In a hotel pan to one side several birds lay opened and deboned, exposed and drying in the kitchen air. Bits of fat and viscera littered the cutting board, the table and the floor, where, beside the table, three more cases of turkeys were stacked. Grub pointed at the turkeys and raised his heavy brows to the Minotaur. The Minotaur unwrapped his tools, selected the thin-bladed flexible boning knife, stroked it quickly back and forth across the sharpening steel to hone its edge, then set to work on one of the birds.

The Minotaur is generally good with tools and has a dexterity to his hands despite limited extension in the fingers and knuckles, despite the thin and almost unnoticeable webs of flesh between the first joints of his index and middle and his ring and pinkie fingers, despite the thickish black-edged nails. He is deft with knives. It is one of the reasons he came to cooking so long ago. Cooking was a timeless craft that he could master.

Under Grub's scrutiny the Minotaur boned the turkey with an expert precision. He set it on its end and cut forcefully down either side of the spine; traced the tip of the knife along the fibulae and down the metatarsals, cutting away the sinew around each joint with minute flicks of the blade; peeled the thick flesh of the breasts away from the ribs; used a fingertip to gently separate the long arrowhead-shaped cartilage at the base of the breastbone from the meat. Completely boneless except for the wings, tips removed because of their tendency to burn, splayed limply on the cutting board, the turkey was ready to be stuffed, trussed and roasted.

"Six days a week, dinner shift. You get Mondays off. That okay?"

"Unnhh," the Minotaur answered gratefully.

Grub gave the Minotaur an apron, showed him where to change in the closet-sized room that led into the employee bathroom, where the Minotaur dinged his horn against a paint-spattered speaker hanging on the wall. Grub agreed to pay him cash under-the-table.

That was nearly a year ago, and Grub has given him fairly regular raises despite the Minotaur's fairly regular catastrophes, such as spilling the clarified butter. Two or three of these accidents bring about the occasional "talk" in the office with the door closed. "Think about it, M," Grub likes to say. "Take the time to think about the thing at hand."

"How you doing, M?" Grub asks tonight from opposite the hot line. The Minotaur cocks his head to see under the stacks of plates and monkey dishes lined up across the top of the heat lamps.

"Unnnh," he says.

"Good," Grub says. "Good."

With Grub as expediter, there is little or no direct communication between the kitchen crew and the wait staff. Grub calls all the orders. The waiters come and go in nervous self-conscious silence. And David more or less handles any problems on the floor. Hernando, the Minotaur, Cecie and JoeJoe function—no, the Minotaur likes to think, they *play*—like a winning team. The Minotaur feels a part of it.

At about nine o'clock things start to slow down. Grub leaves the kitchen for the bar. He'll down two, maybe three Grub-tinies before David closes out the registers for the night. Orders come now every fifteen or twenty minutes, and Hernando likes the crew to use the time to catch up on the cleaning.

The Minotaur is breaking down the bus tubs for JoeJoe, separating the glasses into plastic racks, putting the silver in to soak, when David walks in.

"Hey, M, can I talk to you for a second?"

"Mmm," the Minotaur says, and dries his hands on a towel hanging from his apron string. He sits on the low freezer by the coffee machines while David pours the last of a pot into his personal Grub's mug.

"What are you doing tomorrow?" David asks.

"Unnh unn." Tomorrow is Monday; the Minotaur has no plans.

"I was wondering if you could help me move. I have to be out by Tuesday, and I moved almost all that would fit in my car. I figured if we opened your hatchback I could get the last few things."

The Minotaur agrees to meet David at his apartment around lunchtime. David starts to draw him a map even though the Minotaur had been there before, has given him a ride home several times. In black ink David makes what looks like three overlapping staggered crosses and is about to write down street names when from the dining room comes the clatter and crash of falling silverware and glass. Then the door from the dining room slams open. Where there should be the din of people eating and talking there is a pronounced silence. Timothy, one of the waiters, rushes into the kitchen wide eyed and anxious.

"Something's wrong with Kelly!" he says, almost shouting.

"What?" David asks.

"Kelly. She's having some kind of fit."

David rushes into the hushed dining room. The Minotaur wants desperately to see what's happening but is not able to step out into the room, so he presses the coal-black disk of his eye to the round window in the door.

Kelly lies in the wide aisle between the salad bar and a row of occupied four-tops along the mirrored wall, her body in spasms. One of the customers, an old black man sitting at a deuce near the door, gets up, turns Kelly on her side and puts his coat under her head. The Minotaur sees his mouth move, and David hurries to the front of the restaurant. The other customers seem unsure whether they want to continue eating or to watch. Most crane their necks for a softened view in the gilt-edged mirrors.

Crisis often brings about bonding, or at least the perception of it. By the time the ambulance arrives Kelly is okay, sitting up in the office, embarrassed and ashen. Reluctantly she agrees to go with the ambulance crew. The guests leave the restaurant earlier than usual this night. The waiters and waitresses do their side work, splitting Kelly's responsibilities without bickering. David turns off the intercom. Even the kitchen cleanup is finished ahead of schedule. When the Minotaur walks out of the kitchen at ten-thirty, through the main wait station and into the dining rooms, the restaurant is empty and quiet. Grub has followed Kelly to the emergency room and plans to give her a ride home later. The wait staff sits at the bar figuring tips and talking in hushed tones about the incident. The Minotaur makes himself a Coke; he stands a little closer than usual, listening to the talk.

"God, how humiliating," Adrienne says. "I would die if that happened to me."

"My mom used to have seizures," a tall birdlike waiter named Robert says.

"I thought David was going to shit his panties."

"Well, she fell out right in my section. My tips are totally fucked."

Mike and Shane, the two waiters who mocked David earlier.

"Unnhhh," the Minotaur says, just loud enough to be heard. He wants to be part of the conversation. But when all the waiters and waitresses stop talking to each other and look at him, he doesn't really know what to do next. More than anything he wants them to know that he saw what they saw, that he felt what they felt.

"What's that, M?" Robert asks. "Did you say something?"

Somewhere in the kitchen the Minotaur hears a cooling fan cycle on. In the wait station the time clock moves solidly into the hour. The Minotaur can hear the ice in his glass melting, caving in on itself. The waiters and waitresses look expectantly at him, and their expectation is excoriating.

"Kelly," he says, the *l*s thick and clunky in his mouth, and someone laughs at his effort. "Kelly," he says, shaking his heavy head from side to side, hoping that he won't have to say more, hoping the gesture will suffice. Someone draws deeply on a cigarette; each threadlike strand of tobacco roars as it burns; the exhalation storms his eardrums with gale force. Someone, out of disinterest or pity, works decisively at a calculator, fingertips slamming at the keys, fingernails clicking against the plastic. The Minotaur can hear the current charging through the circuitry.

"Jesus Christ, M, what the hell are you talking about?" Adrienne asks, not really wanting an answer. But the Minotaur can't answer anyway. He doesn't really know what he means, only that he means no harm to Kelly. The silence spills out of the bar where the wait staff sits and the Minotaur stands. It rises from the floor over his thin calves, up the walls, above his waist, into his mouth and lungs, fills the restaurant. It is all the Minotaur can do to move his body through it, out the door and into the night.

CHAPTER 4

*O*ut *of Chaos, out of Eros, out of Earth's prolific and indis-
criminate womb begot.*

The Minotaur dreams of bloodlines:

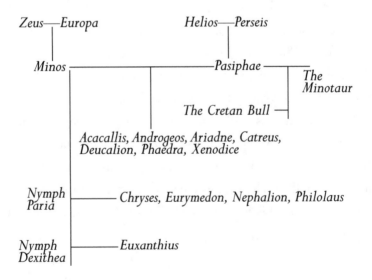

CHAPTER 5

In the mornings before putting on the *briki* to boil coffee, before the cool shower and the talcum afterward, before even rising from bed, the Minotaur likes to lie awhile beneath the window, the sun—if the sun is out—swathing him intermittently as the curtains rise and fall in the breeze—if a breeze happens to blow—or in the damp still air of a cloudy day; whatever the weather the Minotaur likes to lie there in bed in the morning and scratch himself. The Minotaur sleeps shirtless. Over the years he found that no matter how much he altered the necks and shoulders of his pajamas, the garments were binding. Sleep is fitful enough without the encumbrance of fabric, so the Minotaur sleeps shirtless.

The Minotaur scratches the fog of last night's sleep from his face with both hands, rakes the jowly muzzle and the bony expanse of his snout with his nails. He presses hard with his fingertips at the base of his horns. He lows involuntarily, scratching beneath his chin and at his dewlap, lows even louder while stroking the massive neck, its geometry of overlapping muscles and cablelike tendons. The Minotaur scratches until the skin beneath the charcoal-gray fur that covers his meaty shoulders burns, then he scratches still more. He scratches softly at the transitional skin, gray and flaky, where he goes from bull to man or man to bull, depending on the point of origin. It is a scarlike place across his chest, a purplish score dipping beneath his sternum, underlining a man's pectorals from which black rubbery bull's nipples sprout. On the Minotaur's back the transition is less decisive, nothing more than a discoloration of the skin from deep black to gray to pale moon-white human skin. Sometimes this place, this division, throbs, swells, deepens, becomes a chasm within the Minotaur that he will never span, though he will spend eternity trying, becomes a separation between two distinct parts. But sometimes he is able to forget it, to believe for an isolated moment that he is a singular and whole being.

The Minotaur scratches and scratches, his man's belly, the thin—almost womanly—waist with visible hipbones, the wiry thighs. At first appearance there is an incongruity to his body; the lumbering bulk of his bovine head, neck and shoulders is verily grafted onto an if not scrawny then simply adequate trunk and legs. He seems always about to topple. But watching the

Minotaur move through his day, it's possible to detect a hard-won harmony: the wide stance, feet planted apart; the subtleties of balance; the mechanics of muscle, ligament and bone working synergistically to keep this unlikely being upright.

After his shower and two cups of stout coffee he takes the coffee grounds, still steaming, out to the plot of young tomato plants by his front door—three spindly plants tied with baling twine to short stakes made from broom handles. The Minotaur tests the heft of the few green fruits with his fingertips. He is spreading the coffee grounds into the mulch when he hears Sweeny behind him.

"Read the paper today, M?"

"Unnnhh."

Sweeny knows the Minotaur doesn't care much for day-to-day news. The Minotaur knows Sweeny likes to tell bad jokes.

"Seems like one of the matrons of our fine town got herself arrested at the beach last weekend."

"Unnh."

"Indecent exposure."

"Mmm."

"Yep, indecent exposure. She got caught pissing in the ocean. Was hanging her fat ass right off the side of the boat. When they asked her why she was pissing in the ocean the old woman told them that her drunken bastard of a husband had just fell out of the boat into the water and that he was drowning. She figured every little bit would help." Sweeny barely gets the punch line out before he is overcome with wheezing laughter.

"Mmmm," the Minotaur says, going into his trailer. He

closes the door. Through the thin walls he can hear Sweeny still laughing. He hears the clink of the galvanized gate as the old man opens the dog run and calls Buddy. The gate clangs shut.

It's payday. The Minotaur remembers that he has to stop by the restaurant before meeting David. Every other Monday, when the rest of the kitchen crew and the wait staff pick up their checks, Grub has an envelope of cash for the Minotaur. Sealed, always. Small bills, so the Minotaur won't have to go to the bank.

The Minotaur thinks about what to wear. It's important to the Minotaur that he has something to do, so unless Sweeny has a repair job for him or he has errands to run he usually goes to work on his day off, and then he just wears his uniform. Hernando bakes the Black Forest cakes for the coming week on Mondays, and the Minotaur comes in, unpaid, to help ice the stacks of dark chocolate layers. If he's lucky he gets to make the onion soup, twenty gallons at a time—beef stock, half a bottle of cheap sherry and fifty pounds of onions, peeled and chopped. The Minotaur loves onions, always has; he eats them like apples while making the soup, and the pungent juices never even sting his eyes.

The Minotaur decides to wear his uniform pants—the black-and-white checks—and one of his three altered button-down shirts. He remembers, too, that he needs laces for his shoes and some other things. It takes him awhile, but he finds a nearly dry ballpoint pen that writes only after he waves its tip back and forth over a flame on his stove. On the back of an envelope addressed to Resident, his head cocked to one side, eye close to the paper, the Minotaur painstakingly makes a small list:

shoe laces. black
styptic pencil
WD-40
mouthwash
book?

The Minotaur, while scratching in the mornings, often makes himself bleed. The Minotaur is self-conscious about his breath. The Minotaur lacks confidence in his penmanship. Over time the Minotaur has learned to read, has even been able to make the slow laborious transition from one language to another as cultures die off and fade away and as he moves from place to place. But the Minotaur has never been able to rise above rudimentary skills. Most books seem ridiculously small, and the physical act of finding a comfortable sight line over his massive snout frustrates him. Nevertheless the Minotaur is haunted by the idea that books and reading might make those vast stretches of time that loom before him more bearable.

As the Vega pulls out of the drive Buddy charges in the pen, barking that wet bark; the Minotaur can hear the dog's nails scratching at the concrete as he runs. In the front yard Sweeny stands, one hand shoved into his back pocket, the other gesticulating over a rust-colored Ford Maverick. In the driver's seat a gaunt young man in bad need of a shave sits with his mouth open. Standing beside the car, leaning against it for support, a very pregnant woman—girl—wearing shower sandals balances on her substantial hip a crying child in a filthy white pullover and a diaper. Just last week the Minotaur had the guts of the Maverick's transmission laid out on a blanket under the mimosa trees. He changed the pressure plate. The Minotaur gives a finger wave to Sweeny and the couple as he drives past.

Grub is on the phone when the Minotaur gets to the restaurant. The office door is open, and Grub, sitting at the cramped desk arguing loudly about the cost of a case of red wine, winks and smiles at the Minotaur. A radio plays in the kitchen. The Minotaur follows the muted Tex-Mex sounds and the smell of baked cakes back through the restaurant.

"*Qué pasa*, M?" Hernando asks as he spoons white icing from the Hobart floor mixer into a pastry bag. "You helping David move today?"

"Unnnh."

Hernando has the cakes lined up on sheet pans, six per. With the star tip of the bag he begins to pipe a decorative rope around the base of each cake. The Minotaur turns the trays for him.

The big white clock on the wall over the dish machine reads 9:53, and Grub doesn't give out checks or cash until 10:00. From somewhere in the dining room comes laughter, waiters and waitresses here for their meager paychecks. The Minotaur drags a finger up the inside of the mixing bowl and puts it to his fat tongue.

"Mmnnh," he says.

"See you tomorrow, M."

Going back through the dining rooms toward the office the Minotaur feels the hairs on his neck bristle. He meets Shane and Mike, who have come together—in shorts, each wearing a T-shirt advertising a different beer—to collect their pay.

"Hey, wild man," Mike says, unusually friendly. "What's up?"

"Unnh," the Minotaur answers.

"Boss is on the phone. He says to wait a few minutes."

The two waiters go to the bar for Cokes; the Minotaur hesitates, then follows them. They're little more than boys, the Minotaur knows. But boys, more than anything else, boys with their enviable swagger and bravado, their stupidity that is both sweet and malicious, their undeniable allure, make him uneasy. He understands but cannot articulate that these boys embody the qualities of manhood that he can never possess, nor pretend to. Boys remind him of what he was and what he can never be again, remind him of how even the animal in him has diminished.

Shane sits in a booth, his back against the wall beneath an opaque amber-colored false window. He puts his sandaled feet on the padded seat and begins to chew the end of a swizzle stick. Mike grabs a jar of olives from the bar and sits opposite. They talk mindlessly and easily. The Minotaur stands, as he stood the night before, awkwardly against the bar. He thinks it would be best for him just to go back into the kitchen and talk to Hernando until Grub is ready to give out his pay, then to leave here and go help David—probably the kindest person the Minotaur knows right now—move out of his apartment. Instead he steps a little closer and hopes for the opportunity to join the conversation.

"I wonder how Kelly is," Shane says.

"Probably fine," Mike answers. "She's had seizures before. If it happens again, though, I hope it happens in your section."

Shane digs a piece of ice from his glass and flicks it at Mike's head. Mike dodges and retaliates with an olive, which Shane catches in his mouth. *Boisterous boys*, the Minotaur thinks, and wishes for something to say. In the upper dining room someone is talking; it sounds like one of the waitresses.

"She dropped a whole tray of desserts when she fell," Mike says. "Spilled coffee all over the pants leg of this old fucker at one of my four-tops. He was pissed."

"I didn't see that. What I did notice was that black skirt of hers riding almost up to her crotch."

"You're a sick bastard, Shane."

The Minotaur wants to say something. He wants to defend Kelly in some way—although he can't say how or even why—almost as much as he wants to join in Mike and Shane's repartee.

"Unnnh," he says, and both Mike and Shane look at him.

"You say something, wild man?"

Just like last night the Minotaur can't think of anything to say. Embarrassed, he acts hastily.

"Kelly," he finally slurs, and, unable to stop himself, cups both hands in front of his chest, indicating heavy full breasts.

Shane chokes on a piece of ice trying to stifle his laughter.

"What about Kelly?" Mike asks in mock earnestness, and mimics the Minotaur's gesture.

The Minotaur paws the carpet with one foot. He swings his heavy head slowly from side to side, looking at the floor all around the room. What about Kelly? What is it that he can say now to salvage the situation?

"I'm a tit man," he says, and it's all he can do to get it out clearly.

Shane lies down on the seat of the booth, laughing.

Mike feigns seriousness. "What's that mean, M? That you're a tit man?"

Of course the Minotaur can't answer. He doesn't really know what it means to be a tit man. In truth, when the Minotaur dreams of love, and he does as much as any man, he imagines full and giving hips, a soft belly, fleshy thighs rising to an amply haired pubis more often than he imagines breasts, big or small.

"I'm a tit man," the Minotaur says, hoping they will know what it means.

"You are pathetic," Adrienne says from the steps behind him. She snorts, piglike, in disgust and walks away.

The Minotaur moans softly to himself.

A waitress named Margaret, who walked up with Adrienne, glares at the Minotaur and the two waiters. "Grub says the checks are ready. And . . . " She stops, no doubt searching for a valid response to what she has just witnessed. "And you guys are totally inappropriate."

Shane sits up in the booth. He makes his hand into the shape of a gun, thumb back and two fingers extended. He puts the fingertips, the barrel, to the roof of his mouth, cocks the thumb and fires. His head jerks back, eyes wide open.

"They're both prick teasers, M. Don't let them get to you," Mike assures him.

The Minotaur lingers at the bar long enough for Adrienne and Margaret to leave before going to the office for his money. Mike and Shane seem to be in no hurry. Grub, still behind the desk, thumbs through the checks and hands one each to Mike and Shane.

"Thanks, boss. See you tonight."

Grub just nods. Tips are good at his establishment, and he has a stack of applications from people eager to wait tables for him. Grub has little tolerance for a cocky attitude and does not hesitate, even on a busy night, to hand a misbehaving waiter a fifty-dollar bill and tell him not to come back. Rolling his chair back the few available inches in the tight office, his belly expanding into the newly available space, Grub pulls the Minotaur's envelope from the center drawer.

"Here you go, M."

"Mmmm."

"Listen," Grub says, and there is a hesitation. "I heard about the accident with the butter the other night."

"Unnh," the Minotaur says.

"You just need to be careful, okay? For your sake and everybody else's."

The Minotaur recognizes something in the moment. It is the vaguely familiar beginning of closure, the slow and unavoidable decline into change. He nods his head in agreement.

"Have a good day off, and don't spend all that in one place."

In the parking lot Mike and Shane are sitting in Shane's car, parked beside the Vega. The sounds of an electric guitar erupt from speakers in the wide-open doors.

"So, M," Shane shouts over the music. "You got a hard-on for the epileptic's tits? Is that it?"

"Shut up, asshole," Mike says, punching Shane in the thigh. They're smoking marijuana. The Minotaur sees the open plastic baggie on the dashboard, and beside it a slim neat package of rolling papers. Smoke rises out of the car and dissipates. The Minotaur recognizes the smell. He wishes they had parked elsewhere.

"Hey, M, want to join our little bacchanalia?" Mike asks, then draws deeply on the hand-rolled cigarette. A seed sizzles and pops at the burning tip, sending a shower of sparks over Mike's bare legs. He curses, jerks upright in his seat and brushes at the tiny embers, all the while struggling to hold his breath and pinching the joint between his fingertips. When he settles down he offers it to the Minotaur.

"Unnh."

"Come on, wild man. It'll give you a new outlook on life."

"Unnh," the Minotaur says, and unlocks the Vega's door.

"Suit yourself."

The waiters pass the joint between them. Shane says something to Mike that the Minotaur can't hear. Mike turns the stereo off, pivots in the car seat to face the Minotaur, both feet on the asphalt. The Minotaur notices the wiry black hairs sprouting from Mike's toes.

"Somebody told me you're pretty good with engines. That true?"

"Mmmn," the Minotaur answers, looking at his toolbox through the Vega's rear window. He *is* good with engines, and, like everyone else in the world, praise, or sometimes merely recognition, seduces him. He releases the door handle and waits.

"You know Robert who works here, right?" Mike asks. "He's that computer geek. Looks a little bit like a buzzard."

"Unnnh." The Minotaur knows the waiter by his description.

"He's got this motorcycle for sale. A really sweet old BMW."

Top-heavy as the Minotaur is, motorcycles scare him. But he understands the need for unencumbered movement, and to a lesser degree he understands the male need for risk.

"The problem is the bike won't start. And Robert is such

an idiot when it comes to anything not plugged into the wall. I'll bet you could get it running in no time," Mike says to the Minotaur.

Shane plays drums on the steering wheel and the dashboard, rocking his head as if he can hear into the silent radio. The Minotaur looks at his watch. He has to meet David in an hour.

"Unnh."

"Come on, M. You've got plenty of time."

"Mmmn."

"Tell you what. Shane'll drive and I'll buy you lunch. Just come look at the bike and tell me what you think. That's all I'm asking."

"Hey, M," Shane stops drumming long enough to say. "There's a pool at Rob's apartment complex. Hot day like this, there's bound to be tits all over the place."

"Mammaries for everyone," Mike joins in.

"An udder plethora."

"Bring your toolbox."

The Minotaur sits in the center of the backseat so his horns won't tap against the window glass. The windows are electric. Shane claims he doesn't know why the back ones stopped working; he and Mike have their windows rolled down and the radio cranked up. Hot wind and loud music buffet the cramped backseat. The Minotaur struggles to keep his head still. The Minotaur isn't along for the promise of breasts. Nor does he particularly care about the motorcycle. The Minotaur struggles to keep his head still and to come to terms with why he is there. Out of necessity there is a resigned quality to the Minotaur's life, but the resignation is not without a degree of hope, maybe even faith. For as long as the Minotaur can remember—no, for much longer than he can remember—he has risen every day aware of the possibility of change. Some would call him gullible. The truth is, there are days on end when he would gladly barter some of his hope for the arrogant cynicism of people like Shane and Mike. In the backseat the Minotaur's wristwatch pounds incessantly at the thin bones of his arm, resonates up through the joints, rides roughshod over his ribs and battles with the rhythms of his heart.

The motorcycle sits covered with a blue plastic tarp in the parking lot of Robert's apartment complex. Taut bungee cords, hooked in the grommets, weave through the spokes and stretch under the chassis to hold the tarp in place. The Minotaur notices a small pool of oil—tarlike, gritty and iridescent—beneath the crankcase. Rather than going to the door Shane plays a long note on the car's horn.

Robert must have expected it. He comes out right away and is a little surprised to see the Minotaur.

"Hi, M."

"Unnh."

They banter back and forth, Robert, Shane and Mike. As he uncovers the motorcycle Robert makes a weak attempt at a sales pitch. Mike and Shane talk around him. Undraped, the motorcycle, leaning on its kickstand, is impressive. The BMW is almost twenty years old, low to the ground, the color of cinnamon. It conveys a sense of power. It is an animal at rest. Not a svelte or speedy animal, but with its two fat cylinders protruding at right angles on either side of the frame, with its wide gas tank, its solid drive shaft and its drum brake, with the simplicity of its design, it is a willing beast of burden.

Mike gives a low whistle.

"This thing is nearly as old as you are, bud," Shane says disparagingly.

"Shane, my friend," Mike says. "You are the consummate buffoon. Absolutely no sense of style."

"It's kind of a classic," Robert says.

"Style, huh?" Shane says. "Classic."

The Minotaur steps closer to the bike, kneels and cocks his head to get a look at one of the carburetors. "Unnh," he says.

"Where's the key, Rob?" Mike asks.

Shane dislikes the heat. "You got AC in that apartment?"

"Yes," Robert says.

Then Shane asks Robert for a beer. Robert, wanting to keep Mike happy, reluctantly agrees, and Shane follows him inside.

The Minotaur kneels on the opposite side of the bike and runs his finger along the underside of the crankcase, searching for the oil leak. He lays his head nearly on the hot pavement to see along the bottoms of the chrome exhaust pipes. He straddles the motorcycle, checks the play in the clutch and both brakes. When he holds the bike upright the Minotaur is filled suddenly with the potential for movement. It frightens him.

"What do you think, M?" Mike asks.

"Mmmn."

"Listen, there's no sense in both of us roasting out here in the heat. Being a . . . I mean, you're more cut out for it than we are. Besides, you know what you're doing with the bike, and I'm just in the way. Here's the key; you look the bike over good and then come get us. That okay?"

"Unnh." The Minotaur looks at his watch. It's quarter till twelve. David expects him in fifteen minutes.

Mike puts his hand on the Minotaur's shoulder and gives him a wink. "Come on, M. Be a buddy. Help me out just this once and I'll never forget it."

Touch comes so infrequently to the Minotaur that when it happens, sincere or not, it nearly takes his breath away, blinds him momentarily to rational thought and allegiance. Mike wants his help.

There are a few basic principles that the Minotaur learned early. Combustion engines need very little to function smoothly: fuel to burn, a constant spark, oxygen to stoke the fire and a coolant to keep these others in check. Four things. But there is a precise alchemy necessary to translate these four elements into movement. To alter one is to jeopardize the whole.

The engine will not run. The Minotaur puts the key into the ignition and presses his thumb to the start button. The engine turns over once, then fires with a detectable torque to one side as the heavy cam throws the pistons out into the cylinders and yanks them back. The engine sputters, resists the throttle, then stalls. Common sense leads the Minotaur; he checks the easiest things first. He tries the engine again, and the smell of gasoline fills his nostrils, creeps into the back of his throat. It took him decades to get used to this smell. The carburetors are flooded, but that means they are getting fuel. The engine will not run, but it will fire; there is sufficient spark coming from the battery. The Minotaur thinks of the possibilities.

He takes his toolbox from the back of Shane's car, finds the ratchet and the spark plug socket easily because his tools are well ordered. When he takes the plug out of the right-side cylinder and reattaches the wire, he holds it close to the finned cylinder head and presses the start button. A minute white spark arcs back and forth.

On its kickstand the BMW leans to the left. When the Minotaur takes the spark plug from that side its threaded tip is black with carbon and wet from unburned fuel. The plug is fouled. He doesn't even have to check it, but he does anyway. There is no spark when he holds it to the cylinder and presses the ignition. This is why the motorcycle will not start—the Minotaur knows it beyond doubt. But he knows, too, that he is more comfortable here alone with the engine than he will be with the young men in the apartment. The Minotaur tinkers aimlessly until he can muster himself to face them again.

The instant he steps up to Robert's door the Minotaur knocks. He wants to avoid the potential of overheard conversation. Inside, the apartment is nearly frigid. It is also darkened, the blinds closed to thin slits. An air-conditioning unit all but fills the large window at the back of the room. It struggles mightily as it spews, in addition to ice-cold air, a cacophony of rattles and loose-belt squeaks. Shane and Mike sit at the kitchen table, its Formica top chipped and splintered at one corner, the Naugahyde seats in need of upholstery. Shane keeps pulling the curtain aside to look out the kitchen window. They both clutch beers, and there are already empty cans in the sink. After letting the Minotaur inside, Robert returns to the long desk opposite the kitchen table. Chair swiveled to face Mike and Shane, he perches nervously, drinking from an anodized aluminum cup, its yellow color refracted in the condensation coating its surface. A computer that nearly covers the desk top hums and flickers in the half-light.

As clearly as he can the Minotaur explains to Mike about the fouled spark plug. Mike takes the problem seriously. Too seriously. With exaggerated determination he flips through the phone book and locates a motorcycle repair shop, then convinces Robert that he has no hope of selling the motorcycle without a new plug.

"Unnhnn," the Minotaur says, his watch now showing one o'clock; he's wasted too much time.

"Well . . . ," Robert says. "Okay, then. Let's go."

"Aw, man! It's way too hot to go driving all over town looking for a spark plug," Shane protests. "You go."

"It *is* your motorcycle, Rob," Mike says. "And you *are* the guy trying to sell."

"Unh," the Minotaur says, mostly to himself.

"And you guys are going to stay here? In my apartment?"

"Jesus Christ, Robert." Mike feigns offense. "What do you think, that we're going to rip you off?"

"How about this?" Shane offers, looking out the window again. "We'll take a dip in your pool. Stay there until you get back."

"It's really only for residents," Robert says.

"Anybody asks," Shane says, "we moved in yesterday."

"Apartment 3C," Mike adds.

"Unnnhh."

Shane grabs the remainder of a six-pack from the refrigerator before leading them out the back door. The Minotaur doesn't want to be alone in the apartment. He feels a little hostile toward the big computer, its omnipresent humming and the periodic machinations from its bowels. Although he's never told anyone the Minotaur feels hostile toward most things electronic, even the cash register that talks to him at the grocery store. There is a threat in the very existence of such minute and exact circuitry that touches something primal in the Minotaur. He can barely tolerate the small black-and-white television he keeps on the kitchen counter of his trailer. The Minotaur follows Mike out the door, lagging behind and wishing he were helping David, or even at work, where things are more or less predictable.

It's the middle of the day. A summer day. A weekday. The Minotaur is surprised at the dozen or so people scattered around the pool, a painfully blue and painfully rectangular gouge in the earth, made even more cramped by the cement and the chain-link fence that rings it. Shane takes off his shirt as he's walking to the pool. He bunches it in his hands and, just as he jumps in the air from the side of the pool, tosses it back over his head toward the two empty chairs by the gate. Shane lands—knees drawn up, head tucked—with a big splash, whooping as he hits the water. Of the few people already in the water—two clinging to the side and talking, a couple flirting loudly in the shallow end, a woman dressed for competition and swimming the butterfly stroke—only the latter registers Shane's intrusion. She is powerful and graceful, although completely unsuited for the confines of the small unlined pool. Her body undulates in the blue water as her arms sweep the sky once, twice before she turns and kicks off the wall. *It's silly*, the Minotaur thinks, *how seriously she takes herself*.

Mike kicks his sandals off beneath one of the empty chairs,

drops his keys and wallet beside them and dives in. The Minotaur sits. The sun hangs directly overhead, scrutinizing, sweltering. The Minotaur isn't bothered by the heat even though he is unshaded and wearing a buttoned shirt—the long sleeves rolled up his forearms—his work pants and black steel-toed shoes.

When the Minotaur comes among people unexpectedly it is inevitable that his presence is disturbing to some—the woman swimming laps, for instance. When she, after completing a lap, clings to the concrete lip of the pool by the diving board catching her breath, pulls the amber-lensed goggles from her eyes, the rubber strap holding them tight to her forehead, and then sees the Minotaur, she is disturbed. Argus-like, there by the edge of the pool, she scowls with her four eyes. The woman hoists herself from the deep end, water spilling off her broad shoulders, channeling down the hard **V** of her trapezius, taut and dramatic beneath the black swimsuit, and fanning out over the small of her back before riding the hump of her solid buttocks as they rise from the pool. The woman does not look at the Minotaur again, and in not looking he is all she can see. She grabs a towel hanging over the chain-link fence, drapes it around her neck, walks all the way around the pool to avoid passing the Minotaur. She walks, dripping, up the concrete path with palpable indignation. Five thousand years ago the Minotaur would have devoured her, literally. But the Minotaur doesn't remember this.

For most the reaction isn't so strong. Conversations stop abruptly, then begin again awkwardly, with self-conscious determination. Someone says something funny, and people try not to laugh too loudly at it. Most just ignore him.

It is the hottest hour of a hot day. Around the pool people

talk, drink, read or lie quietly in their bathing suits in the baking sun. Some are sheltered behind dark glasses and headphones hooked to compact radios lying beside them. The smells of sweat and coconut oil compete in the dense air. There was a time when the Minotaur was unfazed by the sight of flesh.

When Mike and Shane emerge from the pool the Minotaur gets up from his seat so they can both have chairs. He stands against the fence behind them, his mouth dry, sweat glistening in his bullish nostrils. Mike and Shane rate all of the young women in the water and at the pool's edge according to several variables.

"What do you think, tit man? See anything you like?" Shane asks.

"Lighten up, Shane," Mike says. "Why don't you go get us a smoke?"

Shane rolls his eyes and walks out of the fenced pool area and around the building. In fact there is much around the pool that the Minotaur likes.

"You want to go for a swim?" Mike asks. "Robert's probably got some trunks that'll fit you."

"Unnh." *No.* Chlorine stings his skin. Nor will he bare so much for strangers.

Shane returns with a lit smoke hidden in his cupped hand. The smell of marijuana immediately attracts the attention of the group sitting just down from them. Two girls lie side by side in webbed lounge chairs, one on her belly with the full length of her thin golden back exposed to the sun, the other supine, the fabric of her already scant swimsuit tucked into itself so that as much of her flesh as possible is available. A young man in cutoff denim shorts sits at the foot of the chairs spraying both women with a mist bottle; the water beads on their slick oiled skin. He has a tattoo on his shoulder. When the Minotaur squints the tattoo looks like Pan squatting on his haunches, pipes to his grinning lips. But when the man turns the Minotaur sees that instead it's a bulldog in a spiked collar; *USMC*, it says. On the ground between the two lounge chairs a girl sits cross-legged on a folded towel. She wears a straw hat and completely fills a one-piece floral-print bathing suit. She leans forward, wrists resting on her knees; her ample breasts and the cleft between them are the whitest things in the Minotaur's field of vision. At her thigh lies a fat and tattered paperback.

Shane walks over and offers to share the smoke with them. They accept, and Mike joins the group. The Minotaur finds a twig, sits and begins cleaning between the treads on the thick soles of his shoes, scraping out bits of food and dirt packed in from night after night at work. The Minotaur feels the heat of the sun mostly through the metal disk of his wristwatch.

There is laughter from the group, loud and barbed. The Minotaur knows they are laughing about him. He refuses to look in their direction, concentrates on his task, working the stick in and out of the rubber grooves. They laugh again, and the Minotaur senses someone approaching in his blind spot.

"Oops," she says.

It's the girl in the hat; she's dropped her book by his feet. The Minotaur can't read the title upside down—something about *Love*—but he sees that on the wrinkled, torn and taped cover is a couple from some other time and place embracing on a rocky beach. Written in blue ink on a small red sticker in the corner is *50¢*. The Minotaur does not look up.

"Sorry about that," she says, bending to retrieve the book.

"Unnh," the Minotaur says. He hopes she will go away.

"I'm Christy," she says, sticking her hand out.

"Uunnh," he says. He gives her hand a quick shake, then lets it go.

She smells of patchouli. The Minotaur doesn't know the name, but the scent is familiar, thick and almost solid. Her calves are lean and long, and circling the finely boned ankle is a tattoo of the alphabet: *ABCDEFG* . . . The Minotaur concentrates on not breathing too loudly through his nose.

"Listen," she says. "Why are you over here all by yourself? Why don't you come sit with us? Have a friendly toke, maybe."

The Minotaur loosens what seems to be a small piece of gristle from between the treads, holds it up to his eye on the tip of the stick. Christy kneels at his feet. She takes the twig and flicks it over the fence. Christy moves her head until the Minotaur is looking directly into her eyes.

"Your friends tell me you're a tit man."

He hears Shane giggling.

Christy, kneeling, leans forward, close; she presses her breasts together with her arms. Christy grins slyly.

"Do these," she asks, inhaling, filling and lifting her diaphragm, "meet your approval?"

The Minotaur is slow to anger. Most of the time he prefers to just endure, knowing that each painful moment will inevitably pass away. The Minotaur doesn't answer Christy. The apple-white flesh of her breasts, moving almost imperceptibly with each beat of her heart, is mere inches from his mouth and his flared nostrils.

More laughter.

Christy rises, takes the Minotaur's hand, places it on her

belly just beneath the ladder of ribs. With both of her hands she guides the Minotaur's hand up until it cups her breast. The left breast. The breast that protects her heart. The fabric of her swimsuit is damp and cool, reptilian. The Minotaur cannot feel the heartbeat.

"Of course," she says, "if you need a closer look . . ."

The Minotaur is slow to anger. But when Christy bares her tit, her right tit, and lifts it not like a part of her body but more like an item of merchandise, teasing the Minotaur with its round, chalk-white closeness, when the laughter of Shane and the others storms his eardrums, when the stink of patchouli and sweat and tanning lotion clots in his throat, takes his breath, the Minotaur angers. Five thousand years ago he would have devoured them all. These pitifully arrogant boys and girls would have quaked at the mere mention of his name. One by one they would have been tossed into his chambered pit, oblations to rage or scapegoats to what is most base in man. Five thousand years ago Christy's milk-white breast would not have been so willingly procured for the Minotaur's black mouth. Five thousand years ago he would have welcomed it, would have tasted it on his thick bull's tongue, taken it between the fleshy lips and into his very capable teeth. Five thousand years ago the Minotaur would have bitten her breast off, chewed through her ribs and eaten her heart.

"Unh!" the Minotaur snorts loudly, then stands.

Christy, surprised and afraid, stumbles backward and falls into the pool, her bare breast flopping. The Minotaur takes a deep breath and turns to the others. For a split second they are quiet. There is a flash of fear in Shane's eyes. The potential for chaos exists.

"Be cool, M," Mike says, and laughs nervously.

The man with the tattoo helps Christy get her hat out of the pool. Shane remains silent. There was a time when this would not have—could not have—happened. The Minotaur leaves the pool.

Robert is coming out the door with a single spark plug in his hand as the Minotaur walks up.

"Unnh," he says, grabbing the plug. The Minotaur's head is thick with anger and embarrassment; thoughts race and refuse to be made sense of. But he is used to this state of mind. He walks into the parking lot and twists the spark plug into the cylinder head of the motorcycle.

Mike walks up just as he is about to press the ignition. "Hey, M, Shane was just being his normal jerky self back there."

"Unn," the Minotaur says, and starts the bike. He props it, idling unsteadily, on its kickstand and climbs into the backseat of Shane's car to wait.

CHAPTER 6

"*S*orry," *the Minotaur says* with great effort when David opens the door.

By the time he gets to the apartment, deep in the city's east side, it is raining; summer heat boils up into the sky, liquefies, and returns to earth only a few degrees cooler. Everything steams.

The Minotaur stands on the porch, hot rain riding down the curves of his horns and disappearing in multiple rivulets into the folds of flesh at his neck. The morning's altercation has soured his stomach as well as his mood.

"Late," he says, believing that it's important to acknowledge one's failures.

David, wearing sneakers, slacks and a short-sleeve pullover, the daytime equivalent of his maître d's tux and cummerbund, has the perpetually out-of-place look of a man for whom every-body and everything comes late. He is weary but forgiving.

"Come in out of the rain, M."

Most of what remains in the apartment is stacked or piled in the front room.

"I've taken everything except for the big stuff and my few treasures," David says.

The Minotaur stands in the open door and looks at the empty walls of the small apartment. A blue bookcase, bare, skele-tal, leans to one side against a stack of boxes. Two, maybe three trips, he thinks, even with the hatch open and things tied to the roof. Outside, the downpour intensifies momentarily, then less-ens at the precise moment when the clouds break high above the city skyline. The sun spills through the crack, shafts of bril-liant yellow-white penetrating the gray rain and falling solidly to the earth below. Backlit for an absurdly mythical instant, the Minotaur casts a shadow across the room. David's ottoman, the small upholstered rocking chair with sagging springs and swan's neck armrests, carved heads embedded with faux jewel eyes, the coffee table, an old tattered map with skirmish lines and notes for battle pressed beneath its glass top, the boxes of books stacked and in order, the drab padlocked footlocker—all of David's possessions are consumed in the belly of the Minotaur's shadow. Across the naked wall opposite the door the silhouette of the Minotaur looms, horns stretched from one corner to the other.

"Ooo," David says. "The Devil must be beating his wife."

"Unnh?" the Minotaur asks.

"When the sun shines and it rains at the same time they say

the Devil is beating his wife."

"Mmm."

They decide to wait until the rain subsides before moving anything. David doesn't want his stuff to get wet.

"Come help me for a second," David says.

The Minotaur follows him down a short narrow hall to the bedroom. The tiny closet is empty. The bed stands against one wall and extends into the center of the small room, covering all the available floor space but the narrow aisles along one side and at the foot. The headboard, a shallow arc divided by white enameled bars, rises beyond the stacked pillows and disappears behind heavy drapes on one side.

The Minotaur manages a smile, but it's unrecognizable on his black lips, so David can't tell.

"Unnh."

"Like them?" David asks, knowing right away to what the Minotaur is referring.

David's sheets are illustrated with pro wrestlers—nearly life-size, muscled, outlandishly costumed, garishly colored, names emblazoned beneath them. Hulk, Bonecrusher and The Claw grimace, flex, glare from David's bed.

"A man needs to feel safe when he sleeps," David says, laughing, a little embarrassed.

Again the Minotaur works for a sympathetic smile. They strip the sheets from the bed. David folds them neatly and puts them in one of the boxes in the living room. Together they stand the mattress on its side, along with the sheet of plywood for extra support and the box springs. David has to find a hammer to get the rails unhooked from the headboard.

"Bad back," David says of the plywood.

"Unnh."

By the time they move the disassembled bed into the front room it has stopped raining. At David's direction the Minotaur begins loading boxes into the Vega's open hatchback. David tapes a handwritten sign—*Free*—to the headboard and leans it against a tree. The mattress and box springs will not fit in the car; David hunts some twine so they can tie them to the roof. In less than half an hour the car is full, its aged suspension sagging under the weight.

"I'll put the rest of the boxes in my car, then you can follow me over."

"Unnh."

David's new apartment is only a few miles away, at the edge of a gentrified area where fifty years ago textile mills and mill houses sprawled and the stinking creeks ran the color of the day's dye lot. Up a flight of tight narrow steps are his three rooms and a bath, one of two apartments over a storefront. The storefront window is draped with multicolored beads, and hanging in one corner is an old illuminated sign flickering its crowded message: *Sister Obediah's Psychic Readings—Karma, Past Lives, Tarot, Palms, Dreamwork, Predictions & Forecast on Business Marriage Love Health, Astral Travel. Avbl. For Parties.*

Past Lives. For a few blessed moments the Minotaur dreams of unburdening himself of his history. As for Predictions & Forecast he is less eager.

"She's my neighbor," David says, noticing the Minotaur's careful study of Obediah's supernatural bill of fare.

"Hunh?" the Minotaur responds, not wanting to seem too interested.

"Obediah. She lives in the other apartment, across the hall. I think she has her own stairway down into her store."

"Mmmn."

Getting the ponderous mattress up the staircase is a struggle. The Minotaur bears the brunt of its weight on his substantial shoulder while David backs up one step at a time. The rest of the stuff in the car they unload quickly, hindered only by David's indecision as to where to put things.

"We ought to be able to get everything else this next trip," David says. "I'll just leave my car here."

The Minotaur is hungry. It's nearly five o'clock. There was a time when he ate only once every seven years. He gorged himself, ravenously devoured all that was given to him, then waited anxiously for the next distant feeding. That time is long gone, and the Minotaur cannot recall it. Now, in almost human fashion, hunger gnaws at him every four or five hours. Crawls up from his belly, clouds his thoughts and hammers incessantly at his occipital bone until he concedes to eat.

"Ummnh," he says.

"Let's just get the rest of my stuff, then I'll buy you dinner. Okay?"

Back at the old apartment they strap the bookcase to the roof of the Vega; the ottoman and the rocking chair barely fit into the back, the hatch gaping wide and straining against the taut bungee cords. The Minotaur pulls the car keys from his pocket and opens the driver's door.

"Give me a minute," David says, hurrying back into the apartment.

The Minotaur watches him through the open door. David walks into the back room and comes out seconds later carrying a large box with something wrapped in plastic folded atop it. David hesitates, then looks around before setting the box on the damp porch to lock his door for the last time. He drops the key through the mail slot. As David carries the box to the car, walking carefully, the Minotaur gets out to open the door for him.

"Thanks, M," David says, resting the box on the passenger seat. It's some kind of uniform, the thing in plastic. Gray and woolen. The Minotaur does not recognize the insignia. David drapes the uniform flat over the ottoman in the back of the car.

The large box has its lids interfolded so that its contents— all except for what must be the tip and several inches of the blade of a bayonet protruding dangerously from one corner— are hidden. Despite the narrow bucket seat, despite the fact that the box presses against both the hand brake lever on the center hump and the passenger door handle, despite the precise maneuvering he has to do to ensure that the blade points back between the seats, sharp edge down, David clutches the box protectively on his lap.

"Sorry," David says, eyeing the bayonet. "The handle is pretty fragile. It needs some work, and I don't have a scabbard yet."

The Minotaur is conscious of the blade between the seats as he drives. With his head cocked a little so he can see to drive, he has a pretty clear view of the box with his right eye. David notices him looking.

"It's from the Civil War," David says, momentarily assuming the Minotaur will know to which one he refers. "Eighteen sixty-one to 1865, the American Civil War. More than six hundred thousand Americans were killed—more than in all our other wars combined."

"Mmmm," the Minotaur says, genuinely curious.

"All this stuff, all these things are actual artifacts from different battlefields. Mostly Confederate."

Sensing the Minotaur's interest David eagerly tells him about the contents of the box as they drive. He waxes nostalgic, as if he were actually there some hundred and twenty-five years ago. Reverently, like a devotee or a docent, he displays his sacred loot: medals of valor and honor; documents, battle plans and blood-spattered personal missives; bullets whole and bullets misshapen from impact with bone, each shard a testament of aggression. The Minotaur didn't know David as a teacher—doesn't, in fact, have much experience with teachers of any kind. But listening to David talk passionately about his treasures, the Minotaur feels that the teacher's role must have come naturally to him.

They arrive at the new apartment before David has a chance to show everything. Rather than carry the heavy chair, the ottoman and the bookcase from the parking lot in back of the building, the Minotaur decides to pull into the bus stop and turn the flashers on long enough for them to get David's things to the sidewalk by the front door. The Minotaur cuts the twine with his pocketknife, and they lift the bookcase from the Vega's roof. He and David set the furniture between the door to the apartments and the door to Obediah's storefront. David waits, sitting on the edge of the rocking chair and clutching his box of memorabilia, while the Minotaur moves the car.

"Are you sure you can get that?" David asks when the Minotaur picks up the rocking chair by its arms and pulls it to his chest.

"Unnh."

"Stud," David teases. "I'll follow you with this box, then we'll take the bookcase up together."

David holds the door for the Minotaur, then struggles to keep it open for himself while he bends to pick up the heavy box. The Minotaur moves slowly, up one step at a time, taking care not to scratch the walls with the rockers. David is close behind and patient. Just as the Minotaur nears the top of the flight of stairs the door to the adjacent apartment opens. It's Obediah. It must be.

"Lordgodamighty!" the woman says, as if it is a single word, an incantation or a curse. It would stand to reason that someone so willing to look into the future would not be shocked by looking at the past. But the thin pale woman of indeterminate age, this mock-gypsy with the green silk scarf covering her skull, riding low across her forehead, pulled down to the edge of her manicured brows, her eyelashes so long, thick and black they could be mistaken for the limbs of some mutant insect, this woman who stands in the doorway of apartment number 2, the smell of fried fish wafting from within, who unwittingly looks into the cavernous huffing nostrils and the obsidian eyes of the Minotaur, his bull head looming over the back of the rocking chair as he comes up the steps—she is taken by surprise.

"Lordgodamighty!" she says again, then slams the door.

The Minotaur startles, stumbles backwards. Before he can catch himself the tip of his right horn gouges several inches of the Sheetrock wall. David, too close for safety, refuses to relinquish the space he occupies with his sacred box. He will not willingly move from the path of the falling Minotaur and risk dropping his package. The only thing that prevents David from being crushed is the Minotaur's innate ability to right himself under burden, an ability that holds true even when he's lugging a chair up a narrow stairway. The Minotaur stumbles backward, and at the very instant his horn digs into the plaster the tip of David's bayonet jutting out of the box presses against his scapula. The Minotaur feels the fabric of his shirt resist, then give, feels the edge of the blade ride up his back. According to David this weapon has known flesh before; it was unearthed at Manassas still in the skeletal hands of a Rebel soldier, and around him lay the remains of three Yanks. Today, however, on these stairs, the bayonet is more forgiving. The Minotaur feels it barely scratch the surface of his hide before he stabilizes himself.

It takes them only a few minutes to bring the rest of David's stuff upstairs. David is apologetic to a fault; he insists on putting Merthiolate, a fire-orange antiseptic tincture, on the cut. The Minotaur protests that it's barely a scratch but eventually submits so that David won't feel even more guilty. He sits upright in a kitchen chair with the wide collar of his shirt unbuttoned and one shoulder exposed. The Minotaur winces from the medicine's sting, more because it seems the right thing to do than out of real pain.

When David goes for sandwiches the Minotaur stays at the apartment. He wanders mindlessly in and out of the rooms and eventually out into the hall, where he stands before the neighbor's door. Nothing about the exterior of that door—not its maroon paint chipped away in places to reveal the blue beneath, not its tiny peephole installed just off-center, not even the nameplate, *O. Johnson*—suggests the power of the apartment's occupant. The Minotaur considers knocking on the door, considers Obediah's possible reactions. She could ignore him and not open the door at all. She could throw open the maroon door in rage. Or she could open the door armed with the knowledge of his future. The Minotaur has known his share of clairvoyants and soothsayers. But having outlived most of them by centuries he's come to distrust their claims. Nevertheless, within himself, he feels a change coming—looming, familiar, inevitable change. What he would like from Obediah is validation of his current sense of the impending, a ratification of his fear. With that he might be more ready when change comes.

But instead of knocking the Minotaur slinks quietly down the steps to his car. From his toolbox he takes a half-full container of Spakle paste and a putty knife. He repairs the gouge in the stairwell wall with a little more noise than necessary, so Obediah won't be surprised again. He scrapes the white paste flush with the wall and makes a mental note to sand it smooth the next time he comes over.

The Minotaur is curious at heart, but over the years he has learned to keep his curiosity in check, learned that most of the time wondering is far more satisfying and far less dangerous than knowing. Nevertheless, when David doesn't come back right away, the Minotaur cannot stop himself from going back into the apartment and examining David's possessions, working his way eventually to the box that sits on the kitchen table, the slightest patina of blood gilding the edge of the blade protruding from its closed top.

What the Minotaur finds, what David didn't tell him about earlier, are the photographs. Not the grainy blurred photos of maimed and bloated bodies taken in wartime; those he saw. These photographs, sheathed in plastic, are newer. Men charging away from or toward the camera, rifles flashing. At the bottom of the stack is a picture of a soldier posing alone, standing in full uniform, his weapon held at his chest. Looking closer, head cocked, the Minotaur notices an incongruity. The soldier poses by a rail fence in front of a leafless tree. But in the corner of the photograph, almost out of the frame, is the fender of a car. A Buick Electra, it looks like to the Minotaur, 1980 or thereabouts. Not until he digs further in the box and finds an artificially aged company roster of the First North Carolina State Troops does the Minotaur realize that he is looking at pictures of a younger David. His name is there, near the bottom of the list. He is a sergeant. Suddenly afraid of getting caught the Minotaur puts all the stuff back in the box and sits at the kitchen table waiting.

David returns with the food, and the Minotaur eats all he is given.

"Did you have enough?" David asks.

"Unnh," the Minotaur says, lying.

"Thanks a lot for helping me out. I owe you."

"Unnnh."

David excuses himself and disappears down the hall toward the bathroom. The Minotaur wants to leave but decides he should wait for David to come back. In the meantime he mindlessly flips through an open box of musty-smelling yellowed novels and old history texts. The Minotaur thinks for a moment about pocketing a book.

"I didn't know you were a reader," David says, coming back into the room. The Minotaur feels caught in the act. Water gurgles in the apartment's pipes.

"See anything you like?" David asks. "I've got some real classics."

The Minotaur doesn't respond, only shakes his head slightly.

"Here," David says, moving the top two boxes, then reaching into a third to find the book he has in mind.

Candy. The book is called *Candy.*

"If this doesn't put some levity in your soul, then nothing will." David lays the book in the Minotaur's hand. "Just don't tell anybody where you got it," he says.

When the Minotaur gets into his car the novel slips between the bucket seat and the cracked plastic console that houses an ashtray, two sticky cupholders and the hand brake. Within a half-mile he forgets the book is there.

CHAPTER 7

*B*y *the time the Minotaur* returns to his home the day has worn him thin. It is nearly dusk. The Maverick is gone from Sweeny's front yard, a rectangle of yellowed overgrown grass in its place. Over the rooftops of the house and the trailers chimney swifts by the dozens arc wildly through the fading sunlight, their sharp black silhouettes careening toward, then away from, the earth. Then again and again. It's a hot night, and Sweeny is walking around the backyard in his boxer shorts. No one cares.

"Evening, M," Sweeny says, and follows it with a deep wet belch.

Lucky-U Mobile Estates is a kind of haven. Although defining Sweeny's tenants in terms of similarities is difficult, generally speaking they are all part of a diaspora of sorts. A nebulous group compromised by situation, by strings of bad decisions each perpetuating the next, or compromised simply by the circumstances of their births, these are settlers.

To settle. Settled. Settling. To fix or resolve definitely and conclusively; to agree upon (as in time or conditions). To place in a desired state or in order. To furnish with residents. To quiet, calm or bring to rest. To stop from annoying or opposing. To cause (dregs, sediment, etc.) to sink or be deposited. To dispose of finally; close up. To decide, arrange or agree. To come to rest, as from flight: *The bird settled on a bough*. To gather, collect or become fixed in a particular place, direction, etc. (Of a female animal) to become pregnant; conceive. To become established in some routine, especially upon marrying, after a period of independence or indecision. To apply oneself for serious work. To settle for; to be satisfied with: *To settle for less*.

All of which suggests an intent or a determined quality that is not manifest in their lives. A gritty resignation permeates Lucky-U and its inhabitants, the Minotaur included.

Of the five mobile homes, Sweeny usually has three or four occupied at any given time, using the vacancies to make the necessary—and only the necessary—repairs. Transient in nature, his people come and go, and return tenants are more than welcome. Sweeny almost expects it; he knows all too well the path of false starts and wrong choices and sees Lucky-U as a sort of halfway house or a steppingstone to bigger and better things. It is a hopeful point of view.

Tonight all but one of Sweeny's trailers are being lived in, and quite a lot of that living spills out into the yards. Sweeny barters. Sweeny wheels and deals, with his tenants and almost everyone else. For Mrs. Smith, an aging Japanese woman who came to Lucky-U with her AMVET husband seventeen years ago and stayed behind when he left ten years later, who lives beside the Minotaur and holds the seniority title, Sweeny shops for groceries in exchange for a weekly plate of *potstickers*, the little fried dumplings he'd come to love in the war he had briefly taken part in so many years ago. She never comes out of her trailer, never leaves her bedroom as far as the Minotaur can tell, but spills out in the aural sense. Her bedroom is situated just beyond his kitchen window. All day long and way into the night, whenever the Minotaur is at home, the television plays either stock-car racing or one of the Christian channels.

Beside Mrs. Smith are the newest residents of Lucky-U, who are more often out of their trailer than in. A young couple and its two sons moved in at the beginning of the summer. The parents, seemingly little more than children themselves, chronically unemployed and always at home, seem far more devoted to their own private pursuits than to the raising of their children. Josie, their mother, tans. Every day, in sun or the mere promise of it, she makes the trek into the weedy backyard; portable radio, various tanning oils and a liter of generic cola in hand, she pitches camp at the webbed lounge chair in full recline, turning from belly to back, back to belly at precise intervals, getting up only to reposition the chair for optimal exposure.

The boys' father, Hank, doesn't tan. Not intentionally. But all the hours that Hank spends at his weight bench, a rickety thing of bent tubing and Naugahyde standing a little lopsided at the opposite end of the trailer from Josie's chair, leaning to one side on the sloping yard in the dead center of a semicircle of packed red dirt where the previous tenants' bluetick hound was chained, all that time in the sun keeps him sufficiently golden. And well sculpted, above the waist anyway. Hank never seems to exercise his legs; the Minotaur is acutely aware of disproportion.

At night the whole family gathers in the front yard, where Hank, having removed the screen from the trailer's front window, has positioned the television so it can be seen from outside. They sit on the cracked concrete slab that is the front porch, around a table, a large upended wooden spool made for heavy cable that Hank stole from a previous job, in folding lawn chairs and washed in the light that flickers from the picture tube.

Hank and Josie think it sufficient, when they're actually paying attention, to shriek their parental decrees at eight-year-old Jules and Marvin, who turns seven in a week, from their separate stations, so the entire trailer park knows when it's time for the boys to bathe or eat, and what Jules should stop doing to Marvin, and the consequences of not stopping. Left to their own devices the boys have spent most of the summer months disassembling an abandoned washing machine at the back of the Lucky-U property, Jules ultimately convincing Marvin to climb into the perforated drum for a ride. Compared to their parents the boys are quiet, and seem to talk only to each other. Twice now, hushed and conspiratorial, they have let Buddy out of his run without permission.

The empty mobile home on the opposite side of the Minotaur from Mrs. Smith is under renovation. Sort of. Sweeny has decided to go upscale on this property, maybe charge a little higher rent and attract a different class of tenant, for the sake of balance, of course. It is the only air-conditioned trailer. Sweeny got a mammoth window unit, circa 1975, *Property of Piedmont College* stenciled on the side, as partial payment for a conversion van he sold awhile back. The old air conditioner was far too big for any of the windows in the trailer, so Sweeny spent an entire morning with a Sawz-All cutting a hole through the back wall near the roof. It took the rest of the afternoon for him to build a two-by-four scaffold to hold the air conditioner in place, and he had to wait around until some of the tenants came home to help him hoist it up. When he plugged it in and threw the switch the lights in the rest of Lucky-U dimmed, and the noise from the compressor was nearly deafening. That effort dissuaded him from making other structural changes in the trailer; he decided the rest of his remodeling would be of a more cosmetic nature.

He took the old UPS panel truck he'd bought a few years ago to the flea market that operates every other weekend in the parking lot of the Fox Triple-X Drive-In. He knew a guy there who set up shop alongside the cinder-block concession stand, a guy who sold some pretty high-class furniture. Sweeny got a whole truckload of furnishings—a double reclining settee, an oak-veneer wall unit with mirrored doors, a brass-plated floor lamp, matching swags and more—for less than a thousand dollars.

Outside the trailer Sweeny wanted some sense of delineation. He marked out the property lines with planters made out of truck tires turned inside out, pinked with a sawtooth pattern around the top edge and painted stark white; he's still looking for something to plant in them. He placed lawn statuary of unpainted concrete on either side of the front door and scattered other pieces in the yard: a squat Buddha, a family of absurdly cute deer, a robed caryatid deftly baring one breast and supporting a large urn. A horseshoe pit was already laid out in the side yard; Sweeny set a park bench for spectators and players under a struggling dogwood tree. He's been advertising on one of the late-night cable stations and has put some fliers up at the grocery store. And there is always word of mouth. Community. On good days the Minotaur feels it.

It was D. W. Crews who helped Sweeny lift the air conditioner. D. W. lives with his two brothers in the remaining occupied trailer, which sits at a right angle to Sweeny's house at the far end of the horseshoe. Sweeny allowed the brothers to scrape out a section of the field behind their trailer and pour a load of gravel, so they would have a place to park the stake-bed truck with the hydraulic boom crane and the calipered claw behind the cab, along with the long flatbed on which they haul the calfdozer, the chain saws and their other tools. On the doors of both mud-spattered trucks is *Crews Bros. Logging & Pulpwood Co.*, hand-painted by J. C., the oldest brother. They don't own any other vehicles, so when they have errands or shopping to do they drive one of the big trucks, all three of them squeezed into the cab.

The Minotaur met the brothers—D. W., J. C. and A. J.— shortly after moving in at Lucky-U. The brothers, who like to play horseshoes, have rigged a couple of droplights to nearby clothesline poles so that they can play at night. Sometimes on Saturday afternoons A. J. ties Buddy to the bumper of one of the trucks with a short rope, then sits on the ground picking bloated gray ticks off the dog as it lies passively between his knees. A. J. drops the parasites into an inch or so of gasoline in the bottom of a mason jar, where they die instantly. On the

Minotaur's first Sunday at Lucky-U he was changing the oil in his car while D. W. and J. C. drank beer and pitched horseshoes. The men and the Minotaur looked one another over for a while as inconspicuously as possible, pretending to be focused on the task or game at hand, and when eye contact accidentally occurred each gave a curt and manly nod of the head.

There are very few men who are not drawn to, seduced by, challenged by, even beguiled by things revealed, by the display of things that, as a rule or by design or in the name of decorum, are kept hidden from view. For some men this can be the maze of circuitry and the snug clusters of multicolored resistors in the back of any television set or computer. For others it is the joints, the ligaments and tendons, the organs of living things. Still others are taken in by the impalpable workings of the mind and the emotions, confessed or coerced. And then there are men who are drawn to the open hood of a car, any car. The Crews brothers fall readily into this category.

"She acting up?" D. W. asked that Sunday morning as the Minotaur contorted to get the thin band of the oil filter wrench in place low at the back of the engine.

"Oil change," the Minotaur answered.

"Hmm," J. C. said, craning his neck to get a look beneath the hood.

Close up the first thing the Minotaur noticed were the mosquito bites. Both the men standing over him had bad bites, swollen red welts ringed with yellow, on their faces, foreheads and arms. Both men, however, seemed oblivious to any itching. A. J., the youngest Crews and decidedly the least mosquito-bitten, then walked up, and the four of them talked about car maintenance, then truck upkeep, then finally about the various requirements of chain saw engines. J. C. and A. J. argued about how to best sharpen the loops of the metal teeth. The Minotaur learned a lot about the pulpwood business—how they bought the access rights to rural wooded properties, then went in with their trucks and equipment and cut all the salable trees and saplings. A. J. had the fewest bites because he spent most of his time hauling truckloads of logs from the various work sites to the Cherokee Paper Mill up in the mountains. When he came home he stank of sulfur.

Again, community. Having just arrived in the area the Minotaur had not found a job yet. He spent the mornings and evenings doing repairs for Sweeny and had watched or heard the logging trucks leave just before sunrise and return near suppertime for several days. That Sunday morning D. W. asked the Minotaur if he wanted to ride along the next day to see if he liked logging work, and the Minotaur said yes. At six-thirty the next morning he was sitting in the filthy cab of the crane truck with A. J., who talked nonstop about breeding white mice. He'd heard that science classes at the college bought white mice for lab experiments and that there was always a market for mice as food for pet snakes and such.

"Know what they call them?" he asked the Minotaur just as they pulled off a winding blacktop road on to a rutted treacherous-looking dirt path that cut an all-but-invisible notch out of the high kudzu-draped pines lining the side of the road. In the half-light of dawn the Minotaur didn't even notice the opening. "Know what they call the baby mice?"

"Unnh?"

"Pinkies. They call the little hairless fuckers pinkies. Feed them to the little snakes." All he had to do was convince D. W. and J. C. to let him build the cages along one wall of his bedroom.

The dense green kudzu covered the ground at the base of the trees, climbed the trunks, filled the branches and spread from treetop to treetop, forming an impenetrable cloak between the road and what lay beyond the trees. The Minotaur has seen much in his life, much of what men were capable of doing to each other and to the earth. Little surprises him. But when they pulled through the notch in the thick choking weeds and into the rising sun, the Minotaur was unprepared for what he saw— acres and acres of ravaged earth, hill after mud-red hill, rutted, stripped of all but the thinnest and weakest trees. Nothing green remained. The undergrowth was trampled and torn; some of the tree stumps were jagged and toothlike, others cut clean at ground level, their ringed faces like giant misshapen coins littering the landscape.

"This field is almost finished," A. J. said, then bragged about how they could strip ten acres in a day.

The Minotaur spent the morning helping to steady the logs as they were lifted from the ground onto the bed of the truck, struggling with the heavy iron chain that held them in place. In the brief moments of silence, when the engines were stopped and the chain saw was cooling off, the Minotaur was aware of the absence of other sounds. No birds. No squirrels. No insects except for the incessant mosquitoes. At lunch, while the Crewses sat in the cabs of the trucks, each of them eating three cans of Vienna sausages with saltine crackers and turning the empty cans up to drink the congealed meat-flavored jelly in the bottoms, the Minotaur sat alone, eating an onion in the shade of one of the trucks. He leaned against a back tire and picked at a splinter in his palm. When the snake dropped on him from somewhere overhead his first reaction was to bite its head off. Not until his teeth were halfway through its neck did he realize the snake was made of rubber and had been dropped on him by A. J., who crouched in the back of the truck grinning, his laughter tamed a little by the Minotaur's reaction. The Minotaur spat the rubber snake's head out and forced a smile. He liked a practical joke as well as any man. The Minotaur did not like the pulp-wood business, though. He stayed with the Crews brothers for the rest of that week, then decided to look for kitchen work.

The day has been interminable. The Minotaur is tired from helping David move, weary and still on edge from the rage and embarrassment he felt at the swimming pool. Day to day the Minotaur's existence is tiresome. When he pulls his car to a stop in front of his boat-shaped mobile home and Sweeny belches at him, the Minotaur is glad to be there. It's almost dark. Jules and Marvin have devised some sort of war game with the agitator from the old washing machine and are playing loudly around the trailers. The Minotaur can hear the solid clink of iron against iron, horseshoe against stake, sounding over the roof of the empty trailer, and the loud talk of the Crews brothers.

As Sweeny walks up, the Minotaur hears the rapid *scritch scritch* of Buddy's claws against the aluminum storm door as he tries to get out of the house, then the squeal of stretching springs as the door swings open.

"Buddy!" Sweeny shouts. "Goddammit, Buddy! Come here, boy!"

Sweeny, as he has dozens of times before, offers a leg to

the charging bulldog, bounces on the ball of his foot until the animal leaps up and begins to hump, its jowls frothing, snorting and sucking air, eyes rolling wildly.

"Get off me!" Sweeny says, bringing the display to its familiar halt. Buddy gives only a slight yelp in protest, then limps almost proudly beneath the back porch.

"I love that damn dog," Sweeny says. "Listen, M, that old Belair I picked up last week, I think the universal joint is going bad. Can you look at it one day this week? Maybe go to Bunyan's and get a replacement?"

The Minotaur agrees. He says good night. Inside the trailer he opens all his windows as wide as the cranks will allow so that the sounds of his neighbors' lives will filter in.

CHAPTER 8

The Minotaur taught himself to sew. Years ago, too far back to remember, the Minotaur resolved to cover his nakedness, resigned himself to the continuous struggle of repair and up-keep. Robes and togas were easy to wear. Then, when fashion changed, finding pants and shoes to fit wasn't a problem, but the breadth of his shoulders and the circumference of his bullish neck meant that shirts and coats had to be radically altered to fit him. Often it meant buying two garments and cannibalizing one for the sake of the other.

The Minotaur is comfortable with shears, thimbles and needles. He knows all the important stitches. Sometimes the Minotaur doesn't sleep. Sometimes the dreams are too much to face. This happens most often after a trying day, when the weight of his years and the weight of his difference seem to rest fully on the wide plane between his horns, to spread along the slope of his neck and across his muscled shoulders, to press down on the weakest and most human part of him, threatening to crush his legs. When the Minotaur can't sleep he finds something to mend. Sometimes he sews until morning.

Closing the trailer door, opening the windows to allow the presence of Sweeny, the Crewses and the others in Lucky-U into his night, the Minotaur knows he will not sleep. It's hot in the trailer; the rectangular design with narrow windows placed high in metal walls resists ventilation. But the Minotaur is eager for the sounds of his neighbors, so he doesn't turn on the fans. From a table squeezed into the space between the couch and the slender bar where the Minotaur sits to drink his morning coffee, a lamp made from a liquor bottle shaped like an anchor propped in a coil of thick rope casts more shadow than light. Even in his own home the Minotaur is most at ease in low light. In the bedroom's darkness he undresses. He takes his shirt off, and standing by the window in the faint blue-gray wash from the street lamp that Sweeny got from a disgruntled city worker—the street lamp that stands not quite plumb just above the mimosa trees in the center island of the Lucky-U drive, its commitment to illumination sporadic at best—the Minotaur worms a fingertip through the hole in the fabric, inspecting the damage done by David's sword. The Minotaur lays the shirt out on the bed.

In his pants pocket he finds the list, written this morning, now crumpled. The Minotaur draws the list twice across the edge of his chest of drawers, smoothing the wrinkled paper as best he can. At the foot of the bed the Minotaur places his steel-toed shoes side by side. Naked, he is ready for the bath.

Because the Minotaur's horns and shoulders are broad and the tub is cramped and narrow, with a low shower head, he brings a plastic milk crate into the tub so he can sit sideways, so he isn't forever banging his horns against the fiberglass wall. Because it was a hot day and the heat lingers in the airless trailer far into the night, the Minotaur sits under a cold shower. Because of the day, and because the Minotaur is who he is, he sits on the plastic milk crate sideways in his tub under the cold spray of water for a very long time.

The Minotaur's ablutions are simple and well rehearsed. He doesn't need light to perform them. After toweling himself dry, still naked, the Minotaur sits at the edge of the tub. With a small oval currycomb held to his palm by a worn leather band, he strokes the furred bovine parts of his body. He pulls the metal teeth of the comb over the swells of muscle and ridges of bone—the skull, the long jaw, chin, dewlap, neck, shoulders—gently at first, barely rippling the dense black hair, then deeper, digging all the way to the pigmented skin. The Minotaur draws his fingertips through an open tin of conditioning oil that he buys in bulk from a veterinarian, works the soothing emollient beneath the fur and into the skin, his fingers pressing in tight perfect circles. The Minotaur's skin, raked by the currycomb and stinging, welcomes the cooling oil. His many crevices and folds of flesh are prone to drying and cracking; the Minotaur is slow and thorough. At the place of transition where the Minotaur becomes man, beneath the breastbone where the ribs begin to drop away, he uses a medicinal balm. Over the years, despite his willingness to try new creams and curatives, the line remains tender, painful at times. The temperature of the scarlike ribbon and the flesh around it, bullish gray on one side, milky, translucent and human on the other, always seems a few degrees hotter than anywhere else on the Minotaur's body, as if the fusion is still in process.

The Minotaur's horns require special care as well. From time to time someone, either churlish or simply inquisitive, will ask, "Why don't you just saw the damn things off?" Sometimes he wishes he could. But it's not that simple. Like all horned ungulates the Minotaur needs his horns, no longer as weapons in his case, but rather for visual orientation. The wide-set tips loom like twin guideposts on the perimeter of his field of vision, framing his immediate world and keeping things in perspective. After a bath his horns are easier to groom. With his pocketknife he pares away the splinters on the curved shafts. He shaves and trims the cuticular skin at the base of each. Then, steadying one horn at a time with his free hand and using coursegrained sandpaper in a twisting motion, he readies the horns for finishing. To complete the ritual the Minotaur employs emery cloth to polish each horn to a marble smoothness. Once every couple of months he uses a clear nail hardener, shoplifted out of shame from the cosmetics counter at the drugstore. He uses almost a whole bottle each time, and the lingering smell gives him a headache for days.

The Minotaur finds clean pajamas folded neatly in the bottom dresser drawer. He tends to chafe in the heat, so before slipping the pajamas on he dusts his groin and backside with talcum powder. From the top drawer he pulls a shoebox small enough for a woman's shoes, its top and edges reinforced with duct tape. The Minotaur takes the shoebox and his shirt into the

kitchen and sits at the table. When he lifts the lid, the pincush-
ion—shaped like an apple, with a thin stem and one green leaf—
rests amid spools of thread, almost pulsing in its redness. He
wets a white strand of thread with one rolling swipe across his
fat tongue, pulls it to a point between pliant lips. The Minotaur
cocks his head sharply, threads the needle on the first try, pushes
the thimble on to his index finger and, with a slip stitch, begins
to suture the rip in his shirt.

　　The Minotaur finishes quickly. He looks through his closet
and drawers, even the laundry hamper, for things to mend. Several of his work pants have small tears. He knows of at least
three missing buttons, and a zipper worked free of its teeth and
gaping. By the time the Minotaur sits down to sew again he has
a small stack of projects laid out on the table. It's nearly ten
o'clock, and the sounds drifting in his window from Lucky-U
Mobile Estates are the sounds of night.

　　From the Crewses' trailer comes silence, the horseshoes
resting wherever they fell on the last toss. On weeknights they
go to bed just after dark. On Fridays and Saturdays it's not uncommon for them to stay out in the yard until after midnight,
drinking, working on the trucks and sometimes, though there
is no detectable threat, firing their pistols into the air. But on
weeknights all three Crews brothers turn in early.

　　The Minotaur hears Sweeny call Buddy in for the night,
hears, from Sweeny's back porch, the sounds of kibbled dog food
poured into a shallow metal pot. The Minotaur knows that pot;
he remembers bringing it home from Grub's his second week
of work. When he was hired as a line cook at Grub's many of
the pots and sauté pans hung overhead from steel hooks on a

piece of flatiron suspended above the stove and the grill. They hung there until the Minotaur burned himself one night reaching for a shrimp that had dropped, then reared his head back in pain and punctured one of the saucepans with the tip of his horn. It was a cheap pot, and Grub really didn't even get mad, but the next day they rigged up a different storage system for all the pots. Grub told him to take the punctured one home if he could use it for anything.

Mrs. Smith is watching television—racing, the Minotaur thinks. The Doppler effect is pronounced in the televised races. On the Christian shows, where the measured waves are faith and truth, the science is much more theoretical. Soon she turns it off, and Lucky-U is quiet but for Hank and Josie.

They usually put Jules and Marvin to bed at nine, or begin to, anyway. Sometimes the ensuing battle can last for an hour or more, all of Lucky-U party to each onslaught, before the boys go, pouting, into the closet-sized bedroom they share. Some nights it's Hank and Josie who bicker and yell and cry into the night. About Hank: Did he or didn't he wink at that little slut at the laundromat? About Josie: Can't she at least scoop the cat shit out of the litter box? Tonight, most likely worn out from playing with the heavy washing machine parts, Jules and Marvin go to sleep without protest. Hank and Josie seem at peace. Their trailer is quiet, and from where the Minotaur sits at his kitchen table he sees that the lights are out.

Sometime after midnight the Minotaur struggles with the broken zipper in a pair of his work pants. A dog barks far out in the night, is answered by another. On the stillest nights he can hear snoring, glottal and apneic, from around the trailer park.

Tonight, though, it's the open-throated breathy sounds of love that mingle with the chirping and buzzing of insects, with the painfully hollow rattle of pie pans tied in cherry trees bumped by intermittent breezes; it's love sounds that mix with the electric hum from the light Sweeny erected and spill into the Minotaur's eager ears. Hank and Josie have sex almost as often, and sometimes as loud, as they fight.

There is something heroic about this coupling, about the fervor with which these two well-attended young bodies seek each other out. Heroic, and frightening. The Minotaur has known this act in his life, but he doesn't remember it being so soft and full of easy breath. It stirs a troubled yearning in him.

"Hank. Hank. Hank," Josie calls softly when she makes words at all, and Hank with what seems like superhuman endurance carries on. The pitch and tenor of their lovemaking draws the Minotaur from his task. "Oh. Oh. Oh, my," Josie says. "Mmm. Mmm. Mmm."

And Hank, all pectorals and biceps, deltoids and latissimus dorsi, Hank grunts three times in response, as if utterances of three are sacred. "Uh. Uh. Uh."

If the Minotaur were a different sort he would consider creeping up to the rear of Hank and Josie's trailer to witness what seems to him a conversation of flesh. He would crawl shirtless through the crab grass, crawl through the black night and look with his black eye through the open window.

"Oh, Hank. Oh, Hank. Oh, Hank."

If he were, as he wished, a little bolder, more reckless, he would stand with his dark bull's head obscured by the night, just outside their window, three feet, maybe less, from the tiny single bed on which they perform their gymnastic rites. He would reach out and put his open palm on the moon-white flesh of Josie's bottom, two untanned islands and the channel that splits them in an ocean of gilded flesh. Touch her as she lies atop Hank. Block and tackle of desire. Fulcrum of need.

"Unga. Unga. Unga."

Or if she were on her knees with the mechanical Hank behind working doggedly, the Minotaur would watch the bob and sway of her breasts, the flutter of eyelids rhythmically registering each time she was entered. The Minotaur would watch this movement—the hypnotic fleshy bags, brown nipples, the nipples of a mother, raking the bedspread—if he were different.

The Minotaur is not morally opposed to watching Hank and Josie make love without their knowledge. Not at all. Nor is he afraid of getting caught per se. What he is afraid of is the embarrassment that would follow. Rather than crawl up to the window the Minotaur simply goes quietly outside. He sits hunched forward in the dark on his front stoop listening, reaching far back into the opaque miasma of his time on earth, searching for the thread of memory, some image to cast before the sounds he hears, to give them bodies he can see. Five thousand miles away, and perhaps as many years, a bull-roarer, slat of wood and thong, wails in its orbit. The Minotaur listens. And he sits there on his stoop until Hank and Josie finally separate—"Oh. Mercy. Oh. Mercy. Oh. Mercy"—until they pry their flesh apart and succumb to sleep.

CHAPTER 9

"Sorry," the Minotaur says, but there's no one there to hear him. He's at work. He is chopping herbs. More than anything the Minotaur likes that time in the afternoon before the restaurant opens when his station is set up and ready, the hollandaise and other sauces are made, all the necessary prep work is done and he can take a few sweet minutes to chop the fresh herbs that get sprinkled as garnish over several of the entrees. "Sorry," he says again, articulating carefully, striving for the right tone. The oily scents rise from the cutting board and the methodical blade, fill the deep wells of his nostrils, fill the kitchen itself with an aeonian sweetness. They say Prometheus brought fire from the sun concealed in a hollow fennel stalk. They say tarragon came to be when a flax seed was pushed into the pierced root of a sea onion and planted after dark. The Minotaur simply likes the smell of chopped herbs. "Sorry," he says, but the word gets lost in the staccato sound of the blade striking the board.

Kelly is at work, her first night back since the seizure. The Minotaur saw her folding napkins in the wait station, carefully pressing creases into the starched white linens, making the thin accordion shape that splays fanlike when tucked into the empty water glasses. The Minotaur wants to tell her he is sorry about the seizure, sorry that such a thing had to happen to her, so he practices saying it. "Sorry." The Minotaur wants to tell her this because he knows the power of errant desire, of the body's ability to exert its will, to convince, to do as it pleases despite the mind's protest. "Sorry."

Hernando and the Minotaur share the daily chore of the employee meal. A barbecue, a casserole, a hodgepodge of some kind, heavily sauced to hide the fact that they have cleaned out the walk-in cooler in search of food not quite fresh enough to sell. The Minotaur scrapes the herbs into a stainless-steel bowl and puts a damp paper towel over the top. JoeJoe is on the back dock hosing out the waste cans. On the steps the radio spits a frenetic bass beat. David walks through the kitchen whistling and weaving a wine tool batonlike between his fingers. They're tasting wines at the bar, learning sales tips and what accompanies what from a sweaty ultraserious wine rep who thinks the free corkscrews he gives out should be accepted with more gratitude. David stops long enough to show a new busboy the rack of clean silverware that needs to be wiped dry and put into the bins in the wait stations. It is ten minutes until five. There is an element of hope in the air, the possibility of a good night.

From the cooler the Minotaur takes a box of shrimp thawed a few days earlier for a dinner special that didn't sell. Earlier in the afternoon Hernando made a pot of sticky rice sweetened with vinegar. The Minotaur plans to sauté the shrimp with bell peppers and onions and serve it to the wait staff with the rice and some teriyaki sauce left over from the weekend. Leaning over the sink he peels the shrimp quickly, pinching the twiggy legs between his thumb and forefinger and stripping the shell away with an expert roll of the thumb.

At five o'clock the waiters and waitresses come up from the bar, giddy, feigning much more drunkenness than possible from the few sips of wine they each got. They gather in front of the hot line. While they wait for their meal Hernando explains the specials and the prices. The Minotaur cooks. Adrienne and Margaret, arms crossed alike, same dour expression on both their faces, stand together whispering. Hernando puts a plate in the window, a flounder fillet broiled and topped with halved grapes and toasted almonds, for the wait staff to taste. Robert drops the first bite before it reaches his mouth and begins cursing the butter stain on his shirt. The Minotaur stirs the black gelatinous teriyaki sauce into the pan of shrimp and vegetables. It thins as it heats. From the corner of his eye, his best vantage point, he watches Kelly come through the swinging door, quiet and cautious, her wide eyes, set in a narrow angular face, nervously scanning the room, like a foraging animal, nocturnal and omnivorous. The Minotaur is stricken with an image: Kelly's sharp face in the moonlight, dark supple fur, heavy scent of the rut. She stops to take a bite of the flounder and to listen to Hernando describe the other specials, then goes into the walk-in cooler. She meets Cecie coming out.

"Hey, girl," Cecie says. "You okay?" Kelly nods and says something the Minotaur can't hear. The other waiters and waitresses have avoided the question, have all but avoided her even, out of some combination of pity, shame and fear. Kelly seems to appreciate Cecie's asking.

The Minotaur is at the sink rinsing parsley in a big dented colander. Just before putting the pan of shrimp and rice up for the wait staff, he arranges a bed of parsley sprigs in one corner. With precision and a well-honed paring knife he peels the skin from an orange in a single thin strip. He twists it into a tight spiral in his palm, sets it like a flower in full bloom in the center of the parsley. The white pith is stark against the orange flesh and tiny green leaves. As he lifts the pan to the shelf, turning it so that his orange flower is prominently displayed, Cecie walks by on her way from the cooler. In one hand she carries a huge waxy cucumber, in the other a bunch of radishes, red as candy—a fistful of hearts. Cecie is predictable, and temptation abounds in the kitchen. She stops behind the Minotaur just as he leans to turn the pan around. Standing on her toes and holding the cucumber and radishes to her crotch, Cecie thrusts her hips toward the Minotaur's buttocks.

"Oh, ba-by," she says, punctuating each syllable with the cucumber's blunt tip.

"Ungh!" The Minotaur turns quickly to face Cecie, his horn rattling the pots that hang over her head.

"Damn, M! You've been toting them horns up there for all these years and you still can't control them?" Cecie says.

Normally the Minotaur likes this kind of play with Cecie, looks forward to it even. But not this time.

Although he looms over her by almost a foot, snorting, his hot breath rolling across her face, Cecie isn't afraid of his sudden reaction. She thinks his embarrassment is funny.

"You on the rag, honey?" she asks, gently stroking his biceps in mock concern.

The Minotaur shrugs her off, tries to pretend his reaction was a joke as well, but Cecie isn't so easily duped.

"Anybody got a Midol for Miss M?"

Cecie misjudges the distance as she walks around the table, bangs her skinny hip on the corner. The Minotaur fumbles for a serving spoon, hoping busyness will hide his embarrassment. As covertly as possible he looks around the kitchen to see who has watched the exchange. Adrienne and Margaret are engrossed in their own discussion. Kelly is still in the cooler. Most of the others are too busy spooning out their dinners to have noticed anything, but by the door Mike stands grinning, a glossy red motorcycle helmet in the crook of his arm. Reflected in the dark-tinted face shield, a miniature movie screen, the Minotaur can see an impossibly tiny version of himself at work.

"You walking on the wild side now, M?" Mike asks.

The Minotaur ignores him. By the time Kelly comes out of the cooler and brings a plate up for her dinner, the flower made from the orange peel has unraveled and is coated with thick sticky sauce. The Minotaur watches her push it to one side with the spoon and scrape the remaining rice into a small heap before scooping it onto her plate. The Minotaur stands across from her wiping at nonexistent spots on the stainless-steel countertop.

He wants to say he is sorry. He mouths the word one time, the movement of his lips all but imperceptible. But by the time he builds the courage to give it voice Kelly has taken her plate to the other side of the kitchen, where she eats standing up. Between bites she arranges and rearranges the selections on the dessert tray. The Minotaur watches her move the plates around. The peanut butter pie beside the Black Forest cake. The tiramisú opposite the flan. She moves them again and again, never quite satisfied with how the plates look on the heavy silver tray.

When Kelly goes into the dining room and leaves the tray sitting on the counter, the Minotaur takes an apple from the cooler, lifts his apron to polish it. With the paring knife he cuts a thin disk from one side of the fruit, then a thicker slice from the same side, making a flat surface, on which he turns the apple down, its exposed flesh resting against the countertop. First on one side, then on the other, the Minotaur makes careful lengthwise cuts into the meat of the apple, V-shaped wedges, each wider than the last. Using both thumbs he pushes the wedges out, each telescoping from the other. He cuts a small notch between the wings. Then, with some quick whittling from the first piece of the apple that he cut away, the Minotaur carves the graceful neck and delicate beak of a swan. He dips the pieces in lemon juice to keep the pale apple flesh from oxidizing and turning a rusty brown. He rests the bird on a paper doily amid a nest of mint leaves, then sets the whole thing in the center of the dessert tray. He has just enough time to arrange the desserts around the centerpiece and go back behind the line before anyone notices what he is doing.

"Hey, M," David says as he walks up. "We have a party of

twelve coming in at seven o'clock. Will you make sure Hernando and Cecie know?"

"Unnh," the Minotaur says.

"I don't think Grub is coming in tonight, so if it gets busy I'll expedite at least until the party is served."

The Minotaur checks the coolers beneath the counter to make sure he has enough appetizers and side dishes prepped. He makes a mental note to take a box of puff pastry out of the freezer.

"Listen," David says, checking to make sure the heat lamp is off before leaning his head under it to look at the Minotaur. "Thanks a lot for helping me move my stuff. I'm so glad to be out of that shithole I lived in."

"Mm." The Minotaur is uncomfortable accepting gratitude.

"I brought you something," David says, and reaches into his pocket. This makes the Minotaur flinch, but no one notices.

David extends his balled fist beneath the heat lamp toward the Minotaur. When his fingers unfurl what rests in his palm is a pocked misshapen lump of soft metal the size of a marble. The Minotaur reaches out tentatively, takes the gift from David's hand. Holding it pinched between his thumb and forefinger, the Minotaur cocks his head to see it better.

"Know what it is?" David asks.

"Unnh unh."

"A bullet. A Civil War bullet from the battlefield at Bull Run."

"Mmm."

"That thing's almost a hundred and thirty years old." David says this as if the Minotaur should be impressed by its age.

"Mmmhmm."

"The way it's all warped and twisted I'd say it probably hit a bone. A pretty big bone."

"Thanks," the Minotaur says with difficulty.

"Well, that's about the sweetest thing I've seen all day." It's Shane. He stands by the dish machine and wipes a pretend tear from his eye.

"You're late, Shane," David says. "You've got section four, and do your side work before you eat."

Shane rolls his eyes and starts to say something but decides against it. The Minotaur pulls his apron aside and pushes the artifact deep into his pants pocket. When he cranes his thick neck to see around a stack of plates, looking for Kelly, he sees that the dessert tray is already gone. Whether it was Kelly or some other waitperson who took it out to the dining room, he doesn't know. But he will spend several hours wondering.

The night is busy. Tables come and go. People eat and drink, laugh and spend money. Aside from a waitress named Elizabeth dropping a shrimp cocktail on the floor, its thick catsup-y sauce flecked with horseradish spattering across both the patent-leather shoes of her customer and her own starched white shirt, things go smoothly in the dining room. She spends twenty minutes in the employee bathroom, in her bra, trying to wash the stain out. JoeJoe keeps pretending he is about to walk in on her. Aside from one overcooked rib-eye, and aside from Cecie, sometime after nine o'clock, sidling up to the Minotaur and pressing into his hand a sanitary napkin and two Tylenol, then running away laughing, things go smoothly in the kitchen. The night passes quickly.

At eleven the night is over. David comes back to say that he has locked the door and that there is only a deuce left drinking coffee. Some of the wait staff have already left. Those who remain do their closing side work: breaking down the tea machine and the bar setups, snuffing the flames of the squat glass lamps on each table and refilling the lamps with lemon-scented oil, setting the tables and folding napkins for tomorrow. The tasks are menial and endless. Shortly after the last customers leave, Kelly comes from the dining room holding the dessert tray with both hands. She brings it to the dish area, where the light is good, so she can tell whether the icing has turned dark on the cakes, whether the mousse has begun to separate, whether anything needs to be replaced for the next night. The Minotaur looks around for something dirty, finds a glass and takes it to the dish rack. As long as he is there he decides to break down a tray of glasses from the bar, emptying the butts, toothpicks and other contents into the drain before sorting the glasses into the racks angled at shoulder level in front of him.

"Did you . . . ?" Kelly starts to ask.

The Minotaur concentrates on getting the glasses into the right racks.

"Did you do that?" she asks.

"Hnnh?" He turns to where he can see her, holds to the edges of the bus pan for stability.

"That bird." She points to the apple swan on the tray. The dark red peel has begun to brown around the edges and curl inward, but the bird still looks pretty. "Did you do that?"

The Minotaur nods his head.

"That's really sweet," Kelly says, and puts her hand on top

of his. And puts her hand on top of his. And puts her hand on top of his.

The architecture of the Minotaur's heart is ancient. Rough hewn and many chambered, his heart is a plodding laborious thing, built for churning through the millennia. But the blood it pumps—the blood it has pumped for five thousand years, the blood it will pump for the rest of his life—is nearly human blood. It carries with it, through his monster's veins, the weighty, necessary, terrible stuff of human existence: fear, wonder, hope, wickedness, love. But in the Minotaur's world it is far easier to kill and devour seven virgins year after year, their rattling bones rising at his feet like a sea of cracked ice, than to accept tenderness and return it.

At home in bed the Minotaur doesn't remember what he said to Kelly, if anything. She put her hand on top of his. He tosses and turns throughout the night, maybe sleeps, maybe not.

CHAPTER 10

The Minotaur dreams of the past as if it were tomorrow.
Dreams the lament of the sheet-metal worker. Lament. Lament.
Lament for the thick-hide gauntlets that singe against the heat,
that stiffen and split with age, as if they were still flesh.
For the scratch awl and punch. The need for calibration.
For the blueprint. For the malleable heart. For the brittle heart.
For the shear and the press and everything sharp, tongued out on the lathe.
For the give and take of the ball-peen hammer.
For the arc, struck and sustained. The sliver of fire
that finds and claims for its own a piece of my flesh.
For everything that is not soft, and in my life.
For the meadow near Cnossus, where the hyacinth petals
turn and turn out like so many palms refusing applause.
Think of me, Pasiphae, in your moment of cramped ecstasy.

CHAPTER 11

Anyone walking or driving past Sweeny's the next morning a little after sunrise, anyone seeing the open toolbox in the grass, the lean legs and small feet clad in heavy black shoes protruding from beneath the rear end of the old Chevrolet Belair, anyone not knowing better wouldn't assume the mechanic has horns. The car straddles a wide shallow ditch. The ditch leads into a cement culvert that runs under Sweeny's gravel drive and opens on to a similar ditch on the other side. It's where the Minotaur always works when he needs access to the underside of a ve-hicle, needs to be able to crawl beneath it, tools in hand, and work without constantly bumping his snout against the grimy undercarriage or snagging his horns in the exhaust pipes.

Sweeny was right—the Belair's universal joint is bad, loose and sloppy in its movement. The Minotaur lies beneath the car thinking about the day open before him. Lucky-U is quiet but for Hank at the bench press, his rhythmic grunting punctuated by the solid clang of the barbell dropping into its rack, and Josie rattling the breakfast dishes at the sink.

The Minotaur makes sure his tools are just so in the box before closing the lid and securing the latch. As he carries the toolbox back to the Vega, Hank rounds the corner of his trailer. Of all the residents in the trailer park the Minotaur is most uncomfortable with Hank. It's not that Hank is unfriendly, just decidedly wary. When a greeting is unavoidable Hank makes do with a curt and very manly nod of the head. This morning is no exception, and despite the effort necessary to move his cumbersome head with any degree of subtlety, the Minotaur returns the nod.

Hank wasn't always so reserved. For the first week after he and his family moved in Hank came pretty close to smiling whenever he greeted the Minotaur. But that changed the day the Minotaur gave Josie a jump-start.

The Minotaur remembers the day clearly. He was sitting at his kitchen window stirring sugar into his coffee. He had watched Hank leave earlier in his van, an old empty shell of a work truck with *Scooter's Plumbing* still visible on the sides despite someone's attempt to sandpaper it away. Hank, Josie, the two boys and all their possessions came together in the van. Within a week they bought an ocher-colored bean-shaped AMC Pacer from Sweeny. Hank drove away every morning in the van and usually came back just after lunch, dirtier than when he left. Josie stayed home with the kids.

That morning, as the Minotaur sipped his coffee, inhaling

the acidic earthy scent of the dark brew, he watched Josie come out of the trailer with a lit cigarette clamped between two rigid fingers, the other fingers and thumb of that hand wrapped around an open can of SunDrop, and her car keys, sunglasses and green vinyl cigarette case with a thumb clasp and sleeve for the lighter in the other hand—all in all a laborious undertaking. The two boys came behind.

Issues of fashion have never really concerned the Minotaur, seeming too temporal, or empty, or simply beyond his grasp. But Josie, wearing a knit tube top, blue-jean short shorts and flat-soled shoes of clear crisscrossed plastic, took him by surprise. The Minotaur watched her struggle with the passenger door handle, determined to open it without letting go of anything. She pushed out her bottom lip and blew her bangs away from her face; her hair, eyes, mouth and everything else were more or less the same flecked-wheat color, so that from any distance her features were indiscernible.

The Minotaur understands these tiny personal battles with balance: conquer and relinquish. Josie's sons offered no help. The older stood behind her picking his nose intently, while the younger peed on the back tire. Josie gave in with a sigh that the Minotaur heard from his table, dropped the keys, glasses and cigarettes onto the roof of the car and opened the door with her free hand. She folded the seat forward, and the boys climbed into the back and began fighting immediately over who got to sit in the middle. The Minotaur watched Josie circle behind the car, smoking deeply. The driver's door groaned, a pained sound, when she opened it, and again on closing. The Minotaur watched her adjust her sunglasses and, using her thumbs and forefingers, pull the stretchy fabric of her tube top up and out, twisting her shoulder slightly to situate her breasts within. He watched her find the key that fit the ignition and wiggle it in place. The Minotaur heard the weak four-cylinder engine turn over once, twice and again, losing conviction with each try. There was no fourth cycle. The battery couldn't muster the necessary energy, and all that came from beneath the hood was a pathetic clicking.

Josie got out of the car, remarkably calm, and opened the hood. When she bent forward under it the Minotaur watched pale sickles of flesh appear as her buttocks spilled out of her shorts. The Minotaur turned his head away but then looked again. He couldn't tell what she was doing, but she stayed beneath the hood for a few minutes. Then Josie stood up and, using the same sort of well-rehearsed motion as with her top, slid her index fingers up under the hem of her shorts on either side of her hips and beneath the elastic leg band of her panties; with a wiggle and a roll of her hands she covered the exposed flesh of her bottom with twin swaths of lacy black fabric.

"Unngh," the Minotaur said, more or less involuntarily. He had seen too much. He took his cup to the sink and began washing it.

"Got any cables?"

Josie stood at the door, her face framed by both hands pressed to the sagging screen. It made him uncomfortable to be watched in that way.

When the Minotaur didn't respond right away she asked again. "Jumper cables? I think my battery is dead."

At his best the Minotaur is just adequate with language.

Most of the time he falls well short. Josie standing at his door, the bits and pieces of her flesh both intentionally and unintentionally exposed, the sad and desperate sound of the dying battery, the intimacy of her question—these things were almost overwhelming to the Minotaur. Rather than try to answer he simply nodded yes, although he didn't move away from the sink. Josie continued to stare through the screen into the trailer. Neither of them spoke. After a few minutes of palpable silence the Minotaur went back through the trailer to get his keys out of the glass dish sitting, half full of pennies, on the dresser in the bedroom.

When he came back out Josie was inside the trailer. She stood with her back to the Minotaur, looking at a framed picture on the wall: Jesus surrounded by a herd of doe-eyed children. The Minotaur knew that Sweeny's wife had put this picture in every trailer at Lucky-U before she died. Josie seemed to be mumbling something as she looked at it.

The Minotaur is quiet, surprisingly quiet, when he moves. It occurred to him that there had never been a woman in the trailer with him, not for jumper cables or any other reason. Josie startled, gave a little cry, when she looked over and saw him standing by the door waiting for her. She smiled, embarrassed, and the Minotaur sort of smiled back.

Josie sat in her car, bare legs outstretched, while the Minotaur pulled the Vega into place. When he stepped out to open his hood he saw that the two boys were asleep in the backseat of the Pacer. Josie was busy scraping grease from the chipped maroon polish on her left hand with the nail of her right index finger; her feet were dirty—which momentarily filled the Minotaur with tenderness toward her—and the toe-nails, clearly visible in the open spaces of her shoes, had match-ing polish. Josie sat with her legs parted, enough so that each caught full sun.

The Minotaur tested her battery terminals and found both connections loose. When he pulled the terminals free he saw that acid residue had built up on the posts, making the connec-tions faulty. The Minotaur asked Josie if she had a Coke. She seemed confused by his request but went inside to get one any-way. She looked over his shoulder as he poured a little of the carbonated beverage onto each battery post and terminal, watched it foam and hiss, leaned closer as he spun the wire-bristle-lined cup on the posts, scratching away any buildup not dissolved by the Coke. Josie watched without speaking, and the boys slept in the backseat.

Just as he was about to attach the cables—*Red on hot*, he thought to himself—the toothed clamp open in his fist, Josie asked him a question. "You want a sandwich?"

The Minotaur didn't put the clamp in place. Neither did he answer her.

"I got to eat before my 'poinment anyway them boys ain't gonna wake up I appreciate your help let me fix you a sandwich you ever stick anybody with one of them horns?"

Her leaps were dizzying. The Minotaur followed her inside because he didn't know how else to respond. While Josie made the sandwiches—white bread slathered with mayonnaise, on which she carefully lined up thin slices of overripe banana like mucus-y coins—the Minotaur sat at a table on one of three chairs made from wooden barrels. The red Naugahyde seat let out embarrassing squeaks each time the Minotaur moved.

Because Josie was so precise with the banana slices it took her awhile to finish the sandwiches. It occurred to him that he had never had a banana sandwich before, and new experiences in a life as long as his were rare. However odd the taste might be, he resolved to keep an open mind. The Minotaur didn't speak, and Josie sort of mumbled the whole time. He watched her move around the small kitchen. Despite having birthed two children her body remained firm, held shape. A very functional body, in the Minotaur's view, comfortable in movement. In the white uncompromising light from the florescent tubes overhead, the many scratches and bruises on Josie's legs were clearly visible, a road map of color. She brought the sandwiches to the table on paper napkins, along with two glasses of tea, and sat opposite the Minotaur.

"You didn't answer my question you ever stick anybody with one of them?"

Josie seemed as if she were about to reach out and touch the horns.

The Minotaur shook his big head.

"Hmm," Josie said, and that was the end of conversation. The close space filled to overflowing with the sticky sound of bananas on white bread with mayonnaise being chewed.

Hank pulled up just as the Minotaur was closing the Pacer's hood. The jumper cables hung limply in his hands. Hank seemed tense right away and went into the trailer without acknowledging Josie. The boys stirred in the backseat. Josie thanked the Minotaur, and he went back to his own trailer.

It happened on a Monday. The Minotaur had the day off

from work. He listened to Hank and Josie fight well into the night.

⸺ ⸺

So now, when he has to do anything at all, Hank merely nods at the Minotaur. This morning is no exception. The Minotaur loads his tools into the back of the Vega. Before leaving for the salvage yard he pulls a few old rags from a bag he keeps under the bathroom sink, folds them and stacks them by the toolbox.

Bunyan's Salvage is a destination, meaning that it is impossible to pass it en route to somewhere else; arriving there by accident is difficult. Located at the end of a three-mile stretch of crumbling asphalt (paved and occasionally repaved by Jack Bunyan himself) that cuts through a swampland (known as Bunyan's Slough) infested with mosquitoes, water moccasins and wild pigs, it is the place to go for used auto parts. Jack Bunyan set the pigs out forty-some years ago when he bought the land, claiming that they kept trespassers away better than dogs and that he could always shoot one for dinner if he had to. The pigs thrived, both in actuality and rumor, amid the cypresses, pines and stagnant water.

The Minotaur always enjoys the drive out to Bunyan's. They know him well there, Bunyan and the two men who work for him; even through the layers of grease they all look so much alike that the Minotaur assumes the two men to be Jack's sons. The Minotaur is allowed to wander freely among the junked cars. Scattered throughout the whole of Bunyan's Salvage and the slough are huge granite boulders—some the size of Cadillacs, others bigger than houses—jutting at odd angles from the ground. They constitute a moraine. Glacial deposits. Pushed before or dragged beneath huge rivers of ice, long since melted, the stones are reminders of a time when the earth itself was more tumultuous. There is an ancient ruined quality to the salvage yard that both comforts and saddens the Minotaur. Jack Bunyan fenced in what he could, using chain-link, planks and boards, corrugated tin, anything to keep the pigs in and unpaying customers out. But the lapses in the fence line are many.

This morning, as he pulls through the wide-open cattle gate, the Minotaur sees that he isn't the first customer of the day. Parked in front of the squat cinder-block building with its garage doors open at either end is an old school bus. At least it used to be a school bus. Gone is the dull yellow coat with black lettering. In its place is a paint job with a purpose. Rising up on the sides, as if from beneath the bus itself, are fiery orange flames and an occasional pitchfork and horn. From the top of the bus clouds swirl downward. Around the sides are several scenes of figures acting and reacting. The Minotaur recognizes the scenes as stories from the life of Jesus. The Minotaur is not a Christian. Not then, not now. He recognizes Christ as a recent phenomenon, and separated from the politics and rhetoric, he admires the tenets. But in issues of faith and politics the Minotaur finds it impossible to define himself with the conviction that most people expect. He feels imprisoned by strict categorization.

Beginning on the wheel well of the driver's side of the bus, stretching beneath all the windows and wrapping around the rear is a chronological storyboard: the Nativity, the moneychangers, a healing of the blind and lame, the loaves and fishes, Gethsemane. The Crucifixion spills over onto the levered double door. The whole enterprise culminates on the hood with the Resurrection—Jesus in flowing robes and a golden halo, arms open to greet all as the bus makes its way down the road. In blood-red letters on either side: *The True Light Baptist Church Chariot of Jesus.* Bolted fore and aft on top of the bus are two mercifully mute speakers. The stories painted on the bus are all easily identified by the Minotaur despite the garish colors and the somewhat childish rendering of objects and perspective, recognizable despite the fact that all the figures—the Savior, the disciples, the afflicted, believers and nonbelievers alike, even animals—have the same face. And that face is remarkably similar to the face of the man standing in the door of Bunyan's Salvage, the man who is gesticulating grandly at Jack Bunyan himself.

Not until the Minotaur is standing at the back of the Vega about to lift out the toolbox does he hear the sounds coming from inside the bus. It is a hymn—muted, feeble even, discordant, but definitely a hymn. "Shall we gather at the river/The beautiful, the beautiful river . . ." Looking through the dusty windows of the Chariot of Jesus the Minotaur can tell that most of its seats are occupied.

"Deacon Hinky, I'd like to help you out," Jack Bunyan says. "But I ain't got a water pump that will fit your bus."

Jack gives the Minotaur a wave; the Minotaur tips his horns in acknowledgment and walks back into the acres and acres of damaged automobile carcasses looking for a Chevrolet Belair. The heavy toolbox bumps against his leg with each step.

Back among the boulders, in the privacy of rusting metal and rotting tires, the Minotaur begins to hum. He hums the song of worship he just heard. The farther he gets from the garage and anyone who might hear him the louder the Minotaur hums. When he is certainly out of earshot he attempts to sing. It's the Minotaur's oldest secret, probably the one thing no one has ever known about him. He wishes, sometimes more than anything else, that he could sing. Truly, freely, with rapture, sing. Some nights when he can't sleep—beginning way back when it was just he and the darkness and stone walls for years on end— the Minotaur mouths the words to a song, imagining himself bellowing melodiously, his huge well of a diaphragm powering each precise note. Occasionally the Minotaur lists in his mind all the things he would willingly sacrifice to be able to do this. The Minotaur knows in his heart, and feels in his mouth, the impossibility of this dream. But in the seclusion of Bunyan's Salvage he pretends.

Jack Bunyan has been hauling in junked and wrecked cars for as long as he's owned the property. He began by lining them up behind the garage building, then on the sides and out front. Before long he was spreading out in all directions. So, while there is no intentional order to the cars, generally the farther away from the garage you go the newer the cars get.

The Minotaur wanders, singing, through the disarray of cars, paying little heed to the direction he's going or how far he has walked. He knows that if he just keeps walking he'll stumble upon a suitable Belair. It is about faith.

The first one he finds has no universal joint. In fact the entire drive train is missing. The next Belair is missing not only its drive train but the rear wheels, seats, floorboard, roof, doors and trunk as well. Only the front half of the car, faded and weathered but relatively undamaged, is there. The Minotaur takes a few minutes to climb in and sit behind the steering wheel, trying hard to imagine traveling in such a vehicle. He can't. The concept of having nothing behind him is impossible to comprehend. The sound of an air-powered wrench ratcheting against a lug nut echoes among the rocks and the rusted hulls of the junked cars.

After almost an hour of looking the Minotaur finds what he seeks, and because the old Chevrolet is parked with its front end lying across the engine well of another car, he won't even have to jack it up to be able to crawl underneath.

He sets the toolbox in the weeds by the back wheels. Using both hands he pulls and pushes at the car, making sure the balance isn't precarious. Before crawling under the car the Minotaur looks around, finds a long stick, kneels and sweeps the undercarriage, taking special care to probe behind and over the tops of the wheels. It's not that he is afraid of snakes. In fact the Minotaur finds something provocative in their ancient simplicity. But he would rather not be surprised.

Satisfied that nothing is lurking underneath the car, the Minotaur walks around the outside looking through the dirty windshield. The rear glass is shattered and sunken in. A jagged hole the size of an orange defines the center of the depression. On the floorboard of the Belair a carburetor, its four round mouths bone-dry and gaping, leans against a clotted air filter.

Aside from the occasional blacksnake coiled in tight loops under a front seat and the copperhead sunning itself on a dented trunk, the most common companions the Minotaur has in the salvage yard are wasps. This morning is no exception. In the open glove compartment a gray papery nest hangs by a thin stem, suspended over a crumpled piece of a road map, a grade-school compass still holding its broken pencil and a white porcelain knob from a faucet: *HOT*. Whether the dozen or so wasps clinging to the nest, wings tucked like hard coats over their pinstriped articulated bodies, somber as pallbearers but for the nervous antennae, whether they protect this treasure or are oblivious to it is hard to tell. The Minotaur intends to leave them in peace.

Once, when the Minotaur was looking for a throw-out bearing, one of Jack's sons came into the yard with him to help find it. Without paying attention the man stuck his hand into the grill of an old Ford, looking for the hood latch. He stuck two fingers up to the second knuckles into a busy wasp nest. By the time he pulled his hand out it was coated with stinging wasps— a vindictive glove of sorts. Undaunted by the pain and his swollen hand the man went back to the garage and came out with a Mason jar full of gasoline. The Minotaur remembers vividly how the wasps died. Jack's son sloshed the full pint over them, dousing the nest with the amber liquid, and the insects instantly arched, coiled in on themselves, relinquished their tenacious grasp on the nest and dropped to the chrome bumper and the ground below, dead.

The Minotaur lies on his back on the hard-packed dirt, the earth itself smelling of oil and gasoline, and reaches under the Belair with both hands. Taking care not to snag his horns he grips the undercarriage and pulls himself beneath the car, where he jiggles the universal joint, testing for sloppiness. It seems fine—not too worn, able to bear more mileage. The Minotaur gauges by sight the socket that will fit the rusted nuts holding the shaft and the joint up. When he slips the socket in place the nuts will not budge, despite the considerable leverage he applies. From his toolbox he pulls a can of Liquid Wrench, made to eat away stubborn binding rust, and sprays the area well. In the distance the Minotaur hears a gearbox whine and struggle. The Chariot of Jesus must be leaving.

While the Liquid Wrench works at dissolving years of oxidization, the Minotaur sits in the backseat of the Belair with the door open. He hums a little. He scratches. He lets his big bull's head rest against the seat back and breathes in the stale musty air. Overhead two clearly defined footprints, pressed into and staining the headliner, flank the cracked interior light in the center of the roof. The right foot is missing its little toe. The Minotaur closes the door, and a momentary shiver stirs the wasps on their nest. He fingers the hinged lid of the ashtray in the door handle; it overflows with cigarette butts and will not close completely. Business cards scattered over the floorboard advertise the services of a bail bondsman.

Into the Minotaur's life there come occasional moments of clarity, moments, unpredictable and painfully brief, that arrive at times as a thunderclap and at others as sweetly as a yawn, moments when everything seems understandable, when the whole of his past makes sense to him, his present seems within his control and his future pops and sizzles with a wild dangerous hope. These moments are rare, and their aftermath lies somewhere between excitement and sheer terror.

Sitting in the backseat of the old Chevrolet Belair deep within Bunyan's Salvage, waiting for the rust to dissolve, a sudden and profound silence comes upon the Minotaur, a fragment of time in which the crows and jays close their beaks and hush their bickering. The wind rattles nothing. The wasps cease their shuffling. Everything living or inanimate and capable of sound refuses the charge. The Minotaur spooks, bristles with his most animal instinct. The hairs on the back of his neck rise. His purple scar grows suddenly raw. There is a quickening in his heart, and deeper, in his belly, some ancient knot tightens upon itself.

Then the thunder of hooves on packed earth. Squeal and snort and the gnashing of tusks. Jack Bunyan's wild pigs are running through the junkyard. The stampede is raucous, comes from behind the car. The pigs' eyes roll madly; their mouths are flecked with fear. The herd is wide and without direction. As the porcine surge passes on both sides of the car and floods his field of vision, the Minotaur clings to the backseat door handle. The smells of dirt and swamp water fill the car. The Minotaur can almost feel the coarse and matted hides rub against him through the doors. It's not the pigs that the Minotaur fears. Among animals he walks with human confidence, instills a little fear himself. But these pigs move in the company of something more complicated. Within seconds they are gone.

In that instant before terror subsides, in pursuit of and closing in on the pigs, there comes another hoofed creature. The Minotaur smells it first; the stink of the rut, the stench of familiarity, clots in his throat. Wheezing breath, the clatter of hooves—two hooves—across the trunk of the car, over the roof and onto the hood. Because of the glare from the sun and the clouds of dust stirred by the pigs the Minotaur cannot see clearly. Because the creature pauses only long enough to look through the windshield at the Minotaur in the backseat, to furrow its brow and grunt, either scowling or grinning, then spit between its teeth before leaping to the ground and disappearing in the direction of the pigs, its testicles the size of hen eggs hanging low in their stretched wattlelike sack, nearly dragging the ground—because of the abbreviated nature of the encounter the Minotaur cannot be certain what it was. But he suddenly feels the weight of his five thousand years pressing down upon him. A horrible kinship. A fetid lineage.

The Minotaur sits for a while in the backseat, thinking about what happened. Then, cautiously, he gets out of the car. Lying beneath it the Minotaur thinks he can feel minute vibrations in the earth as the pigs' hooves strike the ground somewhere in the distance, and the subtler but far more resounding hoofbeats of their single pursuer.

The Liquid Wrench has done its work, and he is able to remove the universal joint with manageable difficulty. He carries his toolbox in one hand and the part in the other and walks back to the garage. After laying the part on a section of newspaper, spread out to protect the carpet in the back of the Vega, he looks for Jack or one of the others to pay for what he has taken. They're all standing out behind the garage. The hot lead and the ground from the Hobart welder are stretched out from inside and lie at their feet. A welder's mask, gray and bulbous, its dark lens opaque but for the most insistent light, is perched high on the head of one of the men. His hands are sheathed in leather gloves, the fingers black and rigid.

The men stand around a pair of dog irons, three-footed metal stands meant to hold logs in a fireplace; they are crafted from old crankshafts. The Minotaur gathers from their conversation that they intend to sell the dog irons at the flea market out on the highway. No one mentions the pigs or the stampede. As the Minotaur pulls away from the building he hears the Hobart's diesel engine throttle up; in the rearview mirror he sees the arc struck, the brilliant white light bringing hard resistant edges together.

A mile and a half, maybe less, from the gate of Bunyan's Salvage, the Minotaur rounds a curve. Thinking still about what happened in the Belair he is unprepared for the vision before him. Strewn along the pothole-filled road, a dozen or so wild pigs lie dead or dying on the hot asphalt. The Minotaur can hear their squeals. The smell of burned rubber lingers in the air. A little farther along and off to one side, the rear end of The True Light Baptist Church Chariot of Jesus juts awkwardly from the high weeds and brush lining the road, its back door thrown wide. The front end of the Chariot of Jesus has sunk up to the quarter panels into Bunyan's Slough. Just past the bus he sees old Christians milling about in the road, their mouths gaping in disbelief. Disbelief is his assumption. He counts at least three of the Baptists carrying their own oxygen bottles. Deacon Hinky kneels by the side ditch, as if he is trying to pray the bus out of the swamp. The Minotaur slows his car but does not stop.

CHAPTER 12

G*rub is bringing* his family in for dinner. He calls ahead and asks for popcorn shrimp to be on the special list. Popcorn shrimp—bay shrimp, tiny, pink and fetal, dredged in cornmeal breading, deep-fried and served with hushpuppies—always sell. The FryDaddy is in the Minotaur's station, so it means a busy night. Hernando is making hushpuppy batter. Cecie seems caught up with her salad bar prep work, so the Minotaur asks if she'll chop some pickles and onions for the tartar sauce.

"I'll chop your pickles anytime, big boy."

He gives her a halfhearted wink and lines up three yellow onions in front of the Buffalo chopper. Cecie has them peeled and quartered by the time he gets back with a jar of dill pickles.

The Minotaur takes one of the thick onion wedges into his mouth, crushes it between his teeth. He loves the Janus-like quality of the onion: the cool translucent flesh that belies the burn of its juices. He purses his lips as best he can, as if to kiss Cecie, and she snaps him with a wet dishtowel. It's early. The wait staff isn't there yet.

"How about some slaw, M?" Hernando asks.

"Mmmn."

"Your recipe." Hernando kisses his fingertips. "*Qué bueno.*"

The Minotaur takes a couple heads of cabbage from the cooler, makes quick work of shredding them. In a wide stainless-steel bowl he dresses the slaw copiously with mayonnaise, then with cider vinegar to cut the heavy mayonnaise, then a palm full of sugar to counter the vinegar. The Minotaur finishes the slaw with salt, pepper, some dried scallions and a can of stewed tomatoes drained and chopped. Stirred in, the bits of tomato tend to rise to the top, like vibrant little hearts swimming in the viscous dressing. Hernando agrees that they may as well fry up some shrimp for the employee meal.

A clipboard hangs on the wall in the wait station by the intercom. It's where the staff keeps a running tally of the desserts throughout the shift, so that everyone knows how many orders of each item are left. There is also a list, compiled by the wait staff, of stock items that are running low: sugar packets, lemon skirts, Worcestershire sauce, other condiments, cleaning supplies. The Minotaur regularly checks the list against the supplies because the waiters and waitresses usually forget to update it, and if something runs out it's the kitchen that catches the flak from Grub. Today the only item on the list is coffee filters, but the Minotaur knows that there is just one box of doilies left. Since he is standing at the clipboard the Minotaur takes the time to flip back a few pages to the wait staff work schedule. Jenna's name had been written in for this evening. Jenna has worked three nights a week at Grub's for eight years. During the day she teaches pottery at the high school. Seven years ago, at his company picnic, her new husband won second place in the chin-up contest, then walked out into the muddy man-made lake and drowned. Jenna always smells like clay. A few lines down on the chart Adrienne's name has been furiously crossed out and replaced by Kelly's. David hates it when they switch shifts without asking him, but the Minotaur is glad for the change.

"You ready, M?" Hernando asks.

"Mmmn," the Minotaur answers, then sets up his breading station. An empty trash can is about the right height and fits in the space between the FryDaddy and the grill. He puts a sheet pan on top of it and arranges the shallow containers of flour, egg wash and cornmeal breadcrumb mixture in order of use. It's four-fifteen, and he can hear talking out in the wait station and the buzz and hiss of the tea machine brewing.

JoeJoe has crawled atop the double-stacked convection ovens so that he can reach the screen filters of the ventilation hoods that span the length of the cooking equipment, hanging low. JoeJoe hands a greasy filter to the Minotaur, who stacks it by the dish machine.

"Somebody ought to fast-forward to the fuck scenes," JoeJoe says, handing the Minotaur another filter. The Minotaur smiles. JoeJoe stands the filters upright in the plastic dish racks, three per, and runs them through the machine twice before putting them back in the hood. JoeJoe has done this once a week for the past five years.

oe says, pushing the levered
steam billows around him.
. He checks with Hernando,
it and smoke.
three or four rotting fruits
n the dock, to be discarded
elects the least rotten lemon.
ement, winds up and throws
he highway. They both doubt
hears it land. If the Minotaur
k JoeJoe if he has ever seen
ariot of Jesus riding through
d forget. If the Minotaur had

confidence in his narrative abilities he would tell JoeJoe the story of Deacon Hinky and the swamp. JoeJoe would appreciate it. But even if the Minotaur were a skilled and practiced orator he would keep to himself the encounter he had in the backseat of the Belair, deep in the heart of Bunyan's Salvage. He would not speak of the randy creature that glared at him through the dirty windshield, the hoof and snort of his kinsman.

"Gonna get me some poon tonight, M," JoeJoe says.

The Minotaur finds a small stick—as he has done countless times—and begins to trace the tread patterns on the soles of his shoes, scraping out the inevitable bits of gristle, pieces of vegetables, dirt and other matter that collects there, as JoeJoe tells in explicit detail what he plans to do and with whom. The Minotaur listens only closely enough to know when to nod or give some utterance in response.

"A Russian chick with a skinny ass, and you *know* what they like."

The Minotaur nods as if he actually does know. Whether or not JoeJoe's tales of conquest are true doesn't matter to him. He's not bothered by what would be patently offensive to most. The Minotaur has always felt excluded from the allegiance of men, and this repartee, however coarse and one sided, approximates in his mind what he thinks he is missing.

From time to time the Minotaur tries to fit in. Last summer a guy named Gene waited tables for a while at Grub's. He was there when the Minotaur started. Gene, who had an easy grin and curly yellow hair, regularly claimed to be "born again," but when he wasn't handing out religious tracts with childlike line drawings of suffering nonbelievers, he was trying to sell the porn videos he kept in the trunk of his car. The Minotaur never fully understood what Gene meant by born again, but all the guys at Grub's seemed to like him. One Tuesday night shortly after the Minotaur got the job, business was slow, and Grub let David close an hour early. Hernando had already left. Gene and Mike were the only waiters still there. The Minotaur was covering the pans of rice, vegetables and crepes imperial filling with plastic wrap when he heard the mechanical *thunk* of the time clock and saw, on the periphery, the door from the wait station swing open.

"Party at my house, guys. Wanna come?" Gene said.

Cecie ignored him, but JoeJoe was eager and with some difficulty convinced the Minotaur to give him a ride. The party was Gene, Mike, JoeJoe, the Minotaur and two other men he didn't know. The Minotaur sat in a ladder-back chair between JoeJoe and one of the other men. He had to pass the bottles of Mogen David and the marijuana back and forth, even though he used neither. A bag of generic potato chips made its way around. They sat in a half circle in Gene's stark cramped living room, a wide picture window devoid of curtains or blinds gaping into the night behind them; they sat leaning forward before the console television, the biggest thing in the room. On the screen grainy images provoked, alternately, rapt silence and affected enthusiasm. The Minotaur remembers one woman and two men. They took turns, the men, one inserting ping-pong balls into the woman's vagina while the other knelt, impossibly far away, across the room. She lay on her back, knees bent, feet flat and legs wide apart. Each time the man pushed a ball inside of her the woman hoisted her bottom from the floor, took aim and ejected the white ball in a high slow arc into the waiting mouth of the second man some ten feet away. Then the men traded places. The Minotaur remembers this going on for a long time. Each time Gene and the other guys laughed or cheered for the woman on the television screen, the Minotaur tried to do the same, but he always missed the beat and was still trying to laugh after everyone else had stopped. Each time the room quieted in anticipation or envy or emptiness, the Minotaur searched inside himself for the same. The Minotaur remembers somebody wanting to "fast forward to the fuck scenes." But Gene held tight to the remote control, and the line became a standing joke among them at Grub's. He remembers somebody asking Gene about being born again. Gene said that, like everybody else, he was a situational heathen. A month later Grub fired Gene. He had come to work with a cardboard box full of bootleg copies of a video in which he claimed Jenna had a small role. "Nekkid," he said. "Hot, nekkid and wide open." Two months later Gene was in the minimum-security prison out on the county road. Sometimes Mike or JoeJoe or one of the other guys would ride by and blow his car horn at the prisoners milling around in the yard. In the Minotaur's mind the allegiance of men is pathetic. Is terrifying. Is seductive. Is unattainable.

◆ ◆

"Hi, M. Hey, JoeJoe," Jenna says, opening the back door of the kitchen. The black bow tie hangs loose around her neck. On the ticket book protruding from her apron pocket, a small heart-shaped sticker reads *Kiss Me*. The Minotaur remembers the bumper sticker on her car: *Potters Do It On The Wheel*.

"Mmnn," the Minotaur says.

"Hey, baby," JoeJoe says.

"Hernando wants you, M. I think it's time to feed the waitrons."

"Thanks," the Minotaur stammers. With Jenna he is sometimes willing to make the effort to speak because she is genuinely kind to him, JoeJoe and everyone else in the kitchen and because she doesn't use those irritating intercom speakers unless she absolutely has to.

An old gray mop head lies at the edge of the loading dock, at once limp and shapeless yet stiff, like a dead bird, the potential for fluid movement gone but still apparent. The Minotaur shoves the mop head with his toe. From beneath it a tight knot of roaches, surprised by the sudden light, scurries nervously for the safety of a crevice. One unfortunate insect chooses to run along the bottom edge of the upturned milk crate that JoeJoe sits on. JoeJoe, quick on the draw, aims the lit end of his almost-gone cigarette over the insect's path. Just as the black-clad arthropod is about to escape into the narrow space between the loading dock and the rubber bumpers that protect it from careless trucks in reverse, JoeJoe makes a stab. The ember finds its mark. JoeJoe grinds his cigarette out on the back of the cockroach. It does not die without a struggle. *Fast forward to the fuck scenes*, the Minotaur thinks when Jenna closes the door. It's what he thinks every time he talks to her, and every time it makes him feel small. He nudges the mop head again and it falls—like a dead bird—to the asphalt below.

The handfuls of breaded shrimp begin to spit and sizzle the instant they hit the oil. The Minotaur shakes the baskets so that nothing sticks to the mesh. He checks the warming oven for the pan of hushpuppies Hernando fried for him. Robert walks by with a flat rack full of clean silverware, wet and rattling. He's talking excitedly to Kelly, talking about chrome and speed.

"Over a hundred miles an hour," he says. Kelly seems bored but tolerant. She follows Robert into the wait station but turns, wonder of wonders, to catch the Minotaur's eye before going through the door.

By the dish machine Margaret has the lamps from all the tables arranged on a large oval tray. With both hands and noticeable effort she balances a three-gallon plastic jug of clear fuel and fills each lamp slowly, cursing each time she tips the jug too much, causing it to suck air and splash the lamps, the tray and her with slick droplets of pine-scented oil.

"Why can't the busboys do this shit?"

The Minotaur turns the baskets of fried shrimp out into a pan lined with paper towels. The wait staff gathers on the other side of the hot line; he can almost hear them gnashing their saliva-greased teeth. Cecie slides a pan of the slaw under the window and puts a slotted spoon beside it but then decides tongs will work better. Hernando turns off the radio but keeps whistling the tune as he finds a ladle for the cocktail sauce.

"Grub'll be in about six-thirty," David says, coming into the kitchen. "Hi, M. Hi, guys."

"This look like a guy thing to you?" Cecie asks, pushing her chest out.

"And girls."

The wait staff is ravenous; they fill their plates greedily.

"We've only got two orders of bread pudding left," Hernando says. "Who's going to sell them for me?"

"I will if you'll cut the peanut butter pie for me," Jenna offers.

"You got a deal, chiquita."

David is getting nervous. He gets nervous every time Grub brings his family for dinner. Grub has brought his family in more times than the Minotaur can remember. David flits from the wait station to the kitchen to the dining room while keeping up a running monologue.

"Who's supposed to cut lemons?"

"Brian, that four-top by the door has dirty glasses, and there's a salad fork missing."

"Listen, guys, try to push the Roditys tonight with the shrimp. We've got a whole case in the cooler."

As far as the Minotaur can tell no one responds to any of

David's questions or comments, but it doesn't slow him down.

"Hernando, would you ask JoeJoe to put some toilet paper in the women's bathroom."

"Has everyone finished their side work?"

"Shit! We've only got half a box of mints."

The night begins smoothly despite David's anxiety. Every table has at least one order for shrimp. The Minotaur is busy, but there are plenty of hushpuppies, and he prepped well, so everything goes okay. Nights like this he likes his job, orders coming in and going out like clockwork.

"Grub's here," David says. "I put them in your section, Kelly."

The Minotaur puts two orders of oysters Rockefeller in the oven even before Kelly leaves the kitchen. She comes back through minutes later and turns in the order. Grub and his wife want the oysters. The two older kids are having chicken wings and fried mushrooms. By the time Kelly hauls out a booster seat and serves a Grub-tini, a sweet tea, two virgin daiquiris and an apple juice, the Minotaur has the appetizer order waiting in the window.

"Thanks for your help," she says. "Serving the Big Guy makes me nervous."

David holds the door for her, then carries the tray stand out and sets it up by Grub's table.

When Leon the busboy comes from the dining room, the tray he carries on his shoulder—a large oval piled high with dinner plates and soup bowls, butter dishes and dessert plates, coffee cups, saucers, wine and water glasses, silverware caked with bits of food, stained napkins and tablecloths, ashtrays— blocks the view of his head, so that, seeing him from a distance, it appears that the tray is his head. It's as if the service industry, in an attempt to economize, grafted the tray to the neck of some unfortunate dupe and created the ultimate busser. It all seems to balance on a miracle. The Minotaur can't believe that Leon's tiny outstretched arm and thin girlish body can support the weight bearing down on him. When Leon squats to rest the tray on the shelf by the dish machine and takes a minute to move a piece of parsley and pick a couple of uneaten shrimp from one of the plates to toss into his mouth, the Minotaur thinks he fully deserves them. David disagrees.

"Leon. If you do that again you're going home."

David has a crush on Leon. Everybody knows it.

"Order up," Kelly says.

It's for Grub. David takes the order and reads it out.

"Two popcorn shrimp, extra hushpuppies on both. One crepes imperial. And a kid's chicken."

"The *pequeñito?*" Hernando asks, wondering about Grub's younger son.

"He'll eat from their plates," David says.

Hernando reaches into the cooler beneath the counter with his tongs, places a chicken breast on the grill. By the time Hernando flips it the first time the Minotaur is dusting the shrimp with flour. Hernando flips the chicken a second time, and the Minotaur dips the shrimp in the egg wash, scatters them in the pan of breading and shakes it back and forth. Just before dropping the two orders of popcorn shrimp into the FryDaddy, the Minotaur notices that the oil is a little dark. Once in the hot oil the tiny shrimp buck and spit. The Minotaur smells the burned breading that has settled to the bottom of the rectangular vat.

Leon comes and goes. While David is in the dining room attending to some small crisis, the Minotaur slips the hardworking busboy a few hot shrimp. Grub's order goes up and out with no problems. And until the Minotaur notices Kelly and David huddled over a plate by the ice cream cooler talking in hushed voices, he assumes that everything is fine. David finds a fork and takes a bite of whatever is on the plate, and when he brings it over the Minotaur sees that it's popcorn shrimp, from Grub's order. It's popcorn shrimp, so it is the Minotaur's responsibility, but there is a hierarchy in the kitchen. David brings the plate to Hernando because he is the kitchen manager. Hernando uses his fingers to pick up and taste a shrimp.

"We've gotta change the oil in the FryDaddy, M," he says. "Unngh."

The Minotaur hates the job. He had a feeling the oil was burned and should have changed it when he came in, when the oil was cold. As soon as Hernando makes the call the Minotaur shuts off the power to the FryDaddy. He gives the wire baskets to JoeJoe to clean. The Minotaur and Hernando decide that waiting for new oil to heat will take too long, half an hour or more, and they have orders for popcorn shrimp hanging. They'll double-filter the oil from the vat and top it off with fresh. In a moment of blind stupidity—a familiar moment—and because it is the first thing that comes to mind, the Minotaur pulls one of the empty cleaned pickle buckets from the stack below the dishwasher.

The FryDaddy is a simple appliance. A rectangular well ten inches deep holds the oil. At the front, in the center of a shallow channel, a small round orifice is covered with sediment.

The Minotaur fits the special filter into the perforated cone of the aluminum china cap and hangs it over the mouth of the pickle bucket. The entire front of the FryDaddy is hinged and metal. When the front is opened the stark inner workings of the machine are readily visible: the thin blue wing of the pilot light beating against its ceramic captor, the two-pronged burner that runs beneath the oil vat, now pinging as it cools, the brass valve for draining, the red lever and safety lock. The Minotaur screws a short drainspout into the valve. The bucket and the china cap fit perfectly under the drain.

Orders are still coming into the kitchen. Cecie helps Hernando as much as she can, handing him things from the cooler, turning steaks on the grill when he says it's time. The Minotaur has changed the oil in the FryDaddy dozens of times. He flips the lever to open the drain, but nothing happens; a night's worth of sediment is clogging the hole. An **L**-shaped piece of thick wire with a loop at the top for a handle hangs at the back of the FryDaddy. With it the Minotaur probes for the opening at the bottom of the dark grease.

"Hey, M," Leon says, leaning under the heat lamps.

"Mmmm?" the Minotaur answers without looking up. The wire probe slips into the channel and pushes through the sediment. After several thick gobs of muck are spit out, the hot oil begins to flow freely, staining the paper filter as it fills the china cap and drains into the bucket.

"There's a guy out here asking about the cocktail sauce," Leon says.

"Hmmn?" The Minotaur stirs the oil in the filter to prevent the sediment from clogging. Bending over the bucket the

Minotaur cocks his head to look at Leon.

"Behind you, M," Hernando says, stepping close to open the oven door.

"He wants to know if there's Tabasco sauce in it. He's allergic."

Kelly waits patiently, watching from the other side of the line.

Pain comes first as its acute absence. There is a flash of disbelief, microseconds in length, that renders one, for that blessed time, totally devoid of physical sensation. The Minotaur drains the hot oil into a thick plastic pickle bucket, the same kind of bucket he uses when changing cold oil. But the pickle bucket is not designed to hold hot oil. Because the Minotaur is leaning over the FryDaddy as it drains, and also looking up and talking to Leon, he doesn't see the seam at the bottom of the bucket, just by his right foot, melt, warp and separate, doesn't feel the oil spill out at 375 degrees and pour across his steel-toed work shoe until it washes over the leather upper and seeps to his flesh. The sock, like a black wick, draws the burning oil in deeper. Then the piercing disbelief.

Having lived for five thousand years, having begun in the convoluted belly of deceit and slept in the endless night of the Labyrinth, having eaten rock and bone and, ultimately, crow, the Minotaur is no stranger to pain. He recognizes that fraction of time for what it is. He welcomes it. He clings to the moment for as long as possible.

Although the Minotaur struggles with syntax and articulation when speaking, during times of physical or psychic turmoil, he cries out instinctively. Sometimes the cry is a mournful lowing, a lament. Other times, more rare, the cry is rattling and lusty, even angry. When the hot oil spills into his shoe, seeps into the flesh of his foot, blisters and peels away the first layer of skin and starts on the second, the Minotaur's cry is so complete that it leaves the confines of sound. His black lips roll back to expose worn yellow teeth, bits of food caught between the flat planes. The tongue, thick as a sapling or a boy's arm, falls out, saliva beading at its tip. And the mouth gapes. There is the pretense of sound. Air rattles in the cavernous space, clicks and pops. But that is all.

The Spanish bullfighters call horn wounds *cornadas* and wear their scars like proud badges. The more severe the wound the greater the glory. Even a blunt tip is capable of much damage. What the Minotaur does when he feels the skin of his foot burn and blister is, besides crying out, rear his head suddenly. Hernando, standing behind him, feels the tip of the horn pierce his apron and the fabric of his pants, penetrate deep into the tender flesh of his inner thigh and drive to the bone. The femur does not give way. Hernando's cry is audible.

Chaos, once introduced, is pernicious. Despite Grub's leaving his family at their dinner and coming into the kitchen to help with cleanup, then to help David, JoeJoe and Cecie cook and plate the remaining orders, the night never recovers. Leon, the most expendable, rushes Hernando, a handful of blood-soaked towels pressed to his wound, to the hospital.

"You should go, too," Margaret says, pointing at the Minotaur's burn. He sits with his bare foot, pale and bony, not at all hooflike, in a bucket of ice.

"I'll take you, M," Kelly offers.

"No," he says, avoiding her eyes. Too proud. Too embarrassed.

"Can I look?" she asks.

"No," he says. He won't go to the hospital. He won't let anyone look. At his trailer, in a green ceramic pot shaped like a buoy, an aloe plant thrives. No. He won't go to the hospital.

There is a palpable discomfort in the air. They feed everyone and apologize for the wait. Grub closes the restaurant an hour early.

"How you doing, M?" Grub asks, untying his apron.

"Ung."

Grub sits beside him. The Minotaur is worried.

"Listen." Grub pauses before he speaks again. "I think, tomorrow, I'm going to have the bug guys come in and spray the whole place. We've gotten a couple complaints."

The Minotaur thinks it's a good idea, but he wonders what it has to do with anything. Grub peels the wrapper from a mint-flavored toothpick and begins to scrape the food from beneath his fingernails.

"There are no reservations in the book for tomorrow. I checked with David."

"Mmnn."

"I might as well close tomorrow night. Let the exterminators do a complete spray and give the place time to air out. We'll see how Hernando's leg is, and your foot, too."

The Minotaur nods.

"I'd like for you to come have dinner at my house tomorrow night. Meet my kids, see my wife again. And I want to talk to you a little bit."

The Minotaur says okay, he will. Grub tells him what time

to come, and that he doesn't need to bring anything.

The drive home is painful and slow. The Minotaur tends his burned foot well into the night.

CHAPTER 13

*T*he *morning air* is sweet and cool. If not for his throbbing foot, smeared with aloe jelly and wrapped in gauze, the Minotaur would be content to lie in his narrow bed scratching himself. The Minotaur's keen sense of smell finds the mingled scents of honeysuckle and burned diesel fuel, the latter still in the air from when the Crewses drove out before daylight. Honeysuckle and diesel—and blood. Metallic and sour. Elemental. It takes him awhile to determine the source of the smell. In his distress last evening the Minotaur neglected his ablutions. He did not bathe or groom his horns. On the tip of his right horn—which hangs forever just inside his field of vision precisely opposite the horn seen from the other eye, which together serve as a frame of reference that keeps him oriented in the world—there, staining a good three inches of the Minotaur's polished horn, is a dark patina of blood. Hernando's.

The realization nauseates him not because his horn has never been wetted with blood before, even the blood of those he loves. In fact it is precisely that his horns have wreaked havoc on flesh so many times throughout his life that causes the Minotaur gastric stress. The Minotaur does not bear guilt simply because it would be impossible to carry the burden that is certain to accrue over the span of such a long life, even if that life belonged to someone less monstrous. He exists, day to day, year to year, century to century, in a state of indifference, sometimes blessed, sometimes cursed. What makes the Minotaur's stomach seize is that over the years he has come to recognize cycles within his life. The Minotaur moves from place to place and time to time. He settles in, tries to be as innocuous as possible for someone with the body of a man and the head of a bull. And for a while there is stasis. A decade. Two. Sometimes a half-century. He cooks, he takes care of his body, he minds his business and tries not to mind the business of others. But then things begin to go wrong. More often than not someone gets hurt, and the Minotaur has to move again. He dreads the coming evening, the dinner at Grub's.

The Minotaur has lain in bed later than usual this morning. Cars pass at irregular intervals out on the road, people going about the business of their lives. It's almost eight o'clock. Mrs. Smith's television is on, and someone is winning big. As soon as he swings his feet off the bed and sits up the blood surges to his wound, pounds at the pinkish watery dome of flesh that begins at his instep and sweeps up across his knobby talus. The Minotaur winces and stands.

Through the window the Minotaur watches Sweeny step out of his back door carrying some table scraps in a pie pan for the dog. Buddy comes from beneath the deck, stretches and follows Sweeny into the dog run. As the Minotaur sits on the toilet, unwrapping the gauze from his foot, he hears Sweeny close the gate, then get in his car and drive away. He uses soap and warm water to clean the blood from his horn; he hopes Hernando is okay. The Minotaur limps into his kitchen to make coffee, hoping that the bitter brew will overcome the taste of bile in his mouth.

"Marvin!" Josie screams. "You want eggs or Cocoa Puffs?"

Marvin wants eggs *and* Cocoa Puffs. The Minotaur sits with his coffee and watches the boys play. They have retrieved several beer cans from the wading pool, a green turtle-shaped thing full of beer cans in their backyard. After filling them with sand the boys take turns throwing the cans against the big pine trees at the edge of the driveway. It's a game, but the Minotaur can't tell who's winning because Marvin and Jules get equally excited by the cans that survive being slammed against a tree and the ones that rupture on impact and send a spray of sand into the air. Buddy the bulldog runs back and forth in his pen barking at each thrown can, working himself into a fevered pitch.

The coffee doesn't settle the Minotaur's stomach. From the refrigerator he takes an open box of baking soda, stirs a heaping teaspoonful into a half glass of tap water and chugs it. The Minotaur belches through closed lips. A few minutes later Josie comes on to the porch with a spatula clutched in one hand and a cigarette in the other. She's wearing an oversized T-shirt, thin and white, that says *I'm With Stoopid* in ironed-on red letters and has an arrow pointing to the right. The T-shirt hangs to just below Josie's crotch. The Minotaur convinces himself that it's all she's wearing. He shifts in his seat.

"Eggs is about ready, boys," she says, waving the spatula in the air. The Minotaur watches bits of yellow egg fall around her feet. Josie doesn't wait for Marvin and Jules to respond. Because the Minotaur is watching the outline of Josie's body move under the fabric as she turns on the porch and walks back into her trailer, he doesn't see exactly what happens next. By the time he looks again Jules and Marvin have stopped their throwing game and left bent and torn aluminum cans scattered all over the yard and driveway.

It's not uncommon, on this straight downhill stretch of road defined by curves at both ends, in this hot fly-bitten part of the world, during this time of year, in this particular decade, to hear the pop and rattling sputter of a truck or car decelerating as it nears one curve or the other, the rapid-fire *thrrrraapppt thrrrraapppt thrrrraapppt thrrrraapppt thrrrraapppt* of a combustion engine decompressing, of spent energy pounding its way down the pipes. It's a sound the Minotaur enjoys, more or less, a sound he doesn't usually associate with apprehension.

"Goddammit, Jules! Get away from that dog!" Josie shouts, but it's too late.

Jules clings lizardlike to the dog run's chain-link gate while Marvin swings it back and forth. All the Minotaur can see of Buddy is his piebald behind rounding the corner of Sweeny's house.

Sweeny is a good man, willing to give you the benefit of the doubt, not at all prone to fits of rage or irrational actions. But Sweeny loves that dog.

Time, however abstract the concept, has its own inherent sense of the absurd. The passing of a moment, its coming and going in one's life, holds infinite possibilities. It can be as brief and meaningless as the firing of a single synapse that starts the involuntary twitch of an upper lip. Or it can contain the decimation of whole worlds. The Minotaur cannot entirely follow what happens next. It seems that some glitch in the interaction between time and space has rendered the Minotaur, Josie, Marvin, Jules and everything for miles around Lucky-U Mobile Estates immovable but aware. Everything, that is, except for Buddy and the souped-up Ford Pinto squealing around the curve at the top of the hill.

It comes first as sound. Neither the Minotaur nor Josie nor the boys can see the car, but everyone stops dead in their tracks and listens to its approach. Everyone and everything freezes, is unable to move. The Minotaur knows the Pinto by its sound, knows it belongs to a neighbor's son who seems to do little else with his time but modify the four-cylinder engine and drive train and test-drive the car up and down the stretch of road in front of Sweeny's house. So when the unseen driver throttles the unseen car, its wide rubber slicks barking against the pavement, its throaty intake manifold sucking air directly through a hole cut in the hood, sucking it deep into a cavernous four-barrel carburetor, where it generates a fury that manifests itself in pistons, valves, cams and camshafts, clutch and gears, the Minotaur has a picture in his mind. Enter the piebald bulldog into the picture.

Buddy at full tilt is a ridiculous sight. He's crossing the yard at an angle, heading toward the road. Buddy's short parentheses-shaped limbs swing wildly and seem independent of one another. Despite this fact the dog makes determined progress over the gravel driveway, through the Johnson grass, down into and up out of the side ditch. By the time he reaches the crumbling edge of the asphalt the Pinto is in sight, and everyone witnessing the event knows with unshakable certainty that the two moving bodies will intersect.

They do.

Simultaneously Mrs. Smith drops something inside her trailer and wails; through the window the Minotaur bellows at the top of his lungs; Josie, on her porch, grimaces and so desperately holds back a scream that she farts loudly; the boys, Marvin and Jules, usually overcome by uncontrollable laughter at even the most innocuous instance of parental gas, can only cry where they stand. Buddy doesn't make a sound. Not the impact of his body low on the Pinto's front quarter panel near the bumper, where metal-flake orange flames sprout and begin to weave back to the door. Not his abbreviated but gymnastically impressive flight through the dewy morning air. Not his bouncing halt, belly up. There is no bark, no yelp, no noise at all. In death Buddy looks bemused.

Only after Buddy lies still at the edge of the road do the inhabitants of Lucky-U reanimate, released from their stasis. Forgetting his wound the Minotaur rushes barefoot into the yard. Once there he's not sure what to do, so he just stands looking. Marvin and Jules crawl under their front porch and huddle together, whimpering. Mrs. Smith turns the volume way up. Josie tries to light a cigarette, but her hands shake too much.

The Minotaur limps up, steps onto her porch, realizes he

is shirtless and tries nonchalantly folding his arms across his chest. Josie looks at the dead dog. The Minotaur smells eggs burning in the pan, and the remnants of Josie's fart. Something about the crisis makes him think to kiss her, but he doesn't dare. He looks down at his feet jutting from the faded pajamas. His injured foot throbs. The blister has ruptured. Already the flies swarm at the pinkish liquid pooling beside his foot.

"Unng," the Minotaur says.

"Unnhuuh," Josie replies.

CHAPTER 14

Buddy lies dead by the side of the road. The hot rod Pinto doesn't stop, and in its wake a pall is cast over Lucky-U Mobile Estates. In the sky the sun fades, its brilliance diminished. The unfortunate birds within the boundaries of the trailer park grow lethargic and mute; those flying over struggle mightily until they break through on the other side. All the colors, painted or natural, even the green of the leaves and grasses, seem duller. Josie and the Minotaur stand looking out at the road and the dog's carcass. They stand in silence, the Minotaur shifting in place to keep the slow-moving flies from biting. Josie smokes eagerly, desperately, not letting a single breath into her lungs without its first passing through the smoldering tobacco and tight cotton filter of the cigarette clamped between her lips. The spatula, still clutched in her hand, hangs at the end of a limp arm and rests against her thigh; a drop of grease the color of corn trickles down the swell of muscle. The boys, huddled and whimpering, visible in the narrow sunlit strips between the planks, refuse to come out from under the porch.

The Minotaur sweats when he is nervous, particularly his groin and the hirsute channel between his buttocks. It's a problem that has plagued him since he began wearing clothes. He tends to gall. The Minotaur is embarrassed by the frequency with which he buys medicated powders, sometimes passing up the nearest stores for fear of being recognized. Standing there on the porch with Josie in her too-thin _I'm With Stoopid_ shirt, the day after goring his friend and coworker, having just witnessed Buddy's untimely demise, sweat beading inside his pajama bottoms, welling up and trickling down the delicate skin of the insides of his thighs in fiery stinging rivulets, the Minotaur remembers that he didn't bathe last night.

By this time the sound of the eggs burning in the pan is almost electric. The sizzle nearly fills the unnatural silence accompanying Josie's and the Minotaur's mutual disbelief. His stomach growls, rolls over, and the wet audible belch that follows carries with it the taste of baking soda and coffee. The Minotaur widens his stance just a little, hoping to lessen the burn of the heat rash. Josie, too, shifts her weight. The Minotaur can't help noticing how her buttocks grow taut beneath the fabric, lifting it slightly, clinching. But the sound of her flatulence will not be so easily contained. After a while, in the absence of words, the sounds of the functioning of the two anxious bodies become painful. Josie, without saying anything, goes back inside.

The Minotaur stands there alone for a few minutes more, then begins a slow bowlegged limp back to his own trailer. Exactly why they leave Buddy lying in the ditch the Minotaur can't say. It isn't a decision per se, arrived at or settled upon. In fact, throughout the morning, as the Minotaur goes about his business, washing the *briki*, cleaning himself and bandaging his wound, as they wait for Sweeny to come home, he occasionally looks out the window and thinks about moving the animal, moving him into the yard under a shade tree or wrapping him in a blanket to lie in state on Sweeny's back porch or anywhere out of sight. But as the day passes, minute by minute and hour by hour, it gets harder to take action.

The Minotaur feels the herd mentality settling in. Even though Mrs. Smith never leaves her trailer, and though neither Josie nor the Minotaur speaks a word about the accident, he knows that they all are hurtling toward denial. It is the path of least resistance. If they pretend hard enough that he wasn't killed beneath a speeding car, maybe Buddy will resurrect. Perhaps he'll come swaggering around the corner of the house with a white dove perched on his shoulder, making proclamations about truth and the afterlife.

Hank comes home. He stops the van in the middle of the road and hangs out the window to look at the dead dog. He stomps on the parking brake, and the sound echoes through the trailer park. Hank leaves the door standing open, the van dangerously close to the centerline. The lever-and-cam, pulley-and-hinge quality of Hank's exercised body is apparent even clothed in the filthy teal jumpsuit. He approaches Buddy cautiously, and even from his window the Minotaur can sense the domed muscles of Hank's shoulders and arms and the long muscles of his legs. Hank nudges the dead dog with his toe. He gets back into the van.

Whether there are telltale signs or not, Hank must know that Jules and Marvin had a role in whatever happened because he's yelling even before the van rolls to a stop on the bare patch of dirt in front of their trailer.

"Josie!"

"Marvin!"

"Jules!"

Josie comes from inside, having tucked the tail of her shirt into a pair of lavender corduroy shorts cut on both sides up to the waistband. Marvin appears from the far side of the porch, and Jules struggles up out of the thin opening between two steps. Like good soldiers falling in for inspection they line up. Despite leaning closer to his open window the Minotaur can't make sense of what Hank says, but the tone is clear in his gesticulation. Within moments Jules and Marvin are pointing at each other. Josie adds nothing to the conversation. She stays on the porch when Hank herds the boys inside. The Minotaur knows the sound of a belt against flesh.

Half an hour later, after the boys have stopped crying, the Minotaur sits at the kitchen table cleaning the grease from his shoes and watching Hank throw the heavy barbell up and down and up and down and up. The Minotaur is a little dizzy from the fumes rising from the squat round tin of black shoe polish open on the table. Using an old toothbrush dipped in degreaser he scrubs the seams where the thick rubber soles are stitched to the uppers. The Minotaur cocks his head, snout up, seeking less noxious air. Through the window he sees Hank walking toward him, chest bare, the shirt half of the jumpsuit stripped off and bunched at the elastic waistband. Chest bare and slick with sweat, Hank comes hesitantly.

With each step Hank slows his approach, until he stops in the middle of the drive in front of the boat-shaped trailer. Rocking on the balls of his feet he looks first at the Minotaur's front door, then at Buddy lying stiff legged, already beginning to bloat in the afternoon sun, beside the road. Again he looks back and forth, unable to make a decision.

The Minotaur continues cleaning his shoes. Hank turns and walks away.

It's three o'clock and Sweeny hasn't come home. Abandoned is any idea of moving the dead pet for fear of being caught in the act. In a few hours the Minotaur is supposed to be at Grub's house for dinner. He spends the time polishing the steel-toed shoes to an absurd shine and going through his closet, as if by looking again and again at the several pairs of hound's tooth work pants, two pairs of blue jeans, half a dozen chef's coats and three radically altered and undeniably frayed oxford shirts, he will come upon some combination of clothing that won't embarrass him.

There is still no sign of Sweeny at five-thirty. When the Minotaur drives out of Lucky-U Mobile Estates—wearing clean but faded denim pants, well-shined shoes and a cream-colored button-down shirt with permanent, however faint, sweat stains in the armpits, a shirt that will not button around his massive neck—he averts his eyes to avoid the dog.

The Minotaur is already imagining the flush of shame he'll feel at Grub's front door. Grub wants to have a little *talk*. That was his exact word. The Minotaur is afraid of the outcome. Over the years the Minotaur has learned some things about social protocol. He knows not to show up as a dinner guest without some small gift for the hostess or a contribution to the meal. On the way to Grub's he stops at the MiniMart for a bag of assorted donut holes.

Rachel, Grub's wife, answers the door.

"Hey, M," she says. "Good to see you again. How's your foot?"

Rachel, her voice like clover honey trickling over apples, maternal Rachel with the body of a woman, full and settled into living, Rachel with translucent, pale, ocher skin and ink-black hair, Rachel in purple batik and wooden clogs—Rachel stands in sharp contrast to Grub, a sweet but genuinely unattractive man.

"Umm."

She reaches to shake the Minotaur's hand and seems about to lean forward to kiss him but doesn't really know where on that long expanse of jowl to place her lips, so she stops. Between trying to decide whether to offer his own hand and positioning his head in case she does kiss him, the Minotaur gets confused and drops the bag of donut holes. Fortunately it doesn't rupture.

"Let me take those," Rachel says. "Thank you so much for bringing them. Come on in. Grub is in the den."

The Minotaur limps behind her. He has been to the house

before, but not inside. However, nothing about the sixties split-level surprises him—not the concrete duck wearing a plaid raincoat in the foyer, not the sunken living room and the wall covered in photographs, a framed, matted, specious documentary of the family's lives, not the sign with the neon lips and tongue flashing *EAT EAT EAT* over the kitchen door, not even the elaborate ant farm sprawling over the coffee table, three plastic dwellings thin as paperback novels but tall and wide, full of white sand, a labyrinthine path weaving through each, all interconnected by clear snaking tubes. None of this surprises the Minotaur. It is a house inhabited by children; the Minotaur would know it even if he hadn't met Rick and Raylene, both in that vague place between seven and ten years old. He's seen pictures of the little one, Roger, four years old and the spitting image of Grub.

"Quite a setup, huh?" Grub says, walking in from the den to where the Minotaur stands transfixed by the ants working fervently at their tasks, climbing over and around the tiny green cutouts of tractors and barns and haystacks at the top of the sand, posturing as they greet one another in the plastic tubes, bearing their burdens as if they actually know why.

"Glad you could make it, M," Grub says, then goes on to tell him about how the ants come frozen in a cardboard carton. "U.S. mail," he explains.

They go into the kitchen, where Rachel stands at the stove. Before the Minotaur can protest she shoves a wooden spoon full of something into his mouth.

"Vegetarian chili," she says.

"Mmmm," he answers, and stands by the refrigerator crushing the grainy bulgur and beans against the roof of his mouth. Grub opens the door into the backyard, where the kids are playing. From outside comes the high-pitched whine of a model airplane engine, a single tiny piston whipping furiously in the cylinder.

"Be back in a minute," Grub says. He leaves the door open behind him.

Taped to the refrigerator door is a crayon drawing of what must be a crow and a blood-red sun. The artist's name, scrawled, is the biggest thing on the page: ROGER. Above the drawing a small calendar from the La Leche League is held in place by a magnet shaped like an old-fashioned milk bottle. Here-7PM is written in the circle around tomorrow's date.

The Minotaur asks if he can help do anything. Rachel says no, so he goes outside to find Grub. Roger and Raylene sit on the picnic table watching Ricky, who is standing in the center of the deep treeless yard pivoting in a tight circle. Clenched in the boy's hands is a red oval plastic handle, very like the handle for controlling a kite. But what is attached at the other end, to the two parallel wires extending out twenty-five feet or more from the top and bottom of the handle, is not a kite. It is a model airplane, a Japanese Zero, sputtering through the air in forced orbit.

Since it is useless to try speaking over the loud engine Grub signals for the boy to land the plane. Rick shrugs and continues his own tiny orbit. But within a few minutes the little engine spits and coughs, gasping for more of the white alcohol fuel, then stops. Rick glides the plane to a bumpy halt in the grass. Roger and Raylene run out even before the plane is completely still. The younger boy excitedly opens the hatch over the little plastic seats where the pilots would sit, and out jumps a frog. The frog, confused and dizzied by its experience, leaps again and again. And every time the frog lands it tips over on its back, then struggles frantically to right itself. Disruption of the equilibrium is a new thing to the animal. Roger and Raylene follow the frog, squatting and leaping in mimicry, laughing hysterically each time they and the frog upend.

"Time to wash up," Grub says. Leaving the frog to its lopsided escape and the toy plane parked motionless in the grass, the children head for the door. Relieved of their distraction they all seem a little leery of the Minotaur. What was giddy energy just moments before becomes reticence tinged with fear. The children have never seen the Minotaur outside the kitchen of their father's restaurant or dressed in anything other than dirty chef's coats, and the difference is disconcerting.

"Come on! Come on! Come on!" Grub says. "We'll die of starvation before you kids get to the table."

Rachel has the dinner table set by the time they get back inside. The chili steams from a crock in the center. Small bowls of diced onion, tomato, grated cheddar cheese and sour cream surround the crock. Cornbread muffins shaped like little ears of corn poke up out of a cloth-lined basket. Wedges of iceberg lettuce are lined up in a straight row on a translucent blue platter in the shape of a fish.

"Have a seat, M. Anywhere," Rachel says. "It'll take a few minutes for the kids to get cleaned up."

"You want a beer?" Grub asks.

"Mmmh."

The Minotaur sits at the end of the table simply so his horns won't be a problem. On a plate on the sideboard the assortment of donut holes surrounds a dish of halved strawberries. The children come into the dining room one at a time, Roger, then Raylene; the Minotaur can smell the Ivory soap on their skin. They sit squeezed in on one side of the Minotaur and have to work very hard to keep from looking at him.

"Let's go, Rick," Grub calls.

Rick finally arrives, concentrating and serious in manner. He pulls out his chair and sits with perfect posture, then speaks in his most grown-up voice. "What's for dinner this evening, Mother? I'm feeling quite anthropophagous."

"You are?" Rachel asks without skipping a beat. "Well, I'm sure we've got something that will cure that."

Grub looks at the Minotaur, bemused, raises a brow and offers his palms. The Minotaur smiles back, more or less, unsure of what to do with the oddity of Rick's word. Rachel serves everyone, fixing her own plate last before sitting beside the Minotaur. Rick shifts in his seat.

"If I don't eat soon I may have to pandiculate," he says.

"Not while company is here," Grub answers. "Dig in, M, before the chili gets cold."

The Minotaur shifts in his seat, trying to settle his buttocks in such a way that the chafed areas are separated. Everyone begins to eat.

"Good," the Minotaur says to Rachel, and Grub agrees heartily.

"I dub you Queen of the Chili Pot," he says, winking at his wife.

"Does that make you King of the Pot?" she asks.

"No, dear, I'm merely a knave at your beck and call."

Rick shifts again in his seat. The Minotaur can't be sure because he doesn't want to stare, but he thinks the boy is checking notes under the table.

"I think the chili is missing something, but I'll have to excogitate before I can decide what."

"Rick," Rachel says.

"Eat your dinner, son."

Rick takes a few bites, then jumps up from the table, claiming he's forgotten to wash his hands. When he leaves the room Grub explains to the Minotaur.

"Ricky did real good on his language tests at school. He's convinced himself that he's a genius. Now he's trying to convince the rest of us."

"He's in his room thumbing through his dictionary," Rachel says. "Making another list of words."

The younger kids whisper back and forth, giggling occasionally. The Minotaur likes children. When he catches Raylene and Roger, heads together, peering sidelong at him through their mingled bangs, the Minotaur rolls his top lip up to cover his black nostrils, the thick yellow wedges of his teeth driven into bared gums. Raylene does her best to subdue squealing laughter; Roger does his best to roll his own top lip.

"I do apologize for being so fuliginous," Rick says, returning to the table.

And the meal continues happily. Grub talks about the deck he wants to build out back. Rachel talks about the kids. The kids make faces with the Minotaur. Sometimes they all talk at once; the Minotaur finds contentment in the ruckus. He's nervous; he can't eat much, but he's happy to be there.

"Tomorrow," Rick begins during a lull in the conversation.

"Tomorrow at school . . ." Rick struggles to keep a straight face.

". . . in science class . . ." His eyes are fired with mischief.

"Get to the point, Rick."

". . . fourth period . . . Mrs. Sink has asked me to demonstrate a sigmoidostomy." It's all Rick can do to get the word out before erupting, and the laughter is so consuming that it becomes spasmodic and almost without sound. Rick falls out of his chair, lies beneath the kitchen table laughing. Roger and Raylene laugh simply because laughter is infectious. Equally in the dark, Grub, Rachel and the Minotaur roll their eyes and smile at each other.

"Who's ready for dessert?" Rachel asks. "Did you have enough chili, M?"

"Mmmm."

"You don't eat much for a big fella."

"Mnnh."

She passes the plate of donut holes and strawberries. From the kitchen comes the smell and the sputtering gurgle of brewing coffee. Rick says he has to feed his hamster, Möbius Strip, and do his homework. Grub excuses him from the table. The younger kids seem content to sit and listen. When Rachel goes for the coffee Roger and Raylene huddle together and concoct some secret plan. They leave the table as their mother is returning with a tray of coffee mugs, each cup bearing a grainy, black-and-white, computer-generated photograph of the entire smiling family. When Grub pushes his chair back from the table to get comfortable the Minotaur does the same. After a little while Raylene comes back into the dining room and quietly takes her seat.

"Where's your little brother?" Rachel asks.

Raylene points at the door, and when everyone turns to look the boy's head darts out of sight. He returns within seconds, tentatively. Bit by bit Roger eases around the doorframe. His impossibly tiny sneaker comes first, followed by one skinny leg, then his hip and little cylinder of a trunk, his arm, his shoulder, then half of his thin face. And when Roger is standing fully in the doorway, his face beaming, Raylene snickering in the background, the Minotaur sees the horns. They've stapled together cardboard tubes from empty toilet paper rolls to form blunt tips, held in place by long strands of Scotch tape that crisscross the boy's head and wrap around the paper tubes.

The Minotaur laughs aloud; a wet belch of a noise erupts from his cavernous throat. Roger takes his seat and reaches for a donut hole. The Minotaur knows the *talk* is coming, but he decides that sitting peacefully with this happy family, that talking, drinking coffee and eating with them, that the rare pleasantness of the moment are worth it, whatever the outcome of his conversation with Grub. As they get more confident at interacting with the Minotaur, Roger and Raylene inch closer and closer. When Raylene sneaks up behind him and impales a donut hole on the tip of his left horn, it seems the most natural thing in the world. Rachel scolds her halfheartedly.

It doesn't take long before the excitement of the evening begins to wear the children down. Raylene yawns loudly. And as Grub describes to the Minotaur a boxing match he saw the night before on television, Roger, still wearing the horns made of cardboard tubes, leaves his chair, climbs into his mother's lap, parts the dyed fabric of her blouse, reaches in to take out her breast, seeking to nurse.

"Not now, sweetie," she says, removing the boy's hopeful hand and closing her blouse. The Minotaur is left to imagine the teat, thick as a fingertip and proud, to imagine it smoldering like a dark ember cresting a swell of ivory flesh. The smell of milk, real as can be, metallic and bloody, storms the Minotaur's nostrils.

"That Hispanic kid was so cute," Rachel says, stroking Roger's hair, "until he got his lip split in the fifth round."

"I think it's about bedtime for the Bonzos," Grub says.

Raylene looks as if she's about to protest.

"Say good night to M, Ray," her mother says, cradling Roger as she stands from her chair. "It's time to brush your teeth."

"Night, M."

"Mmm."

Grub and the Minotaur sit quietly for a while after the others leave the room. Finally Grub speaks.

"I want to talk to you for a little bit, M. Let's go into the den." Grub stands, and the Minotaur follows him. "Would you like a beer?"

"Nnnn."

"How's your foot, by the way?"

"Ummn."

"Rick calls this my sanctum sanctorum," Grub says, reaching for the knob. When the door swings open the light that dribbles out is insipid, lifeless, unnatural. "Rachel's name for the room isn't so grand. It used to be the garage."

The Minotaur follows Grub down two low steps into the room. Despite the dark veneer paneling on three walls, despite the painted brick of the fourth, despite the carpet that the Minotaur recognizes as a remnant from the restaurant, despite the leatherette sofa and ottoman sitting opposite a huge gunmetal gray desk, the windowless room retains much of its garage-ness. Along the far wall, standing on top of a squat bookshelf that is empty except for a golf trophy and two stacks of *Restaurants & Institutions Magazine*, is the source of the weak unnatural light. It's a lava lamp, a luminous red mass contained in a narrow cone of glass endlessly dividing and rejoining like torpid and monstrous cells.

When Grub pulls the chain to turn on the twin swag lamps hanging over the desk, the Minotaur sits at one end of the couch. Beside him, on a table, a thing called The Perpetual Wave rocks back and forth, its tiny electric engine whirring and working too hard. Half a yard long, the thin plastic rectangle holds two liquids, one clear as water, the other a heavy viscous blue. Each time the container tips up, the blue substance spills and swirls in wavelike fashion downward. The incessant motion makes the Minotaur a little sick to his stomach.

"I talked to Hernando this morning," Grub says.

"Hnnn?"

"It was a clean puncture, but they want him to stay off the leg for a few days."

Grub just talks for a while, not really saying anything, and the Minotaur grows more and more apprehensive. Finally he broaches what the Minotaur knows is the subject.

"You seem . . . ," Grub begins. He is a tactful and compassionate man. "You seem to have trouble concentrating lately."

"Mm."

"I mean, Lord knows I understand a slump. Ups and downs."

The Minotaur wishes he could unplug The Perpetual Wave. He looks away. On the walls around the room are photographs tracking the life of Grub's Rib: opening night, employee picnics, Christmas parties, local celebrities. The Minotaur looks for his own horned figure among the pictures.

"It's frustrating for me, as a businessman, to have to put the needs of my business first. Especially when I get so close to my employees. Jeez, you guys are as much like family as Rachel and the kids."

The Minotaur rubs at a spot of mud on the heel of his polished shoe.

"You want another beer?" Grub asks, not waiting for an answer before going out the door.

"Unnh," the Minotaur says to himself.

The Minotaur thumbs an untidy stack of papers on the table by The Perpetual Wave. When he realizes that they are tax papers for Grub's employees the Minotaur looks closer. He feels an odd sense of power, holding all this information. He finds Kelly's paper—full name, address and things he probably shouldn't know. The Minotaur clumsily stuffs it in his shirt just as Grub comes back into the room.

"I want to try something new," Grub says. "Just for a while."

"Hnnh?"

"Well, you know how we run the prime rib special on Friday and Saturday nights. And how it always sells out."

It's true, the Minotaur knows these things well.

"When I was at the food show in Chicago I saw something that just might work down here."

The Minotaur is curious. Grub tells him that he wants to run prime rib as a special every night, and maybe even take the T-bone off the menu. As sort of a permanent promotional gimmick Grub wants to rig up a beef station in the main dining room, a heated cart on wheels with a shallow well where whole cooked rib roasts will sit under a hinged dome of plastic, fat caps browned and glistening, the rare meat moist, vermilion, inviting. The beef cart will have a cutting board and a small heated vat of salty Au Jus. It will be wheeled from table to table, the prime rib cut to order for all to see.

"What do you think?" Grub asks.

"Mmm," the Minotaur says, but still isn't sure of his role in the plan.

"I want you to be the beef carver," Grub says hopefully. "It'll get you out of the kitchen for a while. We'll get you a couple new chef's coats and an extra-extra-large hat."

"Hm." The Minotaur tries to picture himself in a white cylindrical chef's toque. The image is absurd. "Hernando?"

"I think you're the better man for the job," Grub says. "Let's try it for a couple weeks and see what happens."

"Not fired?" he asks.

"No, M, of course you're not fired." Grub puts his hand on the Minotaur's shoulder. "Is that why you thought I asked you over?"

The Minotaur feels sweat trickling down his chest, feels the sharp edge of creased paper against his skin. Wishing he hadn't taken the form, he plucks it from his shirt and shoves it between the pages halfway into the novel David gave him earlier.

"Good night," Grub says.

The Minotaur drives back to Lucky-U Mobile Estates with the Vega's windows rolled down. The night air buffets his huge tired head and roars in his ears. He sings. He sings the oldest songs he knows, moving from one to the next, sometimes in midnote. The Minotaur is glad that he still has a job, even if it means being on public display nightly, but the feeling that things are changing for the worse prevails. He sings to mask that feeling; the wavering pitch and the missed notes get lost among the sounds of his traveling.

Buddy's body is still lying beside the road, its four legs pointing skyward. When the Minotaur pulls around the house Sweeny's car sits in its usual place. The kitchen light shines through the window. The Crewses' trailer is dark; the others are lit but silent. Not even the sound of Mrs. Smith's television breaks the uneasy quiet. The Minotaur stands for a moment in the shadow of the mimosa trees, a ragged black hole in the wash of light from the buzzing street lamp. He contemplates knocking on Sweeny's back door but has no idea what he would say.

The darkness of his own trailer welcomes him. When he switches on the anchor-shaped lamp his living space becomes immediately and impossibly tiny. As if his horns stretch from wall to wall. As if with the slightest movement he will gouge the wall, puncture the window screens, shatter the glass. As if. The Minotaur moves carefully through his trailer to the bedroom, where he removes the shoe from his injured foot. The blister has ruptured; the fluid has soaked through the bandage and stained his white sock. The raw wound stings in the open air. The Minotaur bathes, grooms his horns, treats and salves the skin at his division. He tends to his ablutions hoping that each act, each ritual, will bring peace of mind. But in the confines of his trailer the Minotaur grows more and more restless. In his pajamas he walks from one end of the mobile home to the other. Sleep is out of the question. Because he was nervous he didn't eat much at Grub's. The only substantial thing in the refrigerator is a hard-boiled egg. The Minotaur peels it under running water and stands hunched over the sink, clutching a salt shaker in the shape of a cowboy boot. The salt has taken some moisture and will not flow freely. He taps the shaker against the countertop before using it and eats the egg one small salted bite after the other to prolong the experience. In the morning, if he remembers, he'll put a few grains of uncooked rice into the shaker.

There is a black-and-white television sitting on the bar in the Minotaur's kitchen, its screen no bigger than a child's lunchbox. It was there when the Minotaur moved in. Only once, maybe twice, surely no more than three times during his residence, has the Minotaur turned the TV on, corrected the vertical roll and actually sat watching. But something about this night draws him to the deep empty screen.

Watching television, and particularly one so small, is physically challenging for the Minotaur. He has to sit close enough to reach the round dial for changing channels and to twist and bend the wire clothes hanger wrapped in foil that is stuck into the broken antenna, then cock his head back and to the side to fix the little glowing rectangle in his sight. The Minotaur's eyes are tired, and every few minutes he has to turn his head and look through the opposite eye.

He doesn't understand much of what is broadcast. The sitcoms confuse him, both the reruns from twenty years ago and the newer ones. The televangelists with their weeping and pleading stir in him old and dangerous desires. The Minotaur has seven channels, sometimes fewer. As he clicks through the numbers on the dial, everything he comes to is either a sales pitch or a laugh track. Unsure as to what channels he actually receives the Minotaur turns up into the double digits. Eighteen, nineteen, twenty, twenty-one, nothing but hissing static. Thirty-six, thirty-seven, thirty-eight, the same. But at channel forty-three something stops him. The picture rolls, fractures; the sound is barely audible. The Minotaur fiddles with the makeshift antenna. When he finally gets a reasonably clear picture the program goes to commercial. The Minotaur sits before the black-and-white television while an assortment of men and women, all with bare midriffs, demonstrate a wicked-looking contraption called The Abdominizer.

"Are you lonely tonight?" a disembodied voice asks. The camera is fixed on a low table and two glasses of sparkling wine. A thickly carpeted floor leads to a fireplace in soft focus in the background, the fire crackling in shades of gray.

"Me, too." It is a breathy voice accompanied by moody piano music. The camera pans left to the arm and high back of an overstuffed chair facing the fire. All that can be seen of its occupant is one thin leg, clad in a high-heel boot to the knee.

There is something familiar in that voice. The picture goes to static but comes back into view as the Minotaur leans forward to adjust the antenna. When he leans away, there is static again. The Minotaur twists, positioning his body so that the signal stays clear.

"We don't have to be lonely by ourselves." A lean white arm reaches out. The arm is atrophied, but the hand that cups and lifts the wineglass is broad, knuckled and masculine, despite its long painted nails. The Minotaur assumes red.

"We can be lonely together." As the wineglass is lifted to the mouth the camera swings around to the figure in full view: the high black boots, the satiny robe that implies nakedness beneath, the poised hands, the blond hair in ringlets. The face, obscured, refracted in the glass, could be beautiful. When the glass is pulled away the lips are pursed and wet, and the heavy-lidded eyes blink languidly into the camera. The Minotaur lows softly.

"Hi. I'm Hermaphroditus, and I want to be your special friend."

The tectonic plates of the Minotaur's heart pitch and heave. Recognition. Hermaphroditus and the Minotaur, by-products of carnality. Whore's birds. Ancient stepchildren. Siblings of the genus *Erroneous*. A chasm, unbreachable, opens within the Minotaur, and he falls into an all-consuming sadness.

Hermaphroditus peddles a tired old beauty.

"Hermaphroditus Telephone Escorts. I can be anything you want."

"Hermaphroditus is waiting for your call."

"Hermaphroditus Telephone Escorts. Have your credit card ready."

The Minotaur should turn off the television here and now, but he doesn't.

CHAPTER 15

The Minotaur *dreams himself a zygote—dreams
the weight of the yoke across his back—
the whittled ribs and lungs thick with sawdust*

*The Minotaur dreams himself a zygote, formed half—
half formed—no—malformed out of aberrant desire
hammered into life by Daedelus—shortsighted bastard*

*In the dry trough of his birth canal the Minotaur dreams already
of retribution—dreams the sluice gate and the hot wash of shame—
dreams the broadax splinter and pulp*

CHAPTER 16

*B*ut *the Minotaur* does not turn the television off. Nor does he move from his hunched and uncomfortable position, necessary for a clear picture. Rather, he sits bent forward on the frayed couch, his heavy head cocked and drooping, the thin muscles of his lower back taut and aching. Two other commercials follow Hermaphroditus, but neither registers in the Minotaur's mind. When he finally musters the wherewithal to change the channel, once again, hapless fate or poor timing rules the choice.

The Minotaur clicks the dial once, twice. On the third click a blurred image emerges from the static. It is important to note that the bull is a color-blind animal. The Minotaur, however, is blessed with color. Only when tired or weary are his coal-black ocular disks unable to perceive at least the primary colors. But the bull, strictly defined, lives in a monochromatic world, seeing only degrees of gray. When the image of the matador appears on the tiny black-and-white television screen the Minotaur knows that the cape sweeping through the air and over the arena's dirt floor in graceful arcs is red. He knows, too, because he has a man's heart, that the red of the cape has much more to do with the psychology of the audience than with anything inherent in the bull—the bull jet-black but for one ragged patch of white like a cluster of grapes on its haunch, the bull enraged and pawing at the arena floor.

At each pass of the bull the audience roars in approval. "Olé! Olé! Olé!" drowns out the Mexican announcer and the brass horns and the drum. "Olé! Olé! Olé!" drowns out the huffing, wheezing and snorting bull, which cannot possibly understand that the picadors, high on their padded horses, drive the barbed lances again and again into the thick muscle between its shoulder blades to weaken its neck so it cannot raise its head without excruciating pain. The bull was bred for this: kill or be killed. With each pass of the sweeping cape the bull's dark head brushes the brave unmoving matador, its horns seeking despite the pain, eager for any soft target. "Olé! Olé! Olé!" Each pass, each turn and each move are named. Even in the confines of the small television screen, even rendered colorless, the matador's suit of lights—the beaded bolero, the skin-tight pants that define the contours of his muscled thighs and buttocks, that unabashedly pronounce everything male about him—is captivating, seductive. Even in the confines of the small television screen, even rendered colorless, the blood streaming from the pulpy wound on the bull's back glistens horribly.

The matador prances. He stamps his feet and shouts to provoke the bull, which stands laboring for breath before him. Up on his toes, the thin-soled *zapatillas* digging into the dirt, sighting down the long metal blade, the matador steels his heart and profiles for the kill. Because it knows no other option the bull charges. The proud matador stands motionless until the last possible second, solid and fearless as granite, then simultaneously leaps aside and plunges the narrow sword into the wounded flesh between the bull's shoulders. The tip of the blade is curved slightly, hooking downward to ease the passage among the ligaments, cartilage and bone, to find and sever the thick aorta deep in the bull's chest.

When the sword penetrates, the Minotaur's lungs seize. A searing pain climbs his spine. The matador is careless in his arrogance. The sword misses its mark. Rather than sink to the hilt with ease through the animal's viscera the sword stops short. Protruding from the bull's back eight, maybe ten inches, the blade sways wildly back and forth. The bull flings its head from side to side, looping strands of blood-tinged saliva flying from its mouth. The Minotaur feels sick to his stomach.

Outside, on the road, in the dark, the driver of a passing car taps twice on the horn. Inside, in the pale light of the television, the Minotaur watches the matador dance around the bull and pull the sword from the wound. The spectators roar from the wooden stands and stamp their feet, a deafening sound even through the small speaker. Nearing death the animal—stupid and proud—is undaunted. It again accepts the challenge of the matador. The matador—stupid, proud, vastly human—meets its charge and drives the sword home.

To come upon the scene—the matador facing the bull with his arms outstretched and palms turned up—it's possible to think he is attempting to embrace the animal, that he is seeking or offering forgiveness for what has just transpired. But the Minotaur knows differently. When the matador lifts and lowers his hands slowly, the movement mirrored by the bull's head as it follows up and down, the Minotaur knows that it is an action with a purpose. Each time the bull raises its head the blade embedded deep inside its chest cuts and damages more.

Die. The Minotaur wants the bull to die. But the bull is adamant at life. Somewhere inside the massive chest blood gushes. The heavy body begins to sway, but the bull refuses to topple. It tries to make a step toward the open-armed matador; its front legs give way, and the bull pitches forward. Still it will not fall. The matador taunts the dying bull, standing arrogantly mere inches from the once-threatening horns. The cumbersome head is now unable to do more than bob softly as the animal struggles to stay alive. In one final heroic burst of bovine valor the bull staggers to its feet and bellows, the cry choked and muffled by the blood gushing from its mouth and nostrils. The Minotaur feels faint.

He has no idea of the origin of this broadcast—another country, another time. He has no idea of the miles and the minutes, or hours, or maybe years, that separate him from the death of this bull. But when this matador, broken down into minute particles, then shot through time and space to be reconstituted in black-and-white and four inches tall in the Minotaur's trailer, when he steps before the standing bull and hammers his fist down once on the wide bony plate between the animal's eyes, the blow strikes deep in the Minotaur's own heart. The bull goes rigid instantly. Its eyes bulge and roll up, the thin milk-white rims glaring from black pits. Then comes the fall, stiff legged and impossibly slow. The big dead bull leans and leans and leans, a mockery of gravity, held aloft by the raucous fervor of the audience.

"Bravo! Olé! Bravo!"

It falls, though the sound of its body coming to the ground is lost. When the puntillero comes with the short dagger with the three-sided blade, when he stabs it at the base of the bull's skull, severing the spinal cord, the animal's body goes into spasms, legs pedaling the air. And the Minotaur falls to his knees. To be a man means to be capable of this. To be a bull.

CHAPTER 17

*T*he *Minotaur doesn't* use his telephone, never has. As a matter of fact, in the hundred-plus years of the telephone's existence, the Minotaur can count on the fingers of one hand the
number of times he has made or received a call. Though Sweeny
has provided an old rotary telephone in the cramped boat-shaped
trailer, the likelihood of its ringing for the Minotaur is small.
And no matter how distraught, the Minotaur is less likely still
to pick up the receiver and fit his thick-nailed fingertips into
the dial the seven or eleven times necessary to call anyone. Something about the unnatural manipulation of time and space. Something about the disembodied nature of the voices. Something
about the fat sluggish tongue.

Standing in the gravel drive of Lucky-U Mobile Estates in
the tattered blanket of light from the street lamp, images of both

Hermaphroditus and the dying bull reeling in his head—pictures so graphic and tangible as to stink of sweat and blood,
images that boil up deep within the brain, storm the synapses
and slam again and again at the back of his eyeballs, pictures so
incessant that the distinction between them blurs and it becomes
the pale naked body of Hermaphroditus on all fours in the center of the dusty arena that takes the sword, Hermaphroditus
who bellows open-mouthed and retches blood, the sagging
breasts, the withered penis and testicles bobbing and swaying,
and it is the black bull that becomes the tawdry whore of late-
night television, satin robe splitting at the seams, wineglass
wedged in its cloven hoof, breathy solicitations whispered from
its rubbery black lips—standing in the driveway the Minotaur
suffers blurred vision, his heart thumps furiously and he yearns.
He yearns for yesterday. He yearns for two days ago, before
Hernando's wound, before Buddy's death, before Grub's new
plan. And he yearns for even more. The events of the evening
and the past few days have put him in a rare state; the Minotaur
longs to be in the company of another person.

But who? Where to go? Calling anyone is out of the question. His needs are simple; he wants nothing more than to share
space, to breathe common air with another living being. But
there is no one in his immediate world. He can't knock on
Sweeny's door, not tonight, anyway. The Crewses probably
wouldn't wake up. Josie and Hank are out of the question. The
Minotaur gets into his car and rolls the windows down. As he
reaches for the hand brake his thumb rakes the fore edge of the
book he has all but forgotten and catches on a folded piece of
paper. He breathes heavily as he unfolds the tax form to read

Kelly's address in the weak yellow light that falls from the dome in the Vega's roof. He almost laughs aloud at the absurdity of the act. The Minotaur almost laughs because he knows, even as he pulls on to the road and pushes the gas pedal to the floor, the valves slapping and knocking against the rockers as the tired four-cylinder engine struggles to gain speed, he knows that he cannot stop at Kelly's house.

He knows it the first time he drives by. He knows it the second, the third and the fourth. But not until driving past Kelly's darkened house a fifth time does the Minotaur believe it enough to keep driving. With no second destination in mind the Minotaur drives in the hope that the hot night air washing over him will clear his head. He crumples his stolen secret and tosses it out the window on a littered stretch of highway, where it will surely get lost amid all the other trash. When the Minotaur pulls to a stop in front of David's apartment he is no less muddleheaded, and even as he walks to the door he's not sure why he's there. A sign in Sister Obediah's window blinks CLOSED CLOSED CLOSED CLOSED, but he sees thin blades of light between the partially open venetian blinds.

Standing at the window, reading the menu of Obediah's services, the Minotaur wishes he could believe in what she has to offer: a promise woven into the deep lines of his palm, some turn of fate told by a card. But faith is a nebulous thing and charlatans a dime a dozen; it's always been that way. The Minotaur both envies and pities the devout.

The Minotaur hears voices from inside Sister Obediah's. He cocks his head to hear better. A man's voice totally devoid of emotion says something in English, then repeats phrases in another language—a familiar language, old and heavy with diphthongs.

"*Taedium vitae.*"

"Taedium vitae."

"*Taedium vitae.*"

And then Obediah's voice tentatively mimics each phrase after it is spoken, her version a little quieter and less precise, as if she is attaching shadows to the words.

"*Sudum est hodie.*"

The weather is nice today.

"*Quid admisi sceleris?*"

What have I done wrong?

"*Cubitum eamus.*"

Let's go to bed.

Sister Obediah is teaching herself Latin. The Minotaur recognizes the language.

"*Capillus satis compositus est commode?*"

The Minotaur searches his memory for definition.

"*Res male inclinant.*"

He turns his bullish head to press an ear to the glass, forgetting for an instant the cumbersome horns; it is a frequent and disturbing oversight. Almost immediately after the bony protuberance raps against the windowpane, the lights extinguish. All is quiet inside Sister Obediah's. Afraid of being caught looking in her window the Minotaur steps quickly into the stairwell of the apartments overhead. Moths orbit a naked bulb in the ceiling high above; the sounds of their wing beats and of their bodies striking the Sheetrock ricochets in the windowless enclosure.

The Minotaur is halfway up the stairs before he remembers something he has to do. As quietly as possible he slips back out to the Vega and climbs over the front seat so he won't have to open the squeaky rear hatch. From the bottom of his toolbox he pulls a small handmade sanding block, which he puts into his pants pocket. Back in the stairwell the Minotaur smooths the hardened Spakle paste from where he repaired the wall. Then he sits for a while on the steps trying to decide what to say if David answers the door.

He does.

"M?" David asks from the cracked door. As if it could be anyone else standing there with the head of a bull.

"Unngh," the Minotaur answers. As if there were another, a truer answer.

David steps back to let the Minotaur inside.

"Wake you?" the Minotaur asks.

"No," David says. "I was up."

Lights are on in the back of the apartment; the smell of gun oil is palpable. They stand in awkward silence in the doorway of the apartment, and it takes the Minotaur a few minutes to realize that David is not wearing odd pajamas, as he'd first thought. Rather, he is garbed in the Civil War uniform the Minotaur saw in the box the day he helped David move. David is embarrassed. The Minotaur is embarrassed.

"Grub told me," David says. "About the beef cart. You want to come in?"

The Minotaur nods and follows David back to the lighted room.

"There's a battle this coming weekend. A reenactment. I'm just cleaning my Springfield."

"Mmm," the Minotaur says, and looks for a place to sit. The room is large, large enough for the pumpkin-colored sofa and the low coffee table at the opposite end to seem miles away, sitting beneath the open window that looks out over the alley. Old newspapers spread across the tabletop protect it from the oily parts of the disassembled rifle neatly arranged over the covered surface. At one end of the table a thin metal can of gun oil leans against a gym sock with a blackened toe. The Minotaur tries to sit across from the sofa on an upholstered chair with a high curving back, but the arc of the chair back is too tight for his horns. David gets a straight chair from the next room and sets it opposite the couch.

"What am I thinking?" David says when the Minotaur tries to sit in the wooden chair. "You take the sofa."

"Unnh."

"It's been awhile since I've had guests," David says. He picks up the sock and pulls it down over his right hand, then begins to buff the blued breech and trigger mechanism of the gun. David talks about each piece as he polishes it.

The Minotaur doesn't talk about his landlord's dead dog or the accident with Hernando. He doesn't talk about what he saw on the television less than an hour ago. Instead the Minotaur asks David about the upcoming battle, about what role he'll play in it.

David, with boyish enthusiasm, explains it all. David shows him the battle plan and the roster. He reassembles the musket as if it were a performance. David, on his knees, lugs a heavy box of photographs from deep in a closet. He sits beside the Minotaur on the couch and opens the leather-bound album with care bordering on reverence.

Understand this: in his lifetime the Minotaur has had lovers, and they have run the gamut in species, gender and degree of consent and reciprocity. He has known both eager maenads and resistant victims. And the very nature of his existence, the facts and rumors surrounding his progenitors, render him nothing if not open-minded in the area of sexuality. But those lovers were all long ago, so distant, in fact, that the Minotaur cannot remember the last time he was touched by a hand motivated by desire. These days intimacy of any kind is difficult, perhaps impossible. As for the various sexual acts people engage in, the Minotaur has long since stopped entertaining those notions. So when David sits proudly beside him on the couch to show his battle pictures—battalions of men in uniform charging amid billowing gun smoke or writhing in mock death—the Minotaur doesn't withdraw. When David opens the book and his hand comes to rest, accidentally, on his friend's thigh, the Minotaur doesn't pull away. He doesn't flinch when David closes the book and leaves his thin nervous hand where it rests, or even when David, sometime later, walks self-consciously across the room to what the Minotaur thinks is a closet and pulls down a Murphy bed made up with the pro wrestling sheets. Even then the Minotaur does not balk.

This type of transition is more difficult for the human than for the Minotaur. While the Minotaur is willing to follow nearly any path that opens up before him, he doesn't often forge ahead and take decisive action on his own.

David sits on the edge of the bed and, with little more than a nervous glance, gestures for the Minotaur to do the same. His hands, however tentative, are welcome on the Minotaur's tired shoulders and down his spine. The closeness of his face is accepted. But although David may have notions, quiet hopes even, about the things their bodies can do together, once he and the Minotaur lie on the bed together nothing really happens. Once David fits his body snug against the Minotaur's, his head nestled in the sweeping arc that begins as the Minotaur's neck and ends at his horn, once there David seems content, or at least unable to go any farther. They lie all night on the Murphy bed with its sheets tightly tucked, the Minotaur dozing only for moments, if at all. Each time the Minotaur moves—be it an involuntary twitch, a repositioning of his arm, anything, no matter how slight—David's body stiffens. So the Minotaur concentrates on stilling himself.

In the morning it is David who feigns sleep as the Minotaur quietly leaves; the Minotaur can tell by his breathing, which is too deep, too regular. Sitting in the Vega with the door open, on the quiet street, the Minotaur taps the gas pedal with a practiced rhythm until the sputtering engine warms up enough to idle on its own. Just as he is about to pull away from the curb a cinnamon-colored BMW motorcycle pulls out of the parking lot of the apartment building across the street. The shield on the rider's helmet is dark. The motorcycle stops briefly beside the Minotaur's car. When the cyclist revs the engine, pops the clutch and wheelies down the street, the black acidic pit of the Minotaur's stomach roils and torques.

But for the lingering odor of gun oil that refuses to dissipate even with the car windows rolled down—a heavy permeating scent that will stay with the Minotaur until he bathes—he could almost forget the previous evening as he drives home.

Buddy is still dead, still lying belly up by the side of the road in front of Sweeny's house. If the Minotaur were just a little bolder he would take the dog's carcass late in the night and put it in one of the dozens of gunnysacks Sweeny keeps in a bucket in the unlocked shed, sacks he uses in the fall to store and dry all the peanuts growing in the half-acre lot behind Lucky-U's only unoccupied trailer; the Minotaur, if he were even the merest hint of his former self, would take the dead dog way out in the country and throw it in Bunyan's Slough. Instead he looks the other way when turning in the driveway.

CHAPTER 18

By the afternoon the carcass has begun to bloat. The chemical processes of decay taking place inside the dead dog's body demand more and more space. By the following afternoon the body splits open in several places, like an overripe fruit, and swarms of flies suck at the stinking nectar. Stirring momentarily when cars go by, they hover in dark and frantic little clouds, then settle again. As the days pass, the presence of death at work by the roadside, malodorous but quiet, seems less and less an anomaly. To come home and find Buddy's shrinking remains lying by the driveway, a cairn of bones and hide, seems as normal as anything else in the Minotaur's world.

Sweeny acts as if nothing has happened, coming and going as usual, selling cars from his yard and buying others to replace them. The only part of his routine that has changed is that he no longer stands out on his listing back porch in his underwear calling the dog or makes the daily trip to the dog run with the pie pan full of table scraps.

One day the Minotaur is pulling away from his trailer to go to work when he hears Sweeny whistle. Sweeny's whistle is unmistakable. He rolls his loose fleshy lips to manipulate the gale generated from way down in a small but pronounced pot-belly, then forces the wind past where a wedge-shaped piece of tooth is missing from one of his lower incisors; this combination allows for a whistle so powerful it can be deafening. The Minotaur stops the car as soon as he hears Sweeny. He prepares himself for confrontation, or at least for denial. But when the Minotaur makes the effort to turn his cumbersome head in the confines of the driver's seat, Sweeny just smiles and gives a big wave from where he sits. The Minotaur waves back and drives off.

"I ain't seen them boys since that dog was killed," D. W. Crews says to the Minotaur. It's early morning, almost sunup, and several days since the accident.

"You?" D. W. asks.

"No," the Minotaur says with a clarity that surprises him. In fact he hasn't seen Hank or Josie either. He thought that maybe this morning, up early because Sweeny wants him to rebuild a carburetor in a VW bus and carburetors always give him trouble, he might see Hank leave for work, but Hank's van was gone by the time the Minotaur came outside. Only two of the Crews brothers stir, readying for work in the pinkish phlegmy light of dawn.

"What happened to your foot?" D. W. asks the Minotaur after noticing his limp.

"Hurt."

"Hmmm," D. W. says.

"I'll sure enough miss him," A. J. says. He sits on the mud-crusted bumper of the logging truck scratching around and around a sore the size of a quarter beneath his right ear. D. W. climbs into the cab.

"Uhhn?" the Minotaur asks.

"That dog," A. J. answers.

The Minotaur nods but says nothing.

D. W. cranks the truck, and the barely muffled engine sputters and backfires before finding a regular idle. A. J. takes a grease gun from a small metal box welded to the center of the bumper and climbs up between the high metal posts onto the flat bed of the truck. Against the cab an oily cylinder rises out of the center of the bed, and atop it a hydraulic piston and the messy apparatus of a crane stretch toward the back of the truck. A. J., too short to see, reaches along the top of the boom until his fingers find the zerk, the grease fitting, and using both hands he guides the coupler onto the blackened nipple. He pumps the trigger of the grease gun twice, then begins feeling for another zerk. D. W. gives several brief taps on the truck's horn.

After A. J. locks the grease gun back into the box he gets into the truck with his brother. For several minutes the Minotaur watches the two men sit in the idling truck and stare out the windows. A sudden wave of impatience washes over D. W.; he scowls and pounds the horn. When the trailer door opens the Minotaur expects to see J. C. come out, as he does every morn-

ing, wearing dirty blue coveralls and carrying his lunch in a
brown paper bag and a milk jug full of sweet tea. J. C. is in fact
standing at the door, but the Minotaur can't tell what he is
wearing or if he is carrying anything. The Minotaur's view is
blocked by the woman who comes out of the trailer door in
front of J. C. Stern faced but not unpleasantly so, older than
any of the Crewses, she has small pursed lips, almost cartoonlike
in their precise redness, that offset the teased ash-colored hair,
which smells to the Minotaur of aerosol spray net. Looking as if
she just walked from behind the reference desk of the local library, holding the only correct answer to the question, the
woman nods deliberately at the Minotaur and the men in the
truck and marches down the center of the driveway and into
the morning. The sound of gravel crunching beneath her sen-
sible pumps grows fainter and fainter. J. C. climbs into the truck,
and the Minotaur hears D. W.'s curses as they drive away.

By the time the Minotaur gets the VW carburetor disassembled the sun is full in the sky and heating things up. He lays
the parts out in order of removal on an old army blanket: butterfly, jets, bowl and float. The gasket he has to scrape away
from the surface. As the Minotaur leans into the rear of the Vega's
open hatch, reaching for the carburetor rebuild kit, he hears
the door of one of the trailers open.

It's Josie. Mingling with the odors of putrefaction, the
Minotaur smells the bacon grease in the cast-iron frying pan she
struggles to balance in front of her, holding tight with both hands,
trying not to spill the grease on her bare feet as she walks. The
thin T-shirt she wears over her black two-piece bathing suit is
the whitest thing in sight. The trailer door stands wide open,

and Jules and Marvin peer out from inside. Josie is nervous. The Minotaur can tell it from a distance. Through the windshield he can see her look anxiously toward the back door of Sweeny's house. All she has to do is reach the side yard and the shallow ditch lined with chokeberry bushes, where she will pour her unwanted bacon grease, then hurry back to the safety of her trailer. It's an easy task, except that Josie isn't paying attention to where she walks. When she stubs her toe on an exposed root Josie's first instinct is to curse loudly.

"Fuck!"

Her second instinct is to let go of the heavy pan.

Her third is to protect herself from both the falling pan and its hot contents. In a feat of rare athletic prowess Josie simultaneously throws her arms back winglike and leaps several inches off the ground and backwards. The frying pan thuds to the ground, and hot grease sloshes over the sides and congeals almost instantly in the red dirt, but none hits Josie. The problem arises when Josie herself lands. With her feet together and extended behind, Josie is off balance and top heavy. Her thin bare feet planted on the earth act as a pivot, and gravity draws her home.

When Josie falls face down on the ground the Minotaur, forgetting that he has his head inside the narrow hatchback of the car, starts. He remembers where he is the second his horn gouges a hole in the vinyl headliner.

"Fuck!" Josie says, sitting up on her knees. "Fuck! Fuck! Fuck!"

Once out of the Vega the Minotaur doesn't really know what he should do, so he does nothing. It's not until Josie reaches around with both hands to pull the shirt over her head that the Minotaur realizes the smear of greasy red mud sweeping in a ragged irregular crescent from her clavicle down between her breasts to her hipbone is in the vague shape of the Greek mainland and islands. Crete marks her right nipple.

Jules and Marvin laugh. Even before Marvin yanks on the curtain over the door, the curtain printed with overlapping rodeo scenes and matching the rug and toilet-seat cover in the trailer's only bathroom, even before the door slams shut, the Minotaur senses mischief.

He doesn't know what it is about little boys that makes them take pleasure in watching others—even, or especially, loved ones—suffer. He does know that the inclination follows many of these boys into manhood. Jules and Marvin laugh; the Minotaur hears them even through the closed door. Josie leaves the frying pan where it dropped; she bunches the shirt in her hand and wipes away the grease that soaked through to her skin. The half-moons of fabric over her breasts and the wedge covering her pubis are the blackest things in sight.

At his core the Minotaur is a voyeur. His humanity ebbs and flows in a cycle all its own and refuses to be called upon, refuses to be predictable. When he is at his most human the Minotaur is often overcome with shame from the number of times in his tediously long life that he has stood idly by and watched an event unfold, though he is less and less able, as time passes, to influence outcomes. Sometime in the future he'll wish that he had offered Josie help.

Josie flinches when the door to her trailer slams shut. A perceptible spasm shoots through her entire body. When her children laugh, anger and embarrassment jockey for position on her face. Josie heads for the trailer, not exactly running but definitely not walking. Out of the context of her lawn chair turned to the sun in the backyard, Josie looks awkward and uncomfortable pounding on the locked door in her bathing suit and her deep even tan.

"Open this door right now, goddammit!"

The madder Josie gets the louder and more hysterical the laughter of Jules and Marvin becomes. When Josie circles the trailer prying at the windows, looking for an unlocked one, the Minotaur hears the boys running back and forth inside. By the time she reappears from behind the mobile home Josie is raging. The Minotaur, having had some experience with fury in his life, stands behind the car and watches as she curses and rails. When she begins to hurl sticks and the small abundant quartzite rocks at the sides of the trailer, the Minotaur hunkers down, fearing ricochets.

Then Josie just stops. She stops swearing and stops throwing things. The Minotaur can't tell if she stops out of defeat or if she is simply gathering her forces for another charge. She stands in front of the trailer with her arms crossed over her chest, breathing deeply, audibly through her nose.

Feeling that danger has passed, the Minotaur stands from his crouch. In standing he bumps the tray of sockets—arranged first according to the size of the drive, then by dimension, metric on one side, standard on the other, divided by the polished ratchets—balanced carelessly on the lid of the closed toolbox. They spill, a brief hailstorm of steel. The squat cylinders scatter in the grass, catching the sun as they roll and tumble.

The Minotaur is still on his knees gathering up the spilled sockets when Josie walks up. He stands, and just as he is cocking his head to hear her speak the trailer door opens wide and bangs against the outer wall. That's when Josie slaps him. Her tiny furious hand gets lost in the black expanse of his cheek; the intent stings more than the blow. Josie closes the door behind her; the Minotaur goes back to collecting his sockets.

Things have quieted down by the time the Minotaur stops for lunch. Sitting at his table by the window, dipping a whole onion into a saucer of salt, eating white bread after each bite of onion, listening to the occasional car speeding by on the road, the Minotaur can see the dark little clump that was Buddy, and he realizes that the stench of the rotting dog has become almost pleasant. Subdued, the odor has a flowery undertone, as if a tropic wind from a distant orchard of some exotic fruit has been borne across oceans and continents and delivered to the noses of the inhabitants of Lucky-U Mobile Estates.

No sooner does this notion occur to the Minotaur than Sweeny comes from the back door of his house. The Minotaur hears the keys jangling before he actually sees Sweeny; when he does come into view he's swinging the key ring around and around on his gnarled sticklike forefinger.

It's not unusual to see Sweeny squatting to open the padlocked plywood door to the muddy crawlspace beneath his house. Nor is the Minotaur surprised when Sweeny hauls the push mower out into the yard, then reaches in again, half of his body disappearing into the black square mouth, to get the gallon can of gasoline with the yellow spout like a beak. What does seem unusual is that Sweeny puts the lawn mower back under the house and keeps the gas can out. The Minotaur watches him fish in his pockets for something. Not finding it, Sweeny leaves the gasoline on the steps and goes back inside the house; he is absent only a moment. He hooks two fingers beneath the handle on the can and walks around the house and down the driveway.

The Minotaur shoves the last piece of onion into his mouth, folds a piece of bread into fourths and pushes it in as well. He's still chewing when he gets out to the car, where he can get a clear view as Sweeny douses Buddy's rotten carcass with the contents of the can. Half a gallon of gasoline, turning copper in the sunlight, spills back and forth across the body. Sweeny steps back out of the way—too far, in fact. He flicks a lit match, but it is extinguished before it lands; a scant thread of smoke is all it produces. The same thing happens with the second match. Sweeny steps closer, thinks for a moment and takes another step forward.

This time the lit match finds its target. There is more sound than light, a resonating breathy *whoooom*, as if, rather than being propelled outward, all sound is sucked into the explosion, is consumed in the flames along with the dried flesh and viscera, the fur and bones of the dead piebald bulldog. The blast knocks Sweeny back to where he first stood and takes his eyebrows as a toll. Other than that he is unharmed. Sweeny watches until he is sure the fire is well fueled, then picks up the gas can and starts toward the house.

The Minotaur busies himself in the engine compartment of the VW bus when he sees that Sweeny is walking his way.

"Unnh," he says when Sweeny walks up.

Sweeny stands for a while without responding. "Them damn

hippie wagons always need some kind of work, don't they?" he finally says.

"Mmmm," the Minotaur answers, leaning in and squinting to adjust the jets of the carburetor.

"Hurt your foot?" Sweeny asks.

"Mmm."

"Listen, M," Sweeny says. "Couple days, I want you to take a ride with me. Got a deal on something and I need to pick it up. I want you to check it over for me."

The Minotaur agrees. Sweeny watches him work for a few minutes. He kicks around in the grass and finds a quarter-inch socket the Minotaur missed.

"Thanks," the Minotaur says.

"He was a damn sight," Sweeny says.

"Unnh?"

"That dog."

"Mmm."

Sweeny goes back into his house. The smell of burning carrion fills Lucky-U Mobile Estates. Out by the road a black tongue of smoke licks at the sky.

CHAPTER 19

I *want to licksniff kellys big hairy asspussyhole*—the Minotaur
sees it as soon as he sits. It is written upside down but plain as
day in red ink just above the baseboard in the employee toilet.
Little more than a closet between the kitchen and the main wait
station, barely wide enough to accommodate the Minotaur's
horns, the employee bathroom is designated for use by everyone who works at Grub's but in reality is used mostly by the
busboys and the kitchen crew; unless there is a party booked
Grub pretends not to notice when the waiters and waitresses
go up the back stairs to the rest rooms serving the windowless
banquet room overhead. Who can blame them? Even for the
least fastidious among the employees of Grub's Rib the hot,
cramped, smelly bathroom is unpleasant.

The Minotaur spits on the corner of a towel and rubs unsuccessfully at the graffiti with his fingertip. The ink doesn't even smudge. There are dozens of the red pens throughout the kitchen and wait station. Hernando uses them to label things in the freezer. Cecie dates containers of cut vegetables and cheeses for the salad bar. The waiters and waitresses keep the pens around for their own reasons.

The ink is indelible; the message is permanent. It makes the Minotaur angry, inordinately so, for he is not above any of the layers of implication surrounding the obscenity: desire, impulse, action, juvenile prurience, etc. Nevertheless the message makes him angry, and anger chokes his bowels.

"Unnh," he grunts, then stands and reties his apron strings.

The wire brush that he seeks has fallen behind the grill, and by the time the Minotaur gets back to the bathroom Maynard, a sullen teen with horrible acne and a profile very like a chicken's—a boy hired just yesterday to take over the salad bar when Cecie moves up to the hot line—is going into the bathroom with an unlit cigarette pinched between his beaky lips.

"Outside!" the Minotaur says, and pushes past.

Maynard, of course, doesn't argue.

The Minotaur closes the door behind him and kneels. A few swipes with the wire bristles and the obscene message is completely gone, along with a six-inch strip of paint. The act diminishes the Minotaur's anger. He is fortunate in that way.

Coming out of the bathroom with the brush held truncheon-like he meets David. David, whom the Minotaur hasn't seen since that night. David, whose pasty face cannot hide a blush, whose awkwardness and embarrassment are acute.

"Hey, M," David says, a little too loudly for the circumstances. The ballpoint pen in his fingers leaves a blue thread of ink down the wall.

"Hmm," the Minotaur answers, the manifestations of his own guilt—guilt more about being caught with the brush in an act of anger than about anything else—obscured by the dark fur covering his face.

David starts to back out of the narrow hallway so the Minotaur and his horns can get by. Walking backward without paying attention, he doesn't see the laundry hamper overstuffed with stained uniforms and souring towels until his foot tangles in the neck loop of an apron that hangs from a split in the cloth bag, and he falls onto his seat on the floor. The Minotaur puts the wire brush handle into his back pocket and extends his hand to help David up, and David, avoiding eye contact, reaches up tentatively.

The instant their hands touch, the Minotaur knows that it is possible for he and David to never talk about the night in the apartment. Even after thousands of years the human capacity for avoidance, the ability to so completely cloak a moment in denial or shame or fear, to wrap it so tightly inside as to render it fictive, is confounding to the Minotaur. Time after time he has learned that it is quite possible to share the most intimate or horrific of experiences and the very next day have it denied outright. He knows that David will never mention what happened. He knows, too, that it doesn't mean for certain that they will not spend another night together sometime in the future. Such is the way of human interaction. But for now, a precarious period of time—things said or done, unsaid or not done—will shape how their relationship plays out. Doors open and close in the house of ethos with a rhyme and reason all their own. Ultimately the Minotaur will allow David to decide what happens.

"Thanks," David says, brushing off the seat of his pants. He struggles to make light of the situation. "I wondered where that apron went."

The Minotaur works up a smile but doesn't speak. David doesn't know about the motorcyclist the Minotaur saw that morning. The Minotaur isn't sure that it matters—hopes it doesn't.

"Are you ready?" David asks.

Grub borrowed a pickup truck from one of the waiters the day before yesterday and went to a restaurant supply warehouse to buy the beef cart; he has everything ready for the Minotaur to make his debut in the dining room. It's early afternoon, not quite three o'clock, and Grub wants to explain the setup and do a run-through.

"Mmn," the Minotaur says. He doesn't mention the graffiti to David. He doesn't mention his apprehensions about the coming night. The Minotaur goes behind the line to make sure Cecie and JoeJoe know what prep work they're supposed to be doing.

"Hey, M," Grub says, coming in from the dining room. "Do you know where Hernando keeps the carving knife?"

"Mmm," the Minotaur answers. From a low shelf beneath the steam table he pulls a flimsy red toolbox. A brass padlock hangs open on the bent clasp. All the good knives Hernando keeps here. Inside just under the lid is a shallow plastic tray that holds the small tools of the trade: the meat thermometer, its round eye marking increments from zero to two hundred and twenty degrees, several new vegetable peelers, a zester, paring knives, decorative tips for the pastry bags. The eighteen-inch serrated blade of the carving knife will fit in the toolbox only standing diagonally on edge. Hernando keeps it, along with the chef's knife, in a plastic sleeve to protect their edges. The fish knife, especially flexible for following the curvature of fragile ribs, has its own leather sheath. A whetstone lies gray and oily at the bottom of the toolbox.

"Hhun," the Minotaur says, turning the long knife handle-first to Grub.

"You hang on to it," Grub says. "Bring it when you come out. And the sharpening steel, too."

Before the Minotaur can say anything else the back door of the kitchen opens. He sees first one rubber-tipped crutch, then another, before Hernando, dressed in his hound's-tooth work pants and chef's coat, comes into full view.

"*Qué pasa*, guys?" Hernando asks, his tripodal movement through the kitchen remarkably fluid.

"Yo."

"What's up, *hombre?*"

"Hernando! *Como estás*, my man?" Grub asks.

"I'm okay," Hernando says.

The Minotaur nods, somewhat apologetic, and gives Hernando plenty of leeway.

"Hey, M," Hernando says. "I hear you're the star of the show tonight."

"Hmm," the Minotaur says, and rolls his big black eyes.

"You'll do fine."

They talk some more, Hernando and the Minotaur, until it

is clear to them both that there are no hard feelings. Hernando asks about the Minotaur's foot. David brings a stool from the bar and leaves it at the end of the hot line for Hernando, who plans to stick around until the rush is over, doing little but overseeing and making sure that JoeJoe and Cecie can handle their new stations.

Thinking it would be a good idea to promote the new tableside beef carver, Grub ran an ad in the newspaper and bought thirty-second spots during both the gospel hour and the broadcast of a high-school baseball game on a local radio station.

"Grub's Rib. You'll think you've died and gone to prime rib heaven."

Despite Grub's nervous and overly emphatic on-air delivery, by six o'clock this first night, his idea for advertising has proven to be a good call. The restaurant is packed, and there is a twenty-minute wait already.

"You look good, M," Jenna says.

"Oooo, sexy," Shane says.

But the Minotaur doesn't feel good standing there behind the beef cart just inside the main dining room. It is tethered by a short orange cord to an electrical outlet; the Minotaur will have to squat in a precariously tight space and unplug the cord each time he's beckoned to a table. The beef cart is a waist-high thing with a hinged lid of clear plastic that diffuses the light from the heat lamps fixed on a chrome bar hanging above it. The plastic dome all but magnifies the glistening rib roasts, halved and standing on end, their pink flesh unabashedly bared, lined side by side in the perforated pan recessed into the top of the cart. The salt-crusted fat caps and the stacks of curving rib bones have a blood-tinged sheen. The Minotaur doesn't feel good standing there, his prodigious head looming beneath a cloth chef's toque that is draped—absurdly, he thinks—over the flat plane between his horns, but he is grateful to Jenna for saying it. She has the first order of the evening. The Minotaur unplugs the beef cart and follows Jenna to a four-top near the salad bar. He has to roll the cart slowly so as not to slosh the Au Jus from its full and heated well.

It's hard to say what the customers think about having the Minotaur as their table-side carver. For sure, it's not what they expect. When the door opened and the first rush of the evening began there was one couple who walked out of the restaurant as soon as the Minotaur came from the kitchen and took his position behind the beef cart. For whatever reason they were not willing to tolerate a creature half man, half bull slicing their roast. Grub was momentarily worried that maybe this wasn't such a good idea, but no other customers have since walked out. Aside from the occasional gasp and the involuntary flinch when the Minotaur appears unexpectedly and suddenly in customers' fields of vision, most are able to contain their surprise and to limit their reactions to gawking when they think the Minotaur is not aware. Those who can't get beyond the shock and are unable to deal with the Minotaur simply order something else from the menu and avoid him altogether. Little by little, as the night progresses and as one table of customers sees another order the prime rib and sees that prime rib sliced at their table by the Minotaur, the air of tension gives way to something that is not quite acceptance but might be closer to sufferance. Gradually he is overlooked, becoming an unpleasant means to a tender and delicious end.

After Jenna's order, Adrienne and Robert have a party of eight all wanting prime rib. Then Margaret. She's waiting on Mr. Honeycutt, who has come alone every Wednesday night at six-thirty for the past five years, alone, wearing the same ill-fitting toupee and an increasingly gaudy selection of gold jewelry. Honeycutt, who comes in humble and lamblike, is as polite as can be until his fourth Wild Turkey, after which he begins grabbing at whatever waitress he currently has a crush on. This month it's Margaret he asks for. Last week he told her that his penis is thirteen inches long. Mr. Honeycutt owns the Fox Triple-X Drive-In. The waitresses tolerate him because he tips better than anybody else.

The Minotaur sees Kelly. She's in section two, over by the fountain that hangs by a plastic brass-colored chain from the ceiling, an ornate kiosk of sorts about the size of a small waste can, at the center of which a featureless nude heroine stands— or, more accurately, arabesques—while all around her beads of shimmering glycerol perpetually spiral down the thin clear threads that are the bars of her cage. Intermittently and with no discernible pattern, from somewhere inside the base of the fountain, some device attempts to recreate the sounds of trickling and gurgling water. Kelly is busy with drinks and appetizers. She smiled and said hi to the Minotaur earlier, which gave him a fleeting surge of hope, but so far she hasn't needed his services as a carver. The Minotaur thinks for a minute about the obscene message on the bathroom wall, but his imagination proves ungainly, leaping quickly from wondering who wrote it to speculating about the act the graffiti described.

Even from the dining room he can smell the half-dozen prime ribs cooling in their roasting pans on the baker's rack in the kitchen. Deciding how many ribs to cook was tricky. Too many would be a costly mistake, but the whole ribs take two hours at 375 degrees in the convection ovens, then half an hour or more on the cooling racks before they can even be served as rare; once they're gone that's it for the evening.

So far the night is progressing smoothly. The only problem is that Cecie forgot to pound the breasts for the chicken piccata. To do it on the kitchen worktables, where every pot and dish rattles with each strike, is impossible during business hours. From where he stands sentinel the Minotaur can barely hear muted thumping, and he knows that Hernando is inside the walk-in cooler with the door closed, standing over a cloth-draped table swinging a meat mallet down on the vaguely heart-shaped pieces of chicken flesh, pounding at them until they are thin as paper and almost translucent.

"Yo, tit man," Shane says. "I need you in section three. The deuce with the cancerous-looking old fuck in a piss-yellow blazer."

The Minotaur had hoped, unrealistically, to avoid Shane all night. He unplugs the beef cart and wheels it into the smaller dining room. The piss-yellow blazer is easy to spot.

When the Minotaur steps up to the table customers have three choices: King Cut, Queen Cut and the Page. Twelve ounces, eight ounces and two three-ounce pieces, respectively. Grub, if he gets enough requests, plans to add a sixteen-ounce Knight's Choice to the menu.

"You got a end cut?" the old man squawks even before the Minotaur comes to a stop.

"Yes," the Minotaur says slowly. Grub told him to speak

slowly and clearly and to answer questions with words whenever he can.

"I'd like me a ten-ounce end cut, done extra well," the man says. "What about you, Bunchy?"

The overdressed woman with him, Bunchy, says, "Me, too."

Running the length of the beef cart is a thick plastic cutting board eight inches wide, held in place by small steel dowels at each end. A narrow channel with an imperceptible tilt marks the two long sides and one end of the cutting board. At the other end, on the right-hand side, a rectangular hole drops into the belly of the beef cart, where a small bucket catches the blood, juice and bits of fat and gristle that the Minotaur scrapes from the cutting board after carving each order. Unless the customer specifically asks for the meaty rib bones that remain as the Minotaur cuts away the eye of the roast, the Minotaur tosses them into a pan under the beef cart. They'll be slathered with a sugary orange barbecue sauce and cooked for the employee meal.

"Me, too," Bunchy says again, as if things need repeating, the Minotaur being what he is. "I want a end cut well done."

Shane comes from the kitchen, giggling maniacally. The hairs on the back of the Minotaur's neck bristle. He doesn't attempt to explain that there isn't a ten-ounce selection on the menu, nor does Shane offer to clarify.

The Minotaur keeps the carving knife and the two-pronged meat fork crossed on the cutting board. After trying various ways of laying them—side by side at an angle, then straight, knife to the front, fork in back, then the other way—he decides that crossed is more professional looking. The Minotaur was ambidextrous for hundreds of years but has come to favor his right hand for precise work. The knife forms the right side of the **X**. Hanging from a small hook on the frame of the beef cart is the sharpening steel. Before every two or three cuts the Minotaur pulls the thin blade across the steel with a rapid back-and-forth motion, alternating sides with each swipe, not so much because the knife needs to be honed but because he likes the mechanical *shhhick-shhhick shhhick-shhhick shhhick-shhhick* sound of metal against metal, and because he thinks it impresses.

Bunchy seems duly impressed, maybe even a little afraid. She leans against the arm of the old man's chair when the Minotaur stabs the fork into half a rib roast and lifts it onto the cutting board, turning it upside down en route. Because the knife is razor sharp and eighteen inches long, and because the Minotaur is good, two full strokes are all it takes before he uses the blade to lift a piece of meat onto the foil-wrapped platform of the small scale sitting in one corner of the pan. Ten ounces, dead on the nose. He gets another rib and does it again. After ladling out the salty Au Jus, Shane serves Bunchy and the old man.

"Y'all got Heinz 57?" the Minotaur hears the old man ask.

The Minotaur takes a cigarette break. He needs it, needs to feel the smoke bite inside his lungs. On his way to the back dock the Minotaur overhears Maynard telling Cecie about his last job, at Gig's Alley, a seafood house out on the river that specializes in frog legs.

"I crossed them," Maynard says.

"You crossed what?" Cecie asks.

"Every damn frog leg that got fried," Maynard says. "If you don't cross the legs before frying them they come out of the deep fat all splayed out and too ugly to eat."

Cecie winks at the Minotaur as he walks by.

"I seen a lot of legs all splayed out and too ugly to eat," she says. "But they weren't fried."

This makes Maynard laugh. The Minotaur thinks that later, when things slow down, he'll apologize to Maynard for pushing by him in the bathroom.

Just before going out the back door the Minotaur sees Mike and Shane coming out of the walk-in; Shane is gigging strangely, as before. The Minotaur didn't know Mike was working tonight, and the new knowledge churns bile into the back of his throat. Mike must be closing tonight; that would explain why he came in late. Despite the Minotaur's hasty attempt to turn away, his cumbersome head proves sluggish; he and Mike make eye contact. They hold that eye contact long enough for Mike to raise his eyebrows twice, suggestively, and blow a kiss.

Smoking on the back steps, the Minotaur waffles between anger and shame. His hands shake, so getting the lit cigarette between his black lips is a challenge. What exactly did Mike mean?

"I need a beef carver."

It's Kelly; the Minotaur recognizes her voice even through the distortion of the intercom speakers. He flicks the smoking butt toward the trees and underbrush, but it lands short and sends a spray of tiny embers over the pavement.

Grub stands in front of the line, expediting the orders.

"How many imperials you got, Cecie?"

"Three all day," Cecie answers, after scanning the row of tickets hanging across the window.

"Do you have enough crepes?" Grub asks.

"Yep."

Just before the Minotaur goes into the dining room Grub calls out to him. "You're looking sharp out there, M. Keep it up."

Kelly is in her section crumbing a four-top with a small brass-plated tool the size of a pen. All the waiters and waitresses carry the crumbers, and periodically David schedules mandatory preshift workshops to make sure everyone knows how to scrape the tables clean without disturbing the customers.

"Hi, M," she says, making a final sweeping S-curve between half-full wineglasses before raking the crumbs off the edge of the table and into a small tray. "Two Queen Cuts, medium-rare, and a well-done Page, please."

Sometimes, more than anything, the Minotaur wishes he had a facility for idle chatter. As it is he cuts Kelly's order quietly, smiling as best he can when she looks at him. Robert walks up as he's about to wheel away.

"Hey, Kelly, eighty-six peanut butter pie."

"Thanks, Rob," Kelly says. "Thanks, M."

"I need you at table twenty-three, M," Robert says, and the Minotaur follows him through the dining room.

The next couple of hours pass without incident. The Minotaur tries to stay busy even when there are no orders to fill. He's found it best to keep his mind occupied because, like everyone else, mythological character or no, the Minotaur leads a life fraught with incongruity and contradiction. Like everyone else—like most, anyway—he can do little but overlook these issues or displace awareness of them with the trickery of a busy mind. The cannibalistic nature of his new job cannot be denied.

It competes for attention in his mind with the growing feeling that things are about to change for the worse. So when the Minotaur has a few minutes free he cuts orange slices, washes parsley for garnish, trims the fat from the ribs, wipes the beef cart clean again and again with diluted bleach, stays busy. He's standing at the sink shucking oysters for Maynard when Jenna walks in from the dining room.

"Arghhh!" she says to no one and everyone.

"What do you need, Jenna?" Grub asks.

"I'm completely in the weeds, and this jerk at table twelve says his Black Forest cake is stale, and there are no Black Forest cakes cut, and . . ."

"Slow down, babe. We'll take care of it. M, will you . . . ?"

"Mmmm."

Hernando is gone; he left half an hour ago, after he was sure things were set for the night. Hernando usually cuts the cakes, but the Minotaur can do it in a pinch. Jenna brings over a stack of dessert plates. The Minotaur washes the grit and sand from his hands and fills a small bucket with hot water. He marks the cake by rocking the knife lightly over the top—halves, quarters, eighths—wiping the white icing from the blade each time. Before every cut he dips the blade into the hot water and wipes it clean. Shane and Mike walk up behind Jenna, holding dessert plates. When Mike whispers something to Shane and they both giggle like little boys the Minotaur doesn't acknowledge them.

Grub has left the kitchen; the evening rush is over, so he's probably doing paperwork in the office. David is making a fresh pot of decaffeinated coffee and trying not to pay attention to Shane and Mike. Jenna is attempting to make four pieces of cake, four cups of coffee with saucers and two snifters of liqueur fit onto one tray. Just as Jenna gets everything situated Shane, nudged by Mike, kneels in front of the Minotaur and pulls a wilted mangy rose from his apron pocket, an unwanted flower scavenged, no doubt, from the concrete median at the intersection in front of the restaurant, where every day from seven in the morning until six at night a sleepy-eyed man sits in a folding lawn chair, taped to the back and arms of which are hand-scrawled *For Sell* signs, sits beneath a RAM Golf Equipment umbrella with two broken ribs, sits hunched over a five-gallon bucket of plastic-wrapped long-stem roses. Every day he abandons those too wilted or damaged to sell. On his knees Shane pulls the flower from his pocket and offers it to the Minotaur.

"I'm pledging my troth," Shane says with exaggerated emotion. "Here and now."

The Minotaur isn't sure how to respond.

"The very idea of you with another man breaks my heart."

Shane barely gets the words out before laughter overcomes him. Both he and Mike seem to think it is the funniest thing in the whole world.

"Why do you guys have to be such assholes all the time?" Jenna asks. It's a rhetorical question.

"You have a table, Shane," David says, coming through the door. "What are you guys doing back here, anyway?"

"Ohh! *Him!*" Shane says, placing the back of his hand across his forehead. This causes Mike to laugh so hard that he falls to the dirty tile floor.

A wave of scarlet climbs the collar of David's shirt and flows up and across his face. "Get out of the kitchen now!"

They go.

David goes.

The Minotaur cleans up the cake crumbs.

A caul of embarrassment drapes the rest of the evening, distorts time and space. The Minotaur can't seem to see anything clearly. Twice he has to recut orders of prime rib to get the right weight. Mike and Shane hover on the periphery, becoming more and more obnoxious as the night passes.

"Ooh, ooh," Shane says under his breath every time he and the Minotaur cross paths. "Do me, big boy."

Mike giggles, then whistles some song that the Minotaur can't name. Grub overhears this. The rush is over, so he tells David to close both their sections and give them extra side work, which they bitch about but begin doing.

When Elizabeth comes out of the walk-in cooler carrying three orders of pecan pie and complaining that all the cans of whipped topping are empty, and that her customers don't want the pie without topping, Grub is standing right there.

"There's half a case in there, Liz. Six cans."

"I tried them all," Elizabeth says. "Nothing comes out."

She follows Grub into the cooler. He's carrying one of the cans when they reemerge. When Shane enters with a bus tub full of dirty glasses and the parts from the iced tea machine that go through the dishwasher each night, the Minotaur may be the only one who hears him say, "Oh, shit."

The Minotaur would like nothing more than to stay in the kitchen and watch whatever is about to happen. If it weren't Kelly asking for a beef carver he would probably make them wait. But for Kelly he goes immediately.

There are just a few tables remaining to be served. Kelly has a six-top at the round table by the door to the kitchen. She's picking up the salad plates when he rolls up.

"Hi, M. I need a Queen Cut, as rare as you've got, then two medium Kings. I'll be back in a sec with the plates."

"Mmmn," he says, and forks the largest rib onto the cutting board.

The customers talk among themselves, about the beauty of the meat, the skill of the carver. Rarely do they talk directly to the Minotaur. Sometimes they'll ask a question through the waiter or waitress.

"Does he ever . . . ?"

"Will he . . . ?"

The Minotaur has the three orders cut and stacked by the time Kelly gets back. She arranges the warm plates on her serving tray.

"The next is a Queen Cut, and he'd like it in three thin slices, if you can."

That presents no problem. The Minotaur cuts an eight-ounce slice and lays it flat on the cutting board.

David walks up before the Minotaur begins cutting. "They'll be lucky if Grub doesn't fire them," he says quietly to Kelly and the Minotaur.

"Who?" Kelly asks.

"Mike and Shane."

Holding the meat in place with the tips of the fork, the Minotaur easily cuts one thin slice.

"Why?" Kelly says, as if there aren't dozens of reasons.

"The idiots inhaled all the nitrous oxide from the whipped cream cans."

"How does he know they did it?"

"Who cares?"

The Minotaur cocks his head to determine where to place the blade. The second slice will require almost surgical precision.

Shane and Mike come from the kitchen with clean ashtrays and a bottle of oil for the lamps. Grub walks out behind them, angry but in control. "You're not going to get another warning," he says quietly.

Mike seems to take Grub seriously, but Shane smirks as he approaches the empty table beside Kelly's six-top. The Minotaur moves out of nervousness, trying to get out of the way but instead stepping directly into Shane's path.

"Move!"

When the Minotaur moves it is once again into Shane's way.

"Move, faggot!" Shane says. "Goddamn circus freak."

By this time the customers at Kelly's table have stopped talking and eating.

"That's it, boy," Grub says. "Go! You go now. You'll get your check when you bring the uniform back."

Shane turns to face Grub. "You want your fucking uniform back?" he asks, emphasizing the curse word. He unties the apron, wads it into a ball and throws it at Grub's feet, followed by the bow tie. He's made his point. A rational man would stop here. Shane doesn't.

The Minotaur tries to remain focused on the task at hand: an eight-ounce Queen Cut in three thin slices. He guides the blade slowly through one stroke.

Shane takes the crumber from his pocket and flicks it like a knife at David across the room. David ducks. The thin aluminum tool rattles off the mirrored wall.

"I'll give you your fucking uniform," Shane says.

Even Grub seems taken aback when the ruffled tuxedo shirt lands at his feet. Shane stands enraged and shirtless in the weak light of the candles and the sconces on the dining-room walls. He breathes deeply and noisily through his nostrils, his pale muscled chest marked by a cross of dark hairs that defines the channel of his sternum and stretches out around both nipples—nipples, the Minotaur can't help thinking, that look exactly like pencil erasers.

Even most irrational men would stop here.

"Here's your uni-fucking-form, you fat bastard."

It's not too surprising, when Shane unfastens the slacks and drops them to the floor, to see that he doesn't have on any underwear. It's not surprising to the Minotaur, anyway. Kelly's table must be surprised; everyone gasps, and one lady spills her Old Fashioned on the floor. Rationality has taken leave. Utter shock fills the void. Grub, Kelly, the few customers and the rest of the wait staff watch in disbelief.

"You happy, Grub?" Shane asks. "You happy now?"

Shane is angry and nervous; beads of sweat trickle from his armpits, ride his ribs and hipbones down to where they are caught and glisten in his pubic hair. His testicles have drawn high and tight against his body, and the head of his shriveled penis peeks out of the dark thatch like an absurd little snout. The Minotaur can smell him.

Anyone who has worked in a kitchen knows that a dull blade is a dangerous blade. The Minotaur should have taken the time to hone the knife's edge on the sharpening steel before trying such a thin cut. But even with a sharp blade what happens next would distract almost anyone.

"I got your prime rib right here," Shane says to Grub, to the Minotaur, to everybody in the room, hoisting his genitals in one hand and shaking them up and down.

In his lifetime the Minotaur has witnessed the human body in almost every conceivable circumstance, and little shocks him. But context makes a big difference. When Shane stands naked in the middle of Grub's Rib, sweaty, white haunched, so angry and male as to reek of it, the stink is so out of context that the Minotaur forgets he is carving a piece of roast beef with a very big knife. He ponders, for just a second, why he is privy to so much of the messy machinations of the human body, thinks about it until the knife blade angles up through the cooked meat and, uncontrolled, slams edge-first against the longest bone in the Minotaur's thumb on the hand gripping the meat fork.

"Arrrruuunnh!"

The flesh gapes; an inch or more of chalk-white bone is visible.

Shane's last act is to spit a huge phlegmy glob of mucus, drawn from deep within the throat and nasal cavities, onto the floor beside the crumpled uniform. He is out the door before anyone moves. Kelly's six-top walks out moments later. Grub doesn't even try to stop them. The Minotaur clutches a towel to his bleeding wound and snorts with each breath.

"Let me see that," Kelly says.

This time, unlike the kitchen accident, the Minotaur does.

"You need some stitches," Grub says.

"There's an emergency clinic over on Sixty-ninth," Kelly offers. "I'll drive."

Two injuries in as many weeks.

Grub goes to call the police.

As Kelly and the Minotaur leave the restaurant, JoeJoe, Maynard and the busboys argue about who is going to clean up the mess. In the car the Minotaur's black nostrils welcome Kelly's smells: roasted meat, cigarettes, scented oil.

"Are you okay?" she asks. "I can't believe he did that."

"Unnh."

If he were alone he would sing. The cut throbs, and the towel is soaked with blood, but as wounds go the Minotaur has had much worse. To be truthful, if he'd known that Kelly would offer to drive him to the hospital, he may have cut his finger earlier.

Kelly talks a lot.

"You did a really good job tonight, M. Even in the face of, you know."

"Thanks," he says with great effort.

"I wanted to tell you before that I'm sorry about your accident with Hernando."

He wishes he could think of something to say, and that he could say it clearly. Kelly willingly fills his silence.

"I don't know what makes people like Shane act like that. Meanness, I guess."

Kelly has the bad habit of driving the car with one foot on the gas and the other on the brake, of speeding up and slowing down erratically, and it's more pronounced when she talks. If it weren't Kelly this would really annoy the Minotaur.

"They're like birds of prey, almost. They find a weak spot and then peck and peck at it."

Despite the late hour the emergency clinic is busy. Or

maybe it's because of the late hour. It could be that people are more prone to hurting each other in the uncertainty of night. The sterile fluorescent lights and the palpable tension in the room make even the uninjured seem like they're in pain.

They stand while Kelly fills out the forms for the Minotaur; much of the information asked for seems ludicrous. Neither the Minotaur nor Kelly takes notice of the young man who comes alone through the door wearing bicycling shoes with cleats in the soles. But when he begins his clattering walk across the tile floor they turn to look. His black Lycra shorts enhance the musculature of his legs and hips and provide a sharp color contrast to the scraped left knee that bleeds all the way down into his shoe. His left elbow and forearm, and even the knuckles of his left hand, with which he covers that same side of his face—the injured side—bleed freely. Kelly and the Minotaur move away from the reception window to give the man room. He stands quietly at the window, and the nurse does not look up from her paperwork until he reaches his right hand out and with his fingernails scratches softly on the countertop.

"Can I help you?" she asks, without conviction.

With one hand still covering the side of his face, the man opens his mouth and, using the thumb and index finger of the other hand, plucks his own eyeball from the protective bed of his tongue and offers it, like a delicate candy, to the nurse.

She tells the Minotaur and Kelly to sit until a doctor is free.

There are four rows of plastic chairs in the waiting room, two of which are back to back in the center. The chairs are fixed permanently to steel frames. The different-colored plastic in the seat offers only the suggestion of padding. Kelly sits. The Minotaur sits opposite. Chained to a metal shelf high on the corner wall, a television plays without sound. It may be the nightly news, but the screen rolls too often to tell. Every time the picture begins to flip Kelly talks. When it stops she stops.

"Does it hurt?" Kelly asks.

"I don't think I could work in a place like this," Kelly says.

"Did you ever take any classes at Piedmont?" Kelly asks.

"I don't want to be a waitress forever," Kelly says.

Forever, the Minotaur thinks, and strives to communicate a sense of his own dreams. "Someday," he begins, but a doctor interrupts him.

"You have a cut that needs attending?"

Kelly is allowed into the triage room. She winces each time the hooked needle pierces the Minotaur's flesh and the thread is pulled snug. Ten stitches close the wound.

Back in the car Kelly seems thoughtful. After several miles of silence she speaks.

"My step-daddy, he's a . . . He's black."

The Minotaur doesn't know why she is telling him this, but it seems important.

"Mmm."

"I just wanted you to know."

The Minotaur thinks about this for the rest of the trip back to Grub's. He still can't figure out why she told him.

The Vega is the only vehicle in the parking lot. When Kelly pulls up beside it she turns the ignition in her own car off. Neither of them speaks. The Minotaur's breathing is the loudest thing in the car, and it only seems louder when he tries to control it.

He sits holding his injured hand with the other. The local anesthetic is wearing off, and regular jolts of pain shoot from his thumb to his elbow.

"Thank you," he says after a while. Kelly turns and smiles. She pats his biceps once but doesn't say anything. Neither does she start the engine.

The Minotaur takes several deep breaths. This should not be so hard for him.

"M-M-Monday," he finally stutters.

"Monday?"

"Off."

"Me, too." Kelly smiles again, a genuine smile.

But the Minotaur doesn't know what to do next. They might still be sitting there, except that Kelly reaches into the dash, takes out her waitress's apron and from its pocket gets a pen and an order pad on which to write her address. The Minotaur doesn't dare tell her that he already knows it.

CHAPTER 20

Sweeny doesn't mention the black spot that was Buddy when he and the Minotaur pull out of the driveway the next morning. In fact Sweeny doesn't say much of anything for several miles, and then it's just, "Gonna be a hot one." But the silence is fine with the Minotaur; it gives him time to play last night's conversations with Kelly over again and again in his mind. He was tempted, so tempted, to bring along the piece of paper on which she wrote her address, to look at it throughout the day. But it occurred to the Minotaur that he might lose the address, so he hid it beneath the lasso-shaped lamp on the nightstand by his bed.

Besides, the Minotaur has known Sweeny long enough that his fits of quiet aren't surprising; sometimes he's just a slow starter. So they drive in silence. Florida. The Panhandle. All the

Minotaur knows is that Sweeny's cousin's ex-wife has a boy-friend who wants to sell some sort of mobile concession stand, cheap.

After an hour or so Sweeny starts talking, mostly about being hungry and wanting an egg and livermush sandwich, on a hamburger bun with mustard.

"Ain't nothing better," Sweeny says.

The Minotaur is in no position to disagree.

Finding such a sandwich isn't hard. Less than five miles after Sweeny's proclamation he pulls the truck to a stop at a roadside shanty with a hand-painted plywood sign advertising its services: *Beer, Breakfast, Fish Bait, No Gas*. The Minotaur sits in the truck. Sweeny is back in just a few minutes, carrying a brown paper bag with oily stains spreading from the bottom upward.

"I got a couple extra," Sweeny says. "Help yourself."

The Minotaur declines. Sweeny eats noisily; each time he unwraps a new sandwich the truck swerves off the road. It seems all Sweeny needed was food to get him talking. He tells a couple jokes, including one about an umbrella stand and a pretty girl with a big ass, which the Minotaur doesn't understand. He grunts anyway, out of respect and because he didn't take the sandwiches Sweeny offered.

"How come your thumb's all wrapped up?" Sweeny asks.

The Minotaur gives him a condensed version of the story.

"Wasn't that you hobbling around just last week with a gimp leg?"

"Foot," the Minotaur says.

"Shit, boy, that restaurant's gonna kill you. You might ought to get yourself another line of work."

Sweeny talks about Florida and asks if the Minotaur has ever been to the Panhandle. The Minotaur says no simply to avoid having to explain that, in his lifetime, he's been everywhere at least once.

"Good people down there," Sweeny says, and the Minotaur admires, maybe even envies, his faith as expressed in the generalization.

It's a nine-hour drive, maybe a little more because, like the Minotaur, Sweeny avoids the interstates. Grub gave the Minotaur the night off, so there is no rush. Halfway into the trip the Minotaur takes over the wheel. They stop twice for gas and the bathroom, another time for more sandwiches. The Minotaur chooses egg salad. The only other time they stop is when Sweeny makes the Minotaur do a three-point road turn and go back and look at a stand of crape myrtles, high knotty bushes blooming in soft purples and reds along someone's driveway.

"The wife loved a myrtle," he says.

The Minotaur thinks Sweeny may cry, but he doesn't.

"Let's go," he says.

Sweeny talks for the next ten miles about all the flowers and bushes his wife used to tend.

"We never had no kids," he says. "She give them damn flowers everything."

The rolling Piedmont of North Carolina gives way slowly to the low stagnant swampland of its sister state. Farther south the pines and red clay of Georgia acquiesce to the brackish influence of the Gulf of Mexico. Palm trees and mangroves and monkey grass and high tropical weeds appear more frequently as the Minotaur drives.

After the fifth armadillo dead on the side of the road Sweeny brings up the subject of Buddy. It seems the trip is rife with emotion.

"He was a damn sight, that dog."

And that's all he says. He doesn't ask the Minotaur what happened. Nor does he give a rationale for leaving the dog to rot, then burning it with gasoline. But the Minotaur knows that contained within that clipped sentence is a significant feeling of loss.

Because Sweeny's cousin is acting as the intermediary for the whole deal, his place is the first stop. Sweeny has never been to his cousin's house, but despite the absence of a map or any written directions they arrive a little after three. As promised, Golden Gator Retirement Village is impossible to miss for several reasons, not the least of which are the two once-living now-bronzed alligators held by U-bolts to the big wooden sign at the entrance. The village is also notable for its size; a precise grid of narrow, paved, unlined roads with 7½ mile-per-hour speed-limit signs posted at every turn mark out the plots for what must be hundreds of mobile homes, all well groomed in the distinctively Floridian style—tiki lights, twiggy citrus trees with irregular rings of rotting fruit at their bases. Small dirt-colored lizards are everywhere, bobbing their heads up and down in the hot afternoon sun.

Sweeny whistles when they pull into the trailer park. The cab of the truck reeks with envy; the Minotaur can smell it as sure as he smells the salt air from the Gulf, even though they're at least fifteen miles inland.

"Ain't this some spread?" Sweeny says reverently. He asks

the Minotaur to drive around the place before they begin looking for his cousin's. The Minotaur drives, and all the while
Sweeny mutters, mostly to himself, about what he'd do if this
were his place; occasionally he notes ideas he would like to take
home and implement at Lucky-U Mobile Estates. Sweeny is rapt,
and the Minotaur is willing to drive as long as necessary.

After two trips around, and a good half-hour, they make a
right turn past a long row of triple-stacked rural-route mail-
boxes and into the driveway that is their destination.

Sweeny speaks to the decidedly familial (same jaw line and
large ears) man who comes out to greet them.

"Hey, Tommy."

"Hey, Sweeny."

Then they both look at the Minotaur, so he says, "Unnh,"
which seems to satisfy everybody, and they all go inside.

Tommy pours three tall plastic cups full of candy-sweet iced
tea, and they sit around a cramped table while he and Sweeny
converse in that choppy misfiring way peculiar to adult rela-
tives who rarely see one another.

"How you making out?"

"Good as can be expected."

"Good."

"How's work?"

"Going good. You?"

"Can't complain."

And on and on for a while, circling back sometimes to al-
ready-covered ground. Eventually Sweeny asks about the concession trailer they have come to look at.

"Her boyfriend, huh?"

"Yep. She met him at the county fair. He had a regular site there. In spite of it all he ain't a bad fellow."

"How come he's selling?" Sweeny asks.

"Accident."

"What kind of accident?"

"You'll see."

A few minutes later they're all squeezed into the cab of Sweeny's truck and driving toward the Gulf, the Minotaur at the open passenger window with his head turned, one horn out in the wind. Tommy's ex-wife lives with the man who is selling the concession trailer, in a flat-roofed house surrounded by orange groves and reached by a meandering road of rutted sand.

When Sweeny, Tommy and the Minotaur pull up in front of the house the first thing they see is an unfinished ramp of plywood and two-by-fours rising at an impossibly steep angle toward the front door. The second thing they see is an upturned johnboat resting on sawhorses, and this only because of the two little kids of indeterminate gender and age who sit in the rectangle of shade lighting firecrackers and tossing them out into the yard, where a Barbie doll and a GI Joe cower behind a fortress of overripe oranges.

Tommy goes to the door. He waves Sweeny and the Minotaur in.

The Minotaur doesn't expect the wheelchair that sits in the middle of the living room. Even more troubling is that, of the man and woman sitting on the bedsheet-draped couch, the Minotaur can't tell who needs the chair more. Both sit, deep and leaden, unmoving but for their eyes and some amalgam of greeting and grimace that crosses their faces when Sweeny and the Minotaur come in. The eyes—both the man's and the woman's, ringed in deep blue-black, glazed and heavy lidded— betray profound fatigue, an insurmountable weariness.

"You remember Sweeny, don't you, Nat?" Tommy says, and that is all the introduction made.

"Hey," the woman says.

For a few minutes nobody speaks. The Minotaur, trying not to stare, looks instead around the house. Even with the shades pulled it's not hard to see that the house is in a condition of total neglect, a state of dirtiness reached by degrees, as if every day, if not every hour, another chore is added to the list of the impossible-to-do.

"The trailer's out back," the man says with effort. His name is Harold.

"Y'all got to put him in that chair," Nat says. "I can't do it again today. Not yet, anyway."

Nat gestures weakly in the direction of the wheelchair. Harold remains motionless. Harold has become a quadriplegic only recently, so he hasn't fully comprehended the state of utter helplessness in which he exists. When the Minotaur and Tommy lean close to heave him into the wheelchair, Harold's eyes roll with barely contained terror. It subsides.

They have to lift the chair with Harold in it out the back door of the house and down three concrete-block steps and onto a small patio. Because neither of them has any experience at this sort of thing, Harold's useless limbs flop embarrassingly.

There's no denying it, the concession trailer is an impressive thing. It is twenty feet long. A single axle with leveling jacks keeps it steady at each corner. An iron frame welded to the tongue and hitch holds a generator and two pressure tanks for the propane. At the back end a narrow door provides access, and beside it is a shuttered window. The service window, covered by an awning that is pitched when the trailer is in use, takes up the whole of one side.

Tommy pushes Harold over the sparsely grassed lawn while Sweeny and the Minotaur stand back and take in the big picture. On all sides of the trailer bannerlike signs painted in carnival colors advertise the bill of fare. Some—like the yellow ear of corn with a smiling dachshund's head, clutching a ketchup bottle in its very human hands—are cartoon representations. Sweeny reads them aloud.

"*Corn dogs. Sno-cones. Gigamundous pretzels. French fries. Elephant ears—Big & Sweet! Affy Tapples. Cotton candy. And More.*"

Pointing with his head, Harold tells Tommy to remove the padlock hanging open on the door clasp. Tommy opens the door and from the floor of the trailer removes the poles that hold the awning in place. It takes the Minotaur and Sweeny only a couple of minutes to put it up. From a compartment near the base of the trailer Tommy stretches a long power cord across the yard to the back of the house; weaving through patches of long-bladed grass, the orange cord looks like a split in the earth, as if the earth has cracked open and the molten material just beneath the surface threatens to erupt.

"She's a moneymaker," Harold says.

"I bet," Sweeny says. "I'm just not sure I can sell it."

"Always draws, no matter the event. Tell you the truth, I hate giving her up."

It's not hard to tell that Harold hates much about his new situation.

"No way around it?" Sweeny asks.

"Nat's good, but she can't work it by herself."

Harold pauses. All the nervous energy that would normally go into shifting in place or fidgeting with something in his hands is concentrated in the suddenly overburdened muscles and nerves of his neck and head. Beads of sweat from his scalp and forehead trickle down to his ever-dampening collar.

"I don't know yet what I'm going to do. But I sure can't work this trailer."

Sweeny asks the Minotaur to look the trailer over for him. It's why he came along in the first place. Before going inside, the Minotaur lies beneath it to check out the springs and axle and the undercarriage. Lying there with his head under the corn dog trailer the Minotaur hears only snippets of the conversation. He's not sure how the subject comes up, but by the time he crawls out and begins dusting himself off Harold is talking about the accident.

"Oddities of the Natural World," Harold says, and goes on at great length about setting up his concession stand at the Po County Fair, just by the entrance to the dirt track motor speedway and adjacent to a tent displaying, for a mere three dollars per person, what promised to be a life-changing experience, and proof-positive evidence of several things. Most likely Oddities of the Natural World was conceived and created by a taxidermist with a bent for the absurd.

"Y'all wouldn't believe some of the things he had," Harold says.

He is wrong. In fact the Minotaur doesn't doubt him for a second when Harold describes the various glass cases and their contents: a ferret with two heads and two sets of front paws but no tails or back legs, mounted in a permanent tug of war on a pine log; some pointy-faced nocturnal animal shaped around a perfect sphere the size of a bowling ball, tiny limbs splayed far apart and useless; a diorama featuring a blue jay with the paws of an orange tabby cat in place of its own claws, sitting beside a fake pool of water while a field mouse perched on a branch overhead looms from the full height of a crow's legs and black claws. Harold's catalog of memory contains fish things, and nightmarish combinations of animal and mechanical. Harold talks like he's been waiting to tell this story for a long time, making full use of his neck and head for gesticulation.

Harold tells them that the fair wasn't even open to the public yet, that, driven by curiosity, he'd parked the corn dog trailer at his reserved site and left Nat to set the leveling jacks while he went into the Oddities of the Natural World tent.

"Nobody was there," he says. "I ought to have turned around and left right then."

Sweeny gets a couple of lawn chairs from the patio; he and Tommy sit.

The Minotaur steps inside the trailer. It's a small space, but it's well arranged for convenience and a smooth flow of work. A closeable vat of oil for frying the corn dogs and elephant ears, warming boxes, a small griddle and a sink are spaced along the back wall. Overhead are storage cabinets covered with advertisements. At the service window are a countertop, an outdated cash register, napkin holders and plastic bins for the condiments. Beneath it refrigeration units stand empty. By and large the trailer is clean, but the smell of cooked grease is permanent.

The Minotaur switches the equipment on and off, opens

the cabinets, doors and drawers. Most hold what he expects—a disorganized mix of sundries and supplies. But in a small utility drawer under the cash register, empty but for a pad of paper with scribbled notes, a state map and laminated copies of the health department's certification and a vendor's license, the Minotaur finds something he doesn't expect. From inside the pad of paper, one cerulean corner peeking out, the Minotaur pulls a membership card for the Sacred Heart Auto League. It is a trifold thing about the size of a credit card. On the cover, against a blue sky, Christ looms protectively, gigantically, serenely over a miniature crowded highway. His heart, wearing a garland of thorns, beams out like a sun from his chest. Inside the card is the members' pledge:

- I pledge to drive prayerfully and carefully in an effort to insure my own safety as well as the safety of others;
- I further pledge to offer my travel time in a spirit of reparation to the Sacred Heart of Jesus;
- In so pledging I confidently beseech the special blessing of the Sacred Heart as a promise of divine graces and favors.

And so members will know what they get from the transaction, there is a description of the Spiritual Advantages: "As a member of the Sacred Heart Auto League you share in a special Holy Mass offered each morning for all League Members, living and deceased. The Sacred Heart Auto League has Episcopal approval and its members have been favored with the Apostolic Blessings of Pope Pius XII, Pope John, Pope Paul VI, and Pope John Paul II."

The card defines Reparation and Reparation Driving. On the back are the Driver's Prayer and a two-year calendar with half a dozen dates circled in red ink. The Minotaur folds the card open, then closed, then open again. Harold is still talking. Hanging over the tiny sink inside the trailer is a paper towel dispenser. In the chrome surface of its cover the Minotaur catches a glimpse of his reflection, a little blurred but somehow comforting. The membership card for the Sacred Heart Auto League is unsigned. Although he has no specific plans the idea of membership appeals to the Minotaur, as do the promises of guidance and protection. His persistent gullibility draws him to such things. He pockets the card, then goes outside.

"I should've," Harold says. "I should've walked out of the tent then and there. But I didn't. And now . . ."

Harold tells them about a display case the size of a coffin, draped in red satin and sitting on a low table at the back of the Oddities of the Natural World tent. A sign claimed that, for an extra dollar, you could see a living breathing monster, the only one of its kind in captivity.

"What was it?" Tommy asks.

"Hard to say, exactly," Harold says. "I looked around to make sure nobody was watching, but when I pulled off that red blanket I couldn't see anything."

"Nothing?"

"Nothing."

The Minotaur squats on his haunches between Tommy and Sweeny.

"I don't know if it was motion sensitive or what, but the inside of that box was pitch-black until I leaned over and pressed my face to the glass, and then so much happened that I'm not sure what I saw. Somebody yelled, 'Hey, asshole!' from the front of the tent, and the box lit up inside. It might have been a woman. I think she was naked. Could've even been one of them hologram things. All I know is that when the light came on I was looking it in the eyes. There was snakes crawling all over the top of its head, and when it opened its nasty mouth and give the most god-awful screech at the exact same time as that fellow yelled at me from behind, it scared the living shit out of me."

Harold tells how he ran out of the tent and right into a guy wire, which caught him at the neck and threw him flat on his back.

"Next thing I knew I was in the Po County Hospital and couldn't even tell when I was pissing myself."

"How's she look, M?" Sweeny says after a respectful pause. "Mmmn."

"Let's talk price," Sweeny says to Harold.

The Minotaur doesn't want to be part of the negotiations. He wanders around behind the concession trailer and eventually up to the back door of the house, where he finds a garden hose in a loose coil. One end is attached to a muddy spigot jutting from a hole in the house's underpinning. The other is cut off at a jagged angle. The Minotaur picks up the loose end. In a wide-footed stance, his head bent, the Minotaur holds the end of the hose to his pursed lips and turns on the spigot. Nothing happens.

Hoping for nothing more than a glass of water, he knocks on the back door of the house. There is no response from inside.

"Go on in," Harold says from across the yard. "She ain't gonna come to the door."

The transition from the glaring Florida sun to the darkened interior of the house is disconcerting. In momentary blindness the Minotaur stumbles over something plastic and pliable on the floor, almost falls. He picks it up. When his eyes adjust he finds it is the GI Joe doll, singed and shell-shocked, that he holds in his hands.

Nat is still sitting on the couch.

"Water?" the Minotaur asks.

"They's a glass over the sink," Nat answers.

Not until he is halfway around the bar that separates the kitchen from the dining room does the Minotaur see the two children sitting on the floor beside the couch. They barely register his presence, as if a creature of this sort walks through their house every day. A boy and a girl, so pale as to appear almost featureless, no more than eight years old, both skinny and in dire need of a bath. What strikes the Minotaur most is the absence of youth in both children. Their actions and abilities are those of children, but they function with the demeanor of adults: muted, burdened, resigned. The boy and girl play quietly with a broken carpenter's rule, folding and unfolding, folding and unfolding. They eat from a nearly empty container of dry cereal.

There are no glasses over the sink. All the glasses, and what looks like all the plates and bowls and knives and forks and spoons, are stacked precariously in the two wells of the sink, dirty.

"I'm hungry, Mama," the girl says.

Nat doesn't respond.

The two children come from beside the couch. The boy opens one of the cabinet doors, stares into its emptiness, then does the same at the refrigerator. Eventually they both just stand and watch the Minotaur look for a glass.

It takes the Minotaur only a few minutes to wash all the dishes, even taking care to keep his bandaged thumb dry. Once the thin malleable knives and forks and the chipped plastic plates are clean, he looks through the refrigerator and finds little in the way of edible food—half a dozen eggs, a small wedge of hoop cheese from which he cuts the mold, an onion and four hot dogs wrapped in foil. The Minotaur doesn't ask if he can cook for Nat and the children. He just does it. By the time he pulls the frying pan from under the broiler the girl and the boy are standing, side by side and visibly hopeful, next to the table. When the Minotaur slides the big open-faced omelet onto a plate, orange cheese bubbling over bits of frankfurter and trans-lucent onion, they wait as if in disbelief or shock until he mo-tions for them to sit and eat. There may or may not be enough left for Harold and Nat. The Minotaur doesn't want to be part of the negotiations.

⁓

Sweeny, in fact, didn't haggle much on the price of the corn dog trailer. He tells the Minotaur—as they ease on to the high-way, the salty evening wind coming off the Gulf and rocking the trailer and the truck that pulls it—that since there was a con-siderable stock of dry goods and supplies, like the little paper trays for the corns dogs, napkins, packets of mustard, he gave Harold more than the asking price. He says he wouldn't have felt right otherwise. While the Minotaur and Tommy struggled to get Harold back into the house, Sweeny slipped a hundred-dollar bill under a refrigerator magnet when he thought nobody was looking. Sweeny doesn't tell the Minotaur that part; the Minotaur saw it.

It's after dark. They've dropped Tommy off at Golden Gator and are heading home, the Minotaur driving. Because Sweeny can't see well at night the Minotaur will probably drive the whole way. Somewhere in the bowels of Georgia he pulls into a Stuckey's for gas and food and to stretch his tired legs.

They seem to be the only customers. There are no other cars in the parking lot or at the gas pumps. Looking through the wide glass windows, the Minotaur doesn't see anyone, clerk or customer, moving around in the store. If not for all the lights and the *24 Hour* sign flashing over the door, he'd think the Stuckey's closed. Only the pump for the premium-grade gasoline is functioning. A note taped to the front says to pay before pumping, so Sweeny and the Minotaur go in together.

Inside, high open shelves containing assorted necessities—chips and cookies and candy, motor oil, brake and other fluids, antacids and analgesics, half a dozen different souvenirs made from corncobs, miniature Confederate flags and full-size Confederate hats, bread, mayonnaise, bottle rockets and smoke bombs, etceteras ad nauseam—fill the brightly lit store from front to back but do not disguise the fact that it's empty of customers, and possibly clerks. The far wall is lined with reach-in coolers for beer, soft drinks, frozen burritos, milk and the like.

Battling with the bright fluorescent lights on the hierarchy of stimuli inside the store are unidentified sounds coming from somewhere out of sight—a sort of incessant *blip*, a digital *gobble-gobble* interspersed with assorted *boing*s and gulping sounds. Sweeny chooses quickly, a bag of barbecue-flavored pork skins and a quart of chocolate milk, and stands at the counter with money in his hand. After deciding on a hard-boiled egg, a huge dill pickle and a package of saltine crackers, the Minotaur joins him.

Waiting at the register they are closer to the source of the noises. From where they stand Sweeny and the Minotaur can see directly into an open door marked *Employees Only*. Aside from a deep utility sink, a jug of bleach, a bright yellow mop bucket with *CAUTION* stenciled across it and a mop handle held together with duct tape leaning out of view, the room seems empty, and quiet. The electronic cacophony is coming from a smoky little alcove off the back wall, its entrance hidden by a large revolving cigarette display. There, between the men's and women's bathrooms, beside the pay phone and a knee-high canister ashtray that's full to overflowing, the Stuckey's clerk stands at a Ms. Pac-Man video game, stands rigid but for the right arm that works the joystick with practiced facility.

Sweeny rattles the pork skins in the bag. The clerk doesn't turn around.

"Unngh," the Minotaur says, hoping to be heard. But the clerk continues playing.

It's impossible, standing at the counter so far away, for Sweeny and the Minotaur to tell how the clerk is faring in the game, but the *blip*s and *gulp*s continue at an ever-increasing pace, and the clerk's right arm moves faster and faster, so they both get some sense of intensity. Nor can Sweeny and the Minotaur tell much about the clerk from the back, except that the dark hair falling just onto the shoulders of the brown Stuckey's smock and the way the smock drapes the body suggest female.

"Miss," Sweeny says, acting on the assumption. He has to say it twice before the clerk looks over her shoulder. From the Ms. Pac-Man game comes a sinking sound, and the clerk gives an annoyed audible huff. She jabs a cigarette into the ashtray and turns toward them. The Minotaur is counting the change from his pocket and isn't paying attention to the approaching clerk until Sweeny nudges him.

"Hey," Sweeny says. "She's one of yours, ain't she?"

The clerk walks slowly, with a stiff and almost wooden gait. She is out of breath by the time she reaches the counter. Her nametag reads *Hi, My Name Is Laurel*. Laurel has a skin condition. Her thin arms falling from the sleeves, her face—a face containing the ghost of beauty—and even her neck and the wide arrow of flesh dropping behind the buttoned front of the smock, all her visible skin and almost certainly all the skin hidden from view, is flaky, peeling, barklike in texture. Laurel appears to be leaving a trail of something—leaves. There is a ring of thin veiny leaves where she stood playing the video game; there are leaves scattered along the several steps to the cash register. Only when she stands directly in front of them does the Minotaur notice the thin branches woven tightly to her scalp throughout the dark hair and the narrow teardrop-shaped leaves that seem to wilt before their eyes. When Laurel looks at the Minotaur he thinks, he hopes, that it is a glimmer of recognition he sees crossing her face. But instead he sees only millennia of fatigue and a barely concealed need to get back to her video game.

"Will that be all?" she asks.

No, the Minotaur thinks. *That day will never come.* His sadness is sudden and complete. It is as if the Minotaur is looking into the past and the future simultaneously, and both are visions of desolation, of endless and murky emptiness.

"Gas," the Minotaur says, and walks out the door.

Sweeny knows better than to ask the Minotaur about it once they're back on the road. He talks. He tells a joke about a Jew and a DustBuster that makes him laugh for at least five miles.

"I don't know who in the world I'm going to sell this thing to," Sweeny says, speaking of the corn dog trailer weaving along behind them. "Shit, M, if you had any sense you'd buy it yourself."

The thought had not occurred to the Minotaur.

The cab of the truck smells like pork skins for the rest of the trip home. Somewhere near the Georgia border the Minotaur hits an animal, an opossum or raccoon, maybe, something large enough to shatter part of the grill on Sweeny's truck when it gets thrown into the air. Sweeny is only mildly irritated. The Minotaur and Sweeny get back to Lucky-U before sunrise. Sweeny gets out of the truck and directs the Minotaur with a flashlight and some loud whistling while he backs the trailer into place in the front yard. The whole time they're unhitching it and setting the leveling jacks, the Minotaur thinks about what Sweeny said. Just before going to sleep for the couple hours left of the night, the Minotaur wonders what Kelly would think.

CHAPTER 21

The Minotaur dreams himself through the Roman alphabet—
Abattoir
Bovidae, Bull-roarer
Crab claws
Deacon's bench, Dog typhus
Echo, Echoic, Echoism, Echolalia, Echopractic, Echo stop
Furred collar
Gabriel ratchet, Gutting scaffold
Hacksaw, Hamartia, Husbandry
Isthmus of the fauces
Jugs
Kernel smut
-lepsy
Maidenhead spoon, Miter box
Nimbostratus
Odd man out, Omphaloskepsis
Pamphleteer, Penitence, Prodigal
Quickie
Raddle, Roasting ear, Ruminant
Staggered, Scuppernong, Sump pump
Thicket, Tung oil
Ungulate
Valetudinarian, Vestigial
Wattle and daub
Xeno-
Yolk stalk
Zealotry

CHAPTER 22

*S*till *the Minotaur* is disconcerted by automatic doors. This might be taken as a portent for his perpetually diminishing ability to fit in, to function in a world rapidly growing dependent on technology. But he doesn't think that far ahead. Rexall Drugs welcomes the Minotaur with a hydraulic hiss, and he startles. He pulls a list from his pocket:

shoe laces. black
styptic pencil
WD-40
mouthwash
~~book?~~

It's the same list he made a week or so ago, to which he has added

1 spool light blue thread
gauze
candy?

Looking at the list it's not hard to tell that the word *candy* has been labored over—marked through, erased at least once, then written again but fettered by a question mark.

The candy is for Kelly, if the Minotaur can convince himself that it isn't presumptuous. Less directly the blue thread is for Kelly as well. Earlier today the Minotaur looked through his closet, and of the handful of radically altered shirts only the light blue one seemed new enough to wear if he goes to her house. The others were stained or already had several obvious repairs. When he took the blue shirt from the hanger and held it up the Minotaur noticed the seam unraveling over the right shoulder. He noticed, too, the faded ink stain beneath the pocket, but he figured it was the least of many flaws. Not until he got out the sewing box and was sitting at the table did he discover that there was no matching thread—only white, blood-red and black.

So, compelled by the most scant measure of vanity, the Minotaur walks the aisles of Rexall Drugs looking for, among other things, light blue thread. He carries Kelly's address folded in his front pocket, not because he needs it to find her house but because she wrote it. It is proof, of something. The creases in the paper are worn nearly through from overwork. This should not suggest that the Minotaur will get in his Vega and drive to

Kelly's house without hesitation, or even that he will go at all. The Minotaur is just readying himself in case. On the way home from the drugstore he'll fill the tank with gas and get a free car wash.

He carries a shopping basket. In it some unscented talcum powder keeps company with a bottle of store-brand mint-blue mouthwash. The Minotaur is distracted, standing at the end of an aisle holding a spool of thread up to the light to check the color, and doesn't see the boy run around the corner. He does feel the little body strike him at the hip and bounce off. The Minotaur has come to expect certain things—reactions of fear, for example. For him the hardest part of functioning in society is going to a new place, encountering new people and situations, and the Minotaur suspects that this would be true even if he didn't have the head of a bull. He's come to this conclusion by way of deduction. Often when people see him for the first time they are filled with terror. And/or disgust. And/or anger. And/or confusion. And/or . . .

When the Minotaur's unmoving hip sends the boy sprawling across the floor he expects the worst. Clutched in the boy's hand is a toy gun, a space-age weapon that emits a red beam of light and a lethal-sounding oscillating noise whenever the trigger is pulled. And pull the trigger he does, aiming the weapon directly between the black eyes of the Minotaur, who stands over him. But with each blast of the laser it becomes more apparent to the boy that the Minotaur will not die, will not, as expected, dissolve into a smoldering mass or disintegrate into oblivion, that either his weapon is insufficient or the enemy is immortal. Not for the first time the Minotaur witnesses the decimation of faith. In a matter of seconds fear consumes the child, renders him mute and cowering on the floor.

Pity them both.

Pity the child for his loss. He truly wanted his laser gun to kill the Minotaur, believed that it would, even. Each time an act of hope fails, the capacity for experiencing hope itself diminishes. The child will be lucky if he reaches adulthood with even a shred of faith intact.

Pity the Minotaur his plight. Sometimes when he is out in public and he sees a child with even the slightest animalistic trait—a canine sweep to the jaw, wide-set eyes and a broad forehead, something about the way the lips and the teeth work together—he wonders what a child of his might look like. He wonders about the structure of its tiny face, about the smell of its skin, about how it would call out to him. A precious few he has seen were so beautifully zoological that the Minotaur questioned their lineage. But like the mule and other hybrids created to carry out the unpleasant business of humans, the Minotaur is sterile. Any child of his will have to remain imagined. Regarding the Minotaur's own childhood, he has no memory of such, only of darkness and the smell of dry stone. It may be that the Minotaur was brought into existence just as he is now, a horned cumbersome mongrel. So he looks at the trembling little boy lying at his feet not with any sense of threat or anger but with unseeable tenderness and envy.

The Minotaur knows better than to reach out, knows without a doubt that his act would be misconstrued. It all happens quickly. The Minotaur steps back just as the short dumpy man who is the boy's father rounds the corner.

"Sorry," the man says to the Minotaur. On his very kind face the surprise is almost imperceptible.

"I've asked you not to play in the store, Henry. Can you say you're sorry?"

The man's hands are full. He carries a bag of throat lozenges, a roll of masking tape and a heating pad in an orange box with which he tries to conceal a muscle magazine, but the taut rippling pectorals and milk-jug-sized biceps, bronzed and glaring on the cover, are impossible to miss. When he puts everything down to help the boy stand the masking tape rolls out of sight beneath a shelf.

The little boy's fear subsides in his father's presence, but he is still reticent. "Sorry," he mumbles, peeking out from behind the man's legs. The man smiles at the Minotaur.

"Mmm," the Minotaur says, and nods.

Just before he turns to leave the boy speaks again. "What's wrong with him, Papa?"

"Don't be rude, Henry." The man smiles again, gives an apologetic shrug, then gathers his merchandise and leads his son up the aisle.

The Minotaur can't help but overhear them talking in the next aisle.

"Why is he like that, then?"

"For lots of reasons," the man says after a pause. "Tell you what, when we get home, we'll look him up in the encyclopedia and see what we can find."

The Minotaur stops to look at the selection of antiseptic creams; he hears no more of their conversation. The Minotaur isn't insulted by the child's questions. To the contrary, it's what he likes most about children, their unabashed honesty. To an almost visceral degree the Minotaur would like nothing more than to follow the man and his son home, to sit with them on the floor of the boy's bedroom—he struggles but can't imagine what the room would look like—and examine a book to find out why he is like he is. If it were only so simple.

Following them home isn't possible. And even if it were, disappointment is what he would find. No one book can fully explain the whys and whats of the Minotaur's existence. Most of the time the Minotaur is able to forget that his history has been duly chronicled for anyone to see. It has been a long time since his life had any relevance outside his immediate circumstances, and as time passes fewer and fewer people seem to know or care who he is, so he feels cloaked in a tenuous veil of complicated anonymity. Granted, a creature half man and half bull doesn't go unnoticed doing his laundry, buying groceries or going about the business of living. But there seem to be degrees of difference in the world. If most people knew the truth about his life and the things he has done—no matter that he didn't have a choice—his life in the here and now would be much more difficult. Thankfully most people don't know, and while they often replace the truths of his life with rumors and lies, any story they fabricate is okay with the Minotaur. A steady diet of blood and human flesh in the dry black corridors of the labyrinth so long ago thickened his skin. Too, the Minotaur himself is blessed with poor memory.

The man and his son are leaving when the Minotaur comes to check out. There are two security monitors over the clerk's head. On one screen the Minotaur watches the man and the boy walk across the parking lot of the strip mall, get in their car and drive away. On the other he watches himself pay for his merchandise. In his rare moments of personal clarity the Minotaur has some ideas about why he is as he is. He hopes that the man with the kind face tells his son something like the truth—that the Minotaur exists out of necessity, his own and the world's.

The Minotaur is so busy thinking this over that he doesn't remember whether or not he has pumped the Vega's gas pedal the requisite four times before turning the ignition, so he pumps it again. When the four-cylinder engine backfires loudly, then turns over and over without cranking, and the smell of gasoline fills the interior, he knows the engine has flooded. Waiting for a few minutes is the only thing that works. The Minotaur fishes half of a cigarette from the ashtray and pushes in the lighter.

He moves to the passenger seat. As he sits, smoking, the door open and his feet out on the pavement, kicking a bottle cap back and forth with the toes of his heavy black shoes, the Minotaur watches a crow fly out of the afternoon haze, sweep over the parked cars and land on a weathered picnic table chained at one end to a *No Parking* sign on the sidewalk in front of the drugstore. The bird proclaims its arrival with a guttural caw that seems to erupt out of its very blackness, then begins to strut, somewhat suspiciously, around a box of Kleenex abandoned on the tabletop. One sad and nearly leafless tree rising from a lit-tered patch of dirt offers no shade. The crow's shadow mimics its master. Out on the road a squad car drives by the strip mall. The police car does a **U**-turn in the parking lot of a boarded-up Sugar Daddy's Dairy Hut, then pulls into the entrance of the mall. Again the Minotaur turns the key, and again the backfire rattles the storefronts and echoes through the parking lot. The car refuses to start.

The Minotaur is leaning under the open hood loosening the wing nut to remove the air filter when the police car pulls into the empty parking space beside him. He hears the squawking radio before actually seeing the officers.

"Afternoon," the policeman driving the car says with more contempt than conviction.

"Mmm," the Minotaur says, and stands where they can see the air filter, as if it will provide some answers. He can feel cool air spilling from the car.

"Everything all right?"

"Flooded," the Minotaur says with as much clarity as he can muster.

The policeman nods but doesn't reply. Suspicion hangs so heavily in the air that the stifling afternoon breeze has to work around and over it to clog the Minotaur's breath. The Minotaur is filled with guilt when he goes to the back of the Vega to get a screwdriver from his toolbox. Guilt by association. Guilt by default. He knows the policemen are talking to each other.

Using the shaft of the screwdriver to wedge the carburetor's butterfly open, the Minotaur climbs into the driver's seat, pushes the gas pedal to the floor and turns the key. Sucking air and gasoline, the engine begins to sputter and cough. As soon as it catches and reaches an unsteady idle he takes the screwdriver out. He stays beneath the hood operating the throttle mechanism by hand until the car idles smoothly.

"You might want to think about a tune-up," the policeman

says as the electric window closes. The cruiser drives away.

After closing the hood and putting away his tools the Minotaur notices that the crow—still on the picnic table, black as ever, so black that it seems wet—is hard at work pulling the tissues from the box one after another. Each time the bird pinches a thin sheet in its clicking beak and tugs it out with a side-to-side yank of the head, a new tissue appears. And each time the crow responds with renewed determination. The sidewalk is littered with windblown tissues. Tissues hang in the branches of the leafless tree. One thin rectangle catches a gust of wind and boils through the air until snagging on the Vega's antenna. The Minotaur watches the crow pull tissues out of the box until there are no more. Then the bird flies away.

Driving back to Lucky-U Mobile Estates the Minotaur keeps looking in his rearview mirror. He's imagining the corn dog trailer being towed along behind. Only once does it occur to him that he can't afford the trailer, and it doesn't occur to him at all that the Vega might not be up to the challenge.

CHAPTER 23

"*Hey, M*," Kelly says. "I'm glad you came."

"Mmm," the Minotaur says. The candy is jammed under the front seat of the Vega, where it will stay for the time being, but here he stands in Kelly's door with his shirt stitched and his shoes shined. Not two hours ago he was in the corn dog trailer with a tape measure, checking and rechecking widths and heights. For what, he isn't exactly sure, but it seemed important. Not two hours ago he still couldn't say for certain whether or not he would go to Kelly's. But here he stands.

"Come on in," she says.

The Minotaur has never seen Kelly in anything other than her ruffled tuxedo shirt and black pants, usually with her hair back in a ponytail or up in a bun and a short apron tied around her waist. It takes him a minute to adjust to her dark hair falling over her shoulders, her running shorts and comfortably frayed flannel shirt with the sleeves rolled up to her elbows. The shirt is missing some buttons: two at the top and one at the bottom. The gray-plaid fabric does much to emphasize the full sweep of her breasts. The Minotaur tries not to stare.

In the daylight the Minotaur can see that Kelly lives in the smaller half of a clapboard duplex, in a neighborhood of peeling clapboard duplexes, in the shadow of the hoppers, conveyor belts and machinery of the Purina Chow factory. The air is still and everything smells like warm dog food. The Minotaur follows her inside. A canister vacuum cleaner sits in the center of an oval rug made of woven rags. The two rooms visible from where the Minotaur stands—the living room and an eat-in kitchen—are immaculate. He has no doubt that the rest of the house is as clean, and that it stays that way.

"How's your thumb?" Kelly asks.

"Mmm," the Minotaur says, showing her the bandage.

"Want a Coke?" Kelly asks. "Or some tea?"

"Water," he answers.

"Okey-dokey," she says, and does a quick turn on the balls of her bare feet. Her hair sweeps the air like a cloak, and the scent of sweat lingers where she stood. The Minotaur takes it in.

There are two places to sit in the small living room. The white wicker chair looks a bit unsteady for the Minotaur, and the arc of its wing back is probably too tight for his horns. He sits on a futon with a black lacquered frame and a vaguely Oriental cover. Because the room is small, and because the futon faces it, the Minotaur sits and watches the five—no, six—fish move about the aquarium that all but covers the top of an old buffet on the opposite wall. Thirty gallons at least, the Minotaur thinks; he's usually good with capacities. The fish are beautiful. Big as fists, they swim through the crystal-clear water effort-lessly, and their grand tails and fins bring a wonderful air of pomp and circumstance to their movements.

Kelly has lots of books. The only other expanse of wall is taken up by a low full bookshelf. From where he sits the Minotaur can't see the titles, but he can tell that the books are arranged carefully. Nothing is out of place. To be honest the books intimidate him. The Minotaur walks over to the fish tank, cocks his head and leans close to get a better look.

"Those are my babies," Kelly says, handing him a glass of ice water. She stands right beside the Minotaur and tells him about the fish. Goldfish. They're all different types of fancy gold-fish. Kelly talks about each one as if it were her child, as if one strange spring morning she pulled down her panties, raised her skirt, waded into a reedy algae-covered pond, wiggled her hips and released the eggs into water teeming with fish sperm. The results were these well-loved beautiful goldfish swimming back and forth in the Minotaur's field of vision. But the word *goldfish* can be misleading, as can *beautiful*. Most of the fish have very little gold in their coloring. And the characteristics enhanced by breeding and eagerly sought by aquarists could just as easily fall on the other side of that tenuous aesthetic line and into the do-main of the horrific.

"That's a Lionhead," Kelly says of the mottled fish that swims up to greet the finger she presses to the glass. "A calico Lionhead."

The severely humped back and the lack of a dorsal fin seem merely odd next to the craggy raspberry-like growth that crowns the fish's head so fully that it must impair its vision. It is a beautiful fish.

"Mmm," the Minotaur says.

There is a velvety Moor, a black fish with telescopic eyes that she named Othello because it's the only Shakespeare she remembers from high school. The goldest fish is the Celestial, whose eyes seemed to have been attached as afterthoughts, and haphazardly. They hang on the sides of the fish's face and point straight up; the Celestial's eyes are locked on the heavens, and it has difficulty seeing food or anything else below it. There are others. Kelly talks about her fish as if each of their individual deformities of shape and color is the most amazing thing in the world, and the Minotaur takes it all in.

After Kelly says all that can be said about the goldfish there is an awkward silence, helped only slightly by the steady bubbling of the aquarium filter and by the muted sounds of television cartoons seeping through the wall from the adjoining apartment. The Minotaur asks for another glass of water and drinks it too quickly.

"Mmm," he says, giving a sweep of his hand to indicate the house, meaning that he likes it.

"Thanks. I've been here for about a year now. The landlord is a jerk, but he never comes around. That's his niece over there," Kelly says, pointing at the wall. "All she ever does is watch cartoons."

The Minotaur asks where the bathroom is. A short hallway just big enough for a narrow closet and the heating unit leads to a tiny bathroom and the bedroom. Something about the lemon-yellow paint on the walls, the sky-blue porcelain of the tub, toilet and sink and the yellow and black tile on the floor of the bathroom is dizzying. The Minotaur has to close his eyes for a few seconds. He is embarrassed by the force of his urine stream. Hoping to mask the sound the Minotaur reaches to turn on the faucet, but he accidentally knocks over a plastic medicine bottle and what he thinks was a pearl earring, which falls into the drain. Empty, the bottle rattles loudly against the porcelain sink. The Minotaur reads the label before moving it out of the way to look for the earring. Dilantin, for seizures. He can't see the earring.

"Let's go out somewhere," Kelly says when he comes back. "Yes."

Kelly goes to change her clothes. The Minotaur hears a closet door slide open and shut, then a dresser drawer. He hears the rustle of fabric moving over skin, hears snaps and clinking metal. Kelly comes out wearing faded denim overalls and a red crew-neck pullover. The Minotaur doesn't know what the cloth is called, only that the Crews brothers call it long johns. There is no doubt, though, that it is much more appealing on Kelly. She straddles a low covered ottoman to buckle her sandals over bare feet.

"Ready?" she says, smiling at the Minotaur.

He nods and stands. Kelly leans close to the aquarium.

"Bye, guys. I'll be back later."

Just before they walk out the door Kelly remembers something. "Just a sec," she says. On top of the bookshelf is an aqua-colored ceramic bowl with a lid, the handle of which is shaped like a leaping goldfish. Kelly removes the lid, reaches into the bowl and pulls out some money. She counts off a few bills, then puts the rest back and replaces the lid. She folds the bills exactly in half and slips them into her back pocket.

"Now we're ready."

The Minotaur drives. It's assumed that he will. As they pass the Purina warehouses Kelly says she sometimes wishes she lived somewhere else.

"Another town, maybe even another state. You ever feel that way?" She thinks about her question for a minute. "I guess you have, though," Kelly says. "Lived other places, I mean."

The Minotaur is glad that Kelly likes to talk. He lets her lead the conversation. Neither of them has mentioned where they might be going, so he just drives roads that are familiar. When they drive past the closed Dairy Shack, Kelly becomes obsessed with a strawberry milk shake.

"I want one with that chemically fast-food aftertaste."

The Minotaur isn't sure about that particular aftertaste, but there is an Arby's in the next block. Before he even gets his window rolled down at the drive-up menu, the tinny speaker squawks at them. When the Minotaur pauses, not sure that he can make himself understood, doubting both his enunciation and the dubious intercom system, Kelly leans over him and shouts the order.

"Two strawberry milk shakes, please."

Kelly has to brace herself by holding his forearm.

The Minotaur works the plastic straw between his black lips and thick teeth. Kelly slurps unabashedly. He drives through the waning sunlight on the periphery of the city. When they end up at Honeycutt's Putt-Putt, Kelly seems excited.

"I'll warn you now," she says. "I was the Queen of Putt-Putt in middle school."

The Minotaur follows her through the gate and up to a shack not much bigger than a phone booth, painted bright yellow and open halfway down on three sides, where a surly kid with a bad case of acne on his forehead and buck teeth that push his lips out into a beautiful and permanent pout hunches over a guitar magazine. He is obviously annoyed that Kelly and the Minotaur want to rent balls and clubs.

"How many?" the kid asks, despite the fact that only Kelly and the Minotaur are standing in front of him.

There are many odd things about Honeycutt's Putt-Putt, not the least of which is its location adjacent to the Fox Triple-X Drive-In. It's common knowledge that Honeycutt set up the miniature-golf course to give his do-less son-in-law something like a job. It's a well-established rumor that the boy impregnated Honeycutt's daughter on the roof of the low concrete building from which the films are projected and where concessions are sold, during the second run of a movie called *Insatiable*. Giving the boy a job managing the miniature-golf course keeps him in Honeycutt's sight and ostensibly out of trouble.

"How many?" the kid asks again when Kelly doesn't respond immediately.

"Two."

On half of the counter all the putters are arranged by shaft size, from the longest to the shortest, the heads hanging over the front edge. Six recessed wells filled with colored balls—red, yellow, white, green, blue, orange—make up the other half of the counter. Hanging on the wall of the shack behind the boy, two hand-painted signs lay out the rules of the game according to Honeycutt.

Eight stroke maximum per hole. Do not skip holes. Keep balls on course.

No profanity. No alcohol. Only six players per group.

The Minotaur doesn't foresee any trouble with either set of rules. He chooses a club from the middle of the line and picks an orange ball.

"Hey," Kelly says playfully. "That's my color."

"Hmm," he says, and tosses her the ball.

"Call it," Kelly says, and flips a quarter into the air, into the muted tones of twilight. Going up, the coin is hard to see, but as it reaches the apex of its flight the kid behind the counter switches on the lights strung from poles throughout the course. The Minotaur is momentarily blinded.

"Tails," he says.

"You win," Kelly says. "Go first."

Another troubling thing about Honeycutt's Putt-Putt is the lack of a consistent theme. The design of the course and the obstacles created to make each hole challenging seem random. Greeting players on the first hole is the mechanical mouth of a plywood dragon that jerks and squeaks as it opens and shuts. If you're lucky enough to get your ball into the barely big-enough space between the teeth, it drops through a short pipe onto a platform surrounded by the dragon's coiled tail.

The Minotaur misses the first time; his ball bounces off the wedged teeth and rolls to a stop at his feet.

Kelly, of course, makes a hole in one. To be honest the

Minotaur would willingly miss every shot to prolong the game. Kelly talks as she happily wins almost every hole. By the fourth hole she's talking about what she wants to do with her life.

"I'd like to be a physical therapist someday," she says. "But I don't do so well with tests."

"Hmnnn," the Minotaur says, and tells her he knows what she means.

"I've got a friend in Savannah who's getting a massage license."

Honeycutt's Putt-Putt advertises itself as *FAMILY FUN* on the sign by the entrance. Most nights, however, the place is over-run by delinquents who aren't old enough to get into the bars. On the eighth hole, as Kelly is about to putt across a narrow arching bridge over a pool of murky green water, out of which rise two very plastic shark fins, a disturbing noise comes from behind them.

"Mooo."

The call is soft and tentative at first but definitely audible. "Mooooooo."

It's happened before. Without looking the Minotaur knows it's a group of boys. Usually he is alone and just ignores the taunting.

"Moooo."

There are four, maybe five of them, playing three holes behind Kelly and the Minotaur. He truly understands the herd mentality of young men. Without being able to name it he could probably go so far as to guess that testosterone plays a major role; the drive itself is as old as he is. Long ago the Minotaur realized that taunting has less to with him than with those who

feel the need to belittle others in public, and that the best recourse is to ignore it, which he can do without difficulty when
alone.

They play the Statue of Liberty hole and the Frankenstein
hole, which are equally monstrous.

"Moo."

One of the boys makes the sound, then they all giggle as if
it's the funniest thing in the world. But their laughter isn't any
more painful than the animal noises. What disturbs the Minotaur
about the boys taunting him tonight is that they're obviously
embarrassing Kelly. He watches a flush of red climb from beneath the collar of her shirt.

"Moo."

Kelly misses her next putt; the ball ricochets off a rail and
gets stuck under the shingled wall of a miniature windmill that
is supposed to turn but is broken, so it only makes turning noises.

"Stupid little boys," she says, and turns to look.

"Mmm," the Minotaur says, shaking his head. He tells her
that, if ignored, they'll soon be bored with the game. When he
kneels to fish her ball out with the head of his putter the tip of
his horn gets hung momentarily beneath the large wooden shoe
that guards the hole. Kelly takes his arm to help him stand. The
Minotaur is right, of course. A couple of holes later the boys
are laughing at something else.

The other problem with all these bored kids is that their
mischief isn't confined to rude comments and jokes. Holes one
through eight, sixteen, seventeen and eighteen at Honeycutt's
Putt-Putt lie behind and in the shadow of the huge screen of the
Fox Triple-X Drive-In. The rest of the holes are situated along a

high evergreen hedge backed here and there by a fence made of corrugated tin—neither of which is without gaps—running the length of the drive-in, designed to prevent one set of customers from interfering with the enjoyment of the other.

Early on someone discovered that it was possible to sneak through the fence after dark, to crawl out of the incongruous semi-mechanized disarray of the miniature golf course and into the domain of the Fox Triple-X—where squat steel posts rise out of the ground to bear their twin loads of heavy ovoid speakers with hooks to hang on the car windows, rise in perfect rows and mark space with unswerving regularity—to creep in after sundown and turn up the volume on all the unused speakers bordering the fence.

The Minotaur notices it first. Or maybe Kelly does but pretends not to. She is on thirteen, about to putt up an absurdly steep incline. The hole lies in the center of a fake bird nest at the top of the hill. When the ball goes in the hole an even more fake crow, hanging sideways in a tree overhead, lights up and quacks twice. It's impossible to see the screen from anywhere on the Putt-Putt course, but to the perceptive there is a feeling in the air of something huge and pornographic flickering nearby, or overhead, or behind the back.

The projected images are captured and contained by the big white screen, but the accompanying soundtrack is a different story.

"Oh. Yes. Oh. Yes. Oh. Yes."

Kelly whistles as they play.

"Ummph . . . uckme. Ummph . . . uckme."

Kelly looks at the Minotaur and rolls her eyes, feigning

nonchalance. The Minotaur wins the hole by one stroke. There is music—insipid waiting-room music—playing behind the tape loop of dialogue. As they move from hole to hole, still unable to see what actions the dialogue accompanies, things begin to work in concert.

"Suck it. Oh, yes, suck my honeypot."

"In the ass. Now! In the ass."

The grunts and throaty utterances swell.

"Faster harder faster harder faster."

Kelly becomes more flustered as the pitch rises, tripping over her feet, unable to keep score.

"Fat cock in my mouth."

"Yes. Oh, yes. My tits."

The Minotaur grows more and more self-conscious. Compared to these superhuman feats of endurance—it's been half an hour at least—and, most likely, this rich endowment, he is no match. The Minotaur has enough sense to realize that, in this area, he is at best a mediocre performer.

"Fill that cunt! Fill it with your ramrod!"

"Auk! Auk! Gnu! Mmmm!"

At least as embarrassing, if not more so, are the wet, slapping, sometimes flatulent sounds of body against body and of things moving in and out of orifices. These are easily enough imagined. Without being able to see what is happening on the screen, when you divide the number of acts, requests and orifices by the number of voices, it seems that some basic laws of nature are being challenged.

"Come! Come! I'm gonna come."

"Arghh. Squirt, baby."

"Aaaaa. Eeeee."

"Iiiiiiiii."

"Ooooooooo."

"Uuuuuuuuuuuu."

It all culminates just as Kelly sinks her orange ball in the cup on the final hole.

"Let's figure the score in the car," she says.

When they put their clubs back on the counter the skinny kid doesn't even look up. The Minotaur puts the ball he was using into his pocket, to keep as a remembrance. Neither of them mentions what they just heard.

Sitting in the Vega with the doors open, Kelly leans on the dash to tally the strokes. "Still," she says. "I'm still the reigning Queen of Putt-Putt."

Kelly looks at her watch. "I should probably go home, M."

They ride in an almost comfortable silence. Despite everything it's been a good evening. The Minotaur pulls the car to a stop in front of Kelly's house. Feeling more bold than he has in centuries the Minotaur asks the question he's been thinking about all the way home.

"Again?"

"Soon," Kelly answers.

She leans close and kisses him on the snout, then quickly gets out of the car. It happens so fast that he has no time to respond. Long after she is inside the house the touch of her lips radiates warmth over the Minotaur's muzzle.

Back at Lucky-U the Minotaur pulls the candy from under the Vega's front seat, thinking that maybe next time he will give it to Kelly. Then he notices that the lid of the box is punctured.

When he opens it all the candy smells of exhaust fumes. The Minotaur puts a piece in his mouth. It tastes of motor oil. He chews it slowly, then swallows.

CHAPTER 24

Reprieve. Into the Minotaur's life there occasionally comes a reprieve from the inevitable loneliness, relentless and exhausting, that is endured by those who live forever. These moments of reprieve are dangerous times, though. When looking out at eternity it's easy to lose sight of the past, to repeat the same mistakes. If not careful the Minotaur can be seduced by a turn of luck—can be blinded, so to speak. In these sweet and rare moods he's prone to acting hastily.

"What is that thing?" J. C. Crews asks the Minotaur. He's standing by his truck with an oily brown lunch bag clutched in one hand, waiting for his brothers and looking out at the road.

"Corn dogs," the Minotaur says of the concession trailer, trying out the words in his mouth, hoping that they will be explanation enough.

"Oh," J. C. says, apparently satisfied.

Last night the Minotaur dreamed he was washing the Vega. When he woke his palms were damp. This morning he has a hose stretched from the spigot at the back of Sweeny's house and is filling a bucket with soapy water. It's early, and he wants to finish the job before the day heats up.

D. W. and A. J. come out of the trailer together. They're arguing loudly. Something about a half-gallon of curdled milk, but the Minotaur isn't sure what.

"What's that?" D. W. asks, looking at the trailer.

"Corn dogs," J. C. says.

"Oh."

"Morning, M," A. J. says. "Washing your car?"

Creamy white foam swells and begins to spill over the side of the bucket; an imitation-lemon scent fills the air. The Minotaur labors through an explanation of going after the concession trailer with Sweeny. The Crewses are, if anything, patient at listening.

"You ought to buy that thing, M," D. W. says before climbing into the truck. "Being a chef and all."

"Hmm."

"You'd be your own boss," A. J. says.

"And get to do a lot of traveling," J. C. adds.

They drive away. The Minotaur waits for the dust to settle before hosing down the Vega—roof first, hood and hatchback, both sides, then some extra time on the wheels and tires. He fishes a rag, a piece cut from an old apron, out of the soapy water and begins washing the roof with big figure-eight motions. A pair of hummingbirds circles around and feeds in the mimosa blooms overhead, their wing beats impossibly frantic. The Minotaur washes the hood and hatchback, then squirts off

all the soap. He has forgotten a brush for the wheels and goes
to find one in his trailer.

Jules and Marvin are playing on their front porch when he
comes back. They take turns hitting a little metal car with a
hammer. The Minotaur kneels to scrub the Vega's tires. By the
time he finishes washing the car the boys, drawn by the spraying water, the potential for mud, have moved closer to him.
Wearing only cutoff shorts, their skinny trunks and limbs brown
from half a summer of sun, they chase each other around and
around the nandina bushes. Marvin pelts Jules with handful after handful of the small round berries.

Josie's car is parked behind the Vega. The hose will reach,
and the Minotaur feels generous. It takes him only a few minutes to wash her car. As the Minotaur rinses the soapy water
from the roof Jules runs under the cascading spray, then Marvin.
And again. The soap is long gone, but the Minotaur continues
to spray, overshooting the car each time the boys run by. In no
time the pretense of rinsing the car is abandoned, and Jules and
his brother race around as eager giggling targets while the
Minotaur chases them with a stream of water.

"Marvin!"

It's Josie, yelling from inside the trailer.

"Jules!"

It's hard to say whether she sounds any angrier than usual.

"Stop bothering M!" she says. "Get back on the porch."

Reluctantly the kids return, dripping, and resume the de-
struction of their toy. The Minotaur empties the soapy water in
the side yard and washes the bucket out. He disconnects the
hose and loops it around his elbow and extended thumb. After

putting everything away the Minotaur goes back to the Vega, where the box of chocolates, minus one, sits on the seat. He picks a piece randomly and eats it, decides they're good enough, then takes the candy to Jules and Marvin.

The Minotaur is about to go into the trailer when he hears the squeal of braking tires out on the road, then a rattling muffler and the whine of a car in reverse. It's pulling into the driveway, the car he can't see. He hears a flurry of slamming doors—one, maybe two from the car, then Sweeny's front door. Not wanting to seem nosy, the Minotaur waits a few minutes. To give the illusion of purpose he takes a large monkey wrench from the toolbox in the back of the Vega, then ambles up the driveway and around the house.

It's hard to be unobtrusive with a pair of horns, but Sweeny is so busy talking to the three men who circle the concession trailer, opening and closing the door and crawling underneath, that no one notices the Minotaur. By moving close to the trees and bushes he's able to get within earshot.

Exactly what the relationships among the three men are is unclear. They don't look enough alike to be brothers, but there are similarities in demeanor and dress. All three favor a plaid short-sleeve shirt, a little too small, a pocket on each breast, buttoned to the neck. And cowboy boots. One of the men does most of the talking.

"We come up and down this road all the time," he says.

"That so?" Sweeny responds. He's a natural salesman who always lets the customer lead the conversation and never gives a hard pitch.

"Seen this thing sitting here yesterday," the man says.

"Just brought it up from Florida," Sweeny says.

"Y'all handle some pretty good merchandise."

"It ain't hard," Sweeny says. "Folks is always stopping to sell me something. Had a fella come by here the other day trying to sell me a old waterlogged church bus."

The man looks around Sweeny's yard.

"I weren't interested," Sweeny says.

The other two men scrutinize the trailer carefully—so carefully that it makes the Minotaur anxious. They talk mostly to each other, and although he hears only snatches of it the seriousness of their conversation adds to the Minotaur's anxiety.

". . . have to hang a rack right here."

"That'd be no problem."

"Yeah, but if we had . . ."

The Minotaur is not one to impudently abuse his position, that position being one of a creature half man and half bull, a creature potentially frightening to anyone unprepared for him. To the contrary he would much rather go unseen or unnoticed most of the time. But as each moment passes and Sweeny still talks to the three men, the possibility of a deal being struck grows.

"Twenty-five hundred," Sweeny says.

It takes the Minotaur's breath. He has no definite plan. He doesn't have anywhere near that kind of money. But the mere mention of a price makes him act.

"Unngh." It's a grunt more than anything else, and louder than he intended. The man talking to Sweeny looks up and catches the Minotaur's eye, which leaves the Minotaur no choice. He inhales deeply, from the belly up, filling his chest. He holds his head erect, horns straight, then walks toward them.

"Morning, M," Sweeny says.

If fear is what he hopes for, the Minotaur is disappointed. The men acknowledge his presence with little more than nods and furrowed brows. There is a noticeable sag to the Minotaur's shoulders. The man talking with Sweeny joins his friends. The three of them look the concession trailer over again from top to bottom. They speak in hushed tones, but their gestures make some disagreement apparent.

"What you need, bud?" Sweeny asks.

"Unnh," the Minotaur says. Nothing.

He and Sweeny watch the three men. After a few minutes the talker comes over.

"We got to chew on this thing for a little bit," he says, looking Sweeny in the eye.

"She'll set there until she sells," Sweeny says.

"Fair enough."

All three of the men climb into the front seat of their car from the passenger side. When they back out on to the road the Minotaur notices that the driver's door is tied shut with twine.

"Hmm," Sweeny says, and goes back into his house.

Chapter 25

"*I got killed* this weekend," David says. He's balancing a stack of clean ashtrays in his hands and watching the Minotaur fillet a three-foot salmon that hangs off the cutting board at both ends.

"Took a load of grapeshot in the belly."

"Mmm," the Minotaur says. If the blade is good and you're sensitive enough you can feel it riding over each of the ribs coming down the spine. The Minotaur pulls the flesh away from the bones, and the redness of the meat fairly screams against the white plastic cutting board.

David takes the ashtrays out to the smoking section, then comes back with more details.

"I was coming over a ridge of pines fifteen minutes into the battle. Had to sit out the rest of the day."

"Terrible," the Minotaur says. He sometimes wonders why

simulating death is such a common pursuit among men. The two salmon fillets lie side by side. The Minotaur takes a pair of needle-nose pliers and, using his fingertip to locate them, pulls out the sharp transparent bones hidden in the red flesh.

Hernando limps behind the hot line, whistling as he makes roux in a heavy pan.

"Cajun napalm, they call it," Hernando says.

The roux, nothing but flour and butter, bubbling and popping as it cooks to a chocolaty brown, will be used in thickening the étouffée, tonight's special. Hernando shows Maynard a scar from the last time he made this kind of roux: a pinkish and perfect circle the size of a nickel on the back of his hand. The Minotaur has heard Hernando tell the story of getting that particular scar at least a half-dozen times, all different.

Cecie is making crepes. When her back is turned the Minotaur peels one of the thin pancakes from the stack, rolls it into a cigar shape and pretends to smoke it when she turns around.

"I'm gonna fry your ass in this pan if you don't leave my crepes alone," Cecie teases. The Minotaur bites the crepe in half and offers the other half to Cecie. She takes it in her mouth with two quick bites, catching the edge of the Minotaur's thumbnail in her teeth.

When Grub comes in unannounced and unusually quiet, the mood in the kitchen dampens. Grub carries a bag from the hardware store. He smiles and nods to the Minotaur as he walks through to the dining rooms. A little later David comes into the kitchen with the bag, from which he pulls a quart of off-white paint and a small brush. He asks JoeJoe to touch up the employee bathroom. JoeJoe grumbles a little about not being paid to paint walls but then takes the can and brush into the bathroom and closes the door.

Between the big Hobart mixer that sits on the floor at the end of the hot line and the reach-in coolers for the salad station, Grub has put a special table for prepping the cooked prime ribs. The tabletop is sloped; in the center a hole eight inches in diameter drops to a trash barrel standing below. A whole prime rib—the loin, ribs and seasoned fat cap—is roasted in a mesh of cotton string. Before going out to the beef cart the ribs are cut in half on the table, and the crackling fat cap is peeled away with the net and discarded through the hole. The Minotaur readies his beef cart for the night.

"How's your thumb?" Grub asks. It's about four o'clock. The wait staff should start coming in any minute.

"Okay," the Minotaur says, showing him the thumb, bandaged and covered with a latex finger cot.

When he's caught up with his prep work the Minotaur goes out to the wait station to check the schedule, which he's done three or four times already. He wants to make sure that Kelly is still on the shift list. She is; she's closing tonight, so she won't be in until six.

The Minotaur helps Hernando peel crayfish tails for the étouffée. Gradually the kitchen grows busier. The waiters and waitresses attend to their side work responsibilities. Again the Minotaur leaves the kitchen, goes to the bar for a Coke. There he finds most of the wait staff.

"Please, Eva," Mike asks. "Just once. Do it this once."

They all stand around Eva, the new waitress, Shane's replacement, who smiles nervously from within the close circle. Eva is young. Eva is a woman of incongruities. She is short with a thin trunk resting firmly on substantial hips. She has a pretty smile with a desperate edge. Her long jawbone gives way to lots of tiny teeth.

"Maybe later," she says. At least the Minotaur thinks that's what she says, but her voice is so tiny that it's all but contained within the ring of her audience.

"Aw, come on," Mike pleads. "These guys don't believe me. They don't believe you can do it."

Eva has that caught-in-a-trap look.

"I've got to fold napkins," Jenna says, and walks away. It looks like the audience is going to break up.

"Oh, all right," Eva says.

People learn early how to deal with humiliation. Some learn that being embarrassed is sometimes preferable to being ignored. Standing there at the bar with Mike, George, Adrienne, Margaret, one of the busboys and the Minotaur, who is trying to appear disinterested at the ice machine, Eva balls her hand into a tight fist, thumb tucked under her fingers. She puts her fist to her mouth. Eva opens her mouth wide and, starting at the middle knuckles, begins to work her hand between her teeth.

"Yes!" Mike says.

"Jesus."

Somebody whistles.

Eva's thin lips stretch and contort, her cheeks make way and without too much effort her bony little fist disappears inside her mouth nearly to the wrist. She stands there like that, looking to Mike for approval.

"I told you she could do it," he says.

Mike is excited.

"She did it on the radio last week. I knew I recognized her name."

Mike is more excited than anyone else.

"WROC, *Sunrise with Stanky*. It was funny as hell."

Disappointment and embarrassment—they both register to some degree in everyone there.

The busboy makes a crude remark as he and George walk away.

"Sick," Adrienne says. She picks up a tray of lamps and leaves.

Grub walks in and tells everybody to get back to work.

Mike keeps talking about how funny the radio show was, but mostly to himself. He leaves, too. Only the Minotaur is left to watch Eva pull her fist from her mouth. It takes more concentrated work than putting it in, and when the fist comes out the Minotaur is surprised by how dry it is. Eva wipes the little bit of saliva on her pant leg; the wet spot shines on the polyester fabric. The Minotaur can't move his cumbersome head fast enough, so Eva catches him looking at her. She smiles, but it takes effort.

"Bathroom," she says.

"Um hmm," he responds.

The Minotaur feels a freakish kinship with Eva. He hopes she finds other talents.

At five-thirty the Minotaur wheels the beef cart into the main dining room and plugs it in. As with most things the moral dilemma of his current job diminishes each time he stands behind the cart of roasted meat. He's almost gotten used to the way the chef's hat feels draped over the top of his head. Grub has been in the office since the afternoon. David comes and goes from the dining room like a nervous bird.

"Hey, M."

It's Kelly. He didn't see her come from the kitchen. She's standing beside him tying her apron strings in a double-knotted bow.

"Hey," he says.

"Come here," she says. "I've got something for you."

Business is slow; so far there are just three occupied tables in the restaurant, and only one of them has a prime rib order. The Minotaur follows Kelly to the closet behind the bar, where the wait staff stores coats, purses and the like.

"Close your eyes," she says.

He does. In the blackness her smell takes hold. The Minotaur feels something go around his neck.

"Okay," Kelly says.

It's a white kerchief, rolled tight, the ends matched down the center of his chest. He wonders where she found one large enough to circle his bull neck.

"This," Kelly says. "I think you'll like this."

Between her thumb and forefinger she holds a thick ring made of bone, yellowed and beautiful, through which she peers at the Minotaur.

"It's a piece of shank bone," she says, and puts the ends of the kerchief through the hole. She pulls down on the cloth with one hand and with the other pushes the ring of bone snugly up to the base of the Minotaur's neck. "I got a friend who works in a butcher shop."

This makes the Minotaur smile.

"You look like a pro," she says, stepping back. Something on her lapel glints in the light. It's a goldfish pin.

"Thank you," the Minotaur says, happy with the clarity of his words.

The Minotaur looks at himself in the streaked and cloudy mirror of the employee bathroom. The toque, the kerchief with the shank-bone ring and the pristine chef's coat look good, even if adorning a creature with the head of a bull. He ties an apron around his waist and returns to the beef cart. Cecie whistles at him as he walks through the kitchen.

"Fancy," Jenna says, bringing him an order. "Looks good, M."

David, George and almost all the wait staff compliment the Minotaur at some point during the night. Even some of the customers seem to notice. Only Mike says nothing, which is okay with the Minotaur. Mike has minded his p's and q's for the past few days, at least when Grub or David is around.

The night is slow, steady and uneventful. After breaking down the beef cart and running everything through the dish machine the Minotaur goes to the bar, where the waiters and waitresses are figuring their tips. Eva seems to have gotten over her embarrassment. She sits in a booth with Margaret, and they're both laughing about a table Eva served.

"Did you see those nails?" Margaret asks.

"How about the earrings?" Eva says.

"I'm telling you, that was a man in drag," Margaret says, and Eva almost squeals with delight at the very idea.

The Minotaur takes heart in her ability to adapt. He scoops ice into a tall glass and begins to fill it from the soda gun. Mike is in midsentence when the hissing stops.

". . . already working," he says. "Some hoity-toity seafood place out on the river."

He's talking to Adrienne and Jenna, keeping his voice low. It takes the Minotaur a minute to figure out that they're talking about Shane.

"He says he's making big bucks out there."

"I'd hate to come home smelling like fish every night," Jenna says.

"Like greasy meat smells any better?" Adrienne says. "I only made twenty-six dollars tonight, and that's before I tip the bussers."

The Minotaur returns to the kitchen. As he walks by the open office door Grub calls him inside.

"How was your night, M?"

"Mmmn," he says. "Slow."

"Listen," Grub begins. "I've been thinking. I'm not sure this beef cart idea is going to work out with you."

"Hmm?"

"It's not you, but I've had a few customers complain."

Blood surges in the Minotaur's ears. Grub talks a little more, but it's difficult for the Minotaur to understand exactly what he's saying—something about Maynard filling in while the Minotaur was out.

"He did a great job," Grub says.

The Minotaur waits. He waits with roiling familiar gall. He waits for the inevitable change. He sits quietly in the employee bathroom. When he hears Kelly in the kitchen asking if anyone has seen him the Minotaur turns the lights off. Not until everyone has left does he make his way out to the empty parking lot. The clean Vega shines in the light of a gibbous moon. Beneath the windshield wiper a piece of paper lies flat against the glass. It's a note from Kelly.

"See you soon, I hope."

She has signed it with a smiley face.

CHAPTER 26

In the gall of sleep the Minotaur dreams his mother's desire.
She lies with the fishmonger. She lies in his fingers, slick
and silver as kipper. She lies in the migrating eye of the halibut.
The comb of the harlequin cock. She lies with the heifer and the ox.
She lies with Lot's daughters. She lies with the foreskins
of a hundred Philistines. With the drum and with the drummer.
She lies with the milk pail fresh from the udder.
With cloven hoof she lies. She lies with crimson madder
and cadmium yellow. She lies with tyger stripes. She lies
on death death death death death row. She lies
in the stropped shadow of crow's beak.
She lies quiet among clacking looms.
She lies with cornbread and beans,
and with two thieves, and in red clay.
She lies alone.

CHAPTER 27

The Minotaur wakes to the taste of bile creeping up the back of his throat, wakes in the thick wet air of a predawn summer rain. He scratches at his chest with both hands, then along either side of the haired groove that runs down the center of his belly, then beneath the waistband of his pajamas, where he spends five solid minutes scratching his testicles with great pleasure. By the time he rises the sun is up and cooking the moisture out of Lucky-U Mobile Estates. Everything steams. When the Minotaur stands, the bile subsides, but the blood rushing to his limbs causes his injured thumb to throb. The Minotaur fingers the swollen area surrounding the cut on his thumb. It occurs to him that he perhaps should have waited and not pulled the stitches out himself last night. There is also an itching and residual ache deep in the burn-scarred foot.

On the table by the bed sits the shank-bone ring. The

Minotaur picks it up and rolls it in his fingers; he puts it up to one eye and then the other, squinting and looking around the room and out the window, then slips the ring on and off each finger as far down as it will fit. Only on his pinkie does the ring slide beyond the middle knuckle. If Grub takes him off the beef cart he'll wear Kelly's gift—the kerchief and the circle of bone—while working in the kitchen. The decision makes him feel just a little better.

The Minotaur attends to himself in the bathroom, makes his coffee and sits at the table eating pieces of white bread from the plastic bag. He's up early enough to see Hank and the Crews brothers leave. Sweeny's truck isn't in the drive. Nearing seven o'clock Mrs. Smith turns the volume up on her television.

A couple of hours after that Jules and Marvin come outside. Jules, furtive and obvious, carries something in a brown paper bag behind his back; Marvin follows conspicuously close. Conjoined by their secret they move as one to the side of the trailer, where they lean against the underpinning and unroll the bag. Jules reaches in to pull out a small jelly jar, empty and clean. Then from deep in the front pocket of his short pants he takes a jackknife. He pinches a blade and strains to get it open. The blade is long and fatter than any two of his fingers.

The Minotaur cocks his head to get a better view. There is one other thing in the paper bag: a brightly colored and flimsy cardboard box about four inches square. It contains shotgun shells, brass capped and thick as a man's thumb. Marvin digs into the box with his little-boy hand and takes out all he can hold—six, seven, maybe eight shotgun shells. The boys talk, but the Minotaur can't hear what they say. Jules goes behind the trailer, comes back with a scrap of plywood. Using it as a workspace the boys begin to cut open the shells with the jackknife and to pour the gunpowder and the lead shot into the jelly jar.

Again Jules disappears around the trailer. This time he returns with a nail and a piece of a brick. Taking instruction from Marvin he lays the lid from the jelly jar upside down on the plywood. He uses the brick as a hammer, and the nail easily punctures the thin metal lid—one hole, dead center.

When all the shells have been cut open their contents nearly fill the jelly jar. Then it is Marvin who leaves the scene, but only for a few minutes, and when he runs from around the side of the trailer the excitement is palpable. Clutched in his hand is a tightly folded piece of cloth that turns out to be a pair of boy's underwear, and tucked into the little nut pouch is the reason for all their fervor: a packet of firecrackers and a box of strike-anywhere matches. The wind shifts, and the Minotaur picks up the faint smells of sulfur and gunpowder.

Some men are born to lead, to envision, to shape and mold the politics and opinions, the attitudes, the mores, the outcomes of their times, from individual to individual or on a world scale. Others take it upon themselves to intervene rather than to forge, to serve, to help, to intuitively recognize problems or the potential for problems and give whatever is necessary to prevent or at least rectify them. Still others merely exist. Trembling at the thought of the horrible responsibilities that making a decision entails, and willing to let their lives—and, by association, the lives of others—unfold or collapse according to dumb luck, they seek out obscurity. They choose or arrive at insignificance and soon enough become willing to suffer the consequences. There was a time when the Minotaur and his ilk were important, creating and destroying worlds and the lives of mortals at every turn. No more. Now, most of the time, it is all the Minotaur can do to meet the day-to-day responsibilities of his own small world. Some days he can passively witness the things that go on around him. Other days he can't stomach any of it. The Minotaur wants no part of what may happen to Jules and Marvin in the next few hours.

The corn dog trailer glares like an aluminum behemoth out by the road, beckons in a quiet rectangular way. The Minotaur circles it. He kicks at one tire with the toe of his work shoe and realizes the ridiculousness of the action, but he can't stop himself from kicking the other one. He decides to go for a drive despite the lack of a destination. Half a mile from the house the Minotaur meets Sweeny on the road, his truck unmistakable with its shattered grill. As they pass, Sweeny lifts two fingers on the hand that grips the top of the steering wheel. He nods, too; the Minotaur can't see it, but he's ridden with Sweeny often enough to know that a nod accompanies the wave. The Minotaur taps the Vega's horn in response.

He drives. And drives. And drives. By Grub's house and the restaurant, by David's, on the outskirts of town, then through its heart. He drives for an hour, two hours. Well into the third hour no one is more—or less—surprised than the Minotaur when he finds himself standing on Kelly's front stoop looking through the screen door. He isn't known for his boldness. She isn't aware of his presence. Standing there watching Kelly the Minotaur reconsiders his decision. He never goes anywhere unannounced or uninvited. He makes up his mind to leave before she notices him.

Kelly doesn't see the Minotaur because she is preoccupied. She is kneeling, with her back to the door, in front of the aquarium. A five-gallon bucket stands beside her. Through the tight mesh of the screen it's hard to see the clear plastic tubing that hangs over the side of the fishtank, so when Kelly turns in profile to the Minotaur and puts her hand to her face as if she is eating or smoking, but instead takes something between her lips and sucks hard, so hard that her cheeks cave in, the Minotaur is baffled. Kelly misjudges the power of her siphon, draws in a mouthful of water. The Minotaur sees the tube for the first time when she yanks it from her mouth and aims the stream of flowing water into the open bucket, leaning over it at the same time to spit out the contents of her mouth. When Kelly retches and heaves, clear frothy bile drips from her tongue, and the Minotaur winces. His horn raps against the door's metal frame.

Kelly looks up, her eyes red and ringed with tears from nearly vomiting. She smiles. It's weak, a little embarrassed, but it's there. She waves the Minotaur in.

"She's sick," Kelly says, eyeing the tank. "My baby is sick."

The Minotaur looks. Despite the fact that all the fish are bred for various mutations, for odd or frightening body shapes and colors, there's no mistaking the sick fish.

"Dropsy, I think," Kelly says. "I've got to change the water."

She's genuinely upset; the Minotaur can tell. And justifiably so, because at the bottom of the tank, near the front, her calico oranda is bloated, its stomach so distended that the scales stick out pine-cone fashion. It floats upside down, bumping against the glass. If not for the gaping mouth and the minute flicker of desperation in the black eye, the eye barely visible inside a mass of fleshy multicolored ornamentation, he would think the six-inch-long four-inch-wide fish dead.

When the plastic bucket is nearly full she pinches the siphon tube and hands it to the Minotaur; he holds it clamped while she lugs the water—sloshing it only once in the hall—to the tub and empties it. The second time around the Minotaur offers to carry the heavy bucket. Together they empty three-quarters of the tank, then Kelly runs a hose from the sink to refill it. While the other fish move at will in the current from the flowing water, the inverted oranda pitches and rocks helplessly.

"Maybe I should set up a hospital tank," she says. "What do you think?"

"Mmm," he says, having no idea what she means. The Minotaur wants to be helpful but doesn't know what to do.

"Keep an eye on her," Kelly says. "I'll be right back."

The Minotaur kneels and fixes his sight on the sick fish, ready.

From a closet somewhere out of sight Kelly brings a much smaller aquarium—eight gallons, the Minotaur decides—empty of water but holding several things. He recognizes the clear plastic box stuffed with cotton batting and charcoal as a filter. The long thin cylinder made of glass and topped with a dial must be for heating the water.

"Let's do it in here," she says, carrying the aquarium into her bedroom. She squats to set it on the floor, then moves a stack of neatly folded laundry off the top of the dresser to make space for the aquarium there. Kelly sets up the hospital tank, fills it with warm water.

"Salt," she says.

Kelly comes back from the kitchen with a box of salt and a puzzled look.

"I can't find my measuring spoons."

"How much?" the Minotaur struggles to ask.

"A tablespoon for every five gallons," Kelly says. "I think that's it."

The Minotaur cups his palm and uses the other thumbnail to pry open the spout on the saltbox. With practiced concentration he pours a small white mound into the creased depression of his hand; he scatters the salt over the surface of the water, then repeats the process, making a slightly smaller mound.

Kelly opens the top drawer of the dresser—the sock drawer—and takes out a black lacquered chopstick that the Minotaur has seen her wear wound in her hair. She stirs the salt into the water with it, wipes the chopstick dry on her T-shirt and puts it back in the drawer. In the mirror the Minotaur can see himself standing behind Kelly. In the mirror the Minotaur can see the wrought-iron bed, its thin bars painted eggshell white; he can see the wicker nightstand and the incense burner made of jade. In the mirror the Minotaur can see the clock that sits on the nightstand, its round face emerging from the belly of a plaster Buddha. Ten o'clock. How can that be? It takes him a second to realize he's seeing a reflection. It's two o'clock. He should be at work in an hour and a half.

Through the bedroom wall, from the adjoining apartment, comes the sound of TV cartoons. *Boing. Screeeech. Schhhplattt.*

An explosion and canned laughter. There's something else the Minotaur can see in the mirror: the closet door, mirrored itself. The reflection of him and Kelly caught between the two mirrors grows smaller and smaller infinitely into the distance.

When the filter is hooked up and air is bubbling in the corner of the hospital tank, Kelly goes for her sick fish. The Minotaur isn't the least bit surprised when, instead of using a net, she reaches in with her hand and gently scoops up the oranda. The big fish more than fills her palm. Carefully, lovingly, Kelly eases the fish into its infirmary, places it upright at the bottom of the tank.

"We have to watch her for a while," Kelly says.

"Mmm."

The Minotaur goes into the kitchen and returns with two ladder-back chairs, one painted blue, the other red. He and Kelly sit in front of the tank. For a precious few minutes the oranda remains plumb and upright as a fish should. But very soon it begins to list a little to its right. After a half-hour, the Minotaur and Kelly watching quietly, the fish lies on its side at the bottom of the tank desperately sucking water through its gills. Twenty minutes later it's dead. There's no gaping mouth, no life in the tiny black eye. Dead.

Kelly cries. She puts her forehead to the glass and sobs. The Minotaur can think of nothing to do, so he sits upright in the chair with his hands resting on his thighs. The woven cane seat creaks with his every move, and the harder he tries to sit still the more his body twitches. He should be at work in forty-five minutes.

"I've had that oranda for almost three years," Kelly says. "I can remember the day I bought her."

She pulls the back of her hand beneath her nose, which leaves a glistening stripe of mucus from wrist to knuckles.

"Sorry," he says.

Mustering his courage the Minotaur makes a gesture of compassion. He reaches out and puts his hand on her shoulder. Kelly, of course, is too upset to notice the sweat from his palm seeping through her T-shirt.

Kelly turns in her seat, leans forward, lays her head on the Minotaur's shoulder and sobs mightily. The Minotaur, of course, is unaffected by the clear watery snot that seeps through his shirt. The human ability to attach so much emotion to things not human is baffling to him—baffling, enviable and tinged with hope.

Kissing is difficult for the Minotaur. It's something he has little experience with. There are the rubbery black lips and the bristly snout to work around. There is the tongue, thick, long and unruly. It's difficult enough to control in speech, and making it adhere to the subtle intimacies of a kiss is nigh impossible. The great distance between his mouth and his eyes and the blind spot in his vision are also disconcerting; the Minotaur simply cannot see anything directly in front of his face. Kissing the Minotaur is perhaps even more difficult, for all those same reasons. It may be that kissing is a privilege of the fully human and should be left to them.

Apparently Kelly feels differently. It's not hard to guess who makes the first move toward an embrace. As well, it's not hard to see how moments of acute emotion can blur at the edges, how a particular feeling, say grief, can spill over—or metamorphose, even—into something different, say desire. One minute Kelly is crying on the Minotaur's shoulder with her arms around his thick bullish neck, and the next her brackish mouth is seeking his. The Minotaur is surprised, but he doesn't pull away. No, he welcomes the insistent warmth of her kiss along the underside of his long chin, where his bull skin is the softest, then up to his lips.

"Unng," the Minotaur says.

"I know," Kelly answers.

Kelly turns her blue ladder-back chair to face the Minotaur; he turns the red chair. There, in front of the hospital tank with its bubbling airstone and its lifeless patient, they kiss again. What would compel a woman to kiss a man with the head of a bull? Pity? Curiosity? Genuine attraction? Maybe Kelly recognizes the freakish parts of her own self and is drawn to the Minotaur through that alliance. Most likely it is a fluctuating merger of all these things that moves her.

She doesn't balk when the Minotaur responds to her tongue with his own fat organ, which, despite his tentative probe with just the tip, nearly fills her mouth. Kelly stands and pulls the T-shirt over her head, reaches back with both hands to unfasten the frayed cotton bra.

"Oh." It's all the Minotaur has time to say before she leans into him.

She takes a horn in each hand and pulls him close. The skin of her belly is warm against his black snout, as are the heavy breasts hanging on either side. Kelly strokes the back of his head, scratches at his leathery ears and around the base of both horns. When she backs away and lifts her breasts, pushes them together toward his mouth, the Minotaur cocks his head just enough to see them wholly—the spidery blue veins, the nipples the color of milk chocolate, from which curly black hairs sprout—before going to work with his tongue.

The Minotaur has had lovers in his lifetime. That is not to say that he is an accomplished or even sensitive lover, but just that he isn't completely ignorant of pleasure, and pleasuring. But a first encounter, a new intimacy, is usually awkward, wrought with apprehension and false starts. Forgiveness, or at least tolerance, is necessary. Kelly winces when the flat plains of his thick front teeth accidentally clamp down on her right nipple.

"Ouch," she says. "Not so hard."

Kelly reaches to unbutton the Minotaur's shirt, and he pulls her hand away. But Kelly is insistent, and this time when she takes the button in both hands he doesn't stop her. After pulling the shirttail out of his pants Kelly unfastens each button slowly.

Much to the Minotaur's surprise Kelly doesn't turn away in disgust at the sight of his division, that purplish scarlike line along his chest where he goes from one thing to another. Rather, she seems drawn to it. With her index finger she traces the path of the scar beneath his left arm and under the pectorals to the other arm. Kelly then licks her fingertip and runs the scar in the opposite direction, circling each black nipple in passing. The last time anyone saw, much less touched, this place on his body is so far gone that the Minotaur has no clear memory of it. Sweet rapture is Kelly's soothing tongue along the full length of the purple scar.

"Ummha," the Minotaur says. He's saying, *Thank you*. He's saying, *What have I done to deserve this?* He's also saying, because he can't help but see the clock in the mirror, *I'm supposed to be at work soon*.

Kelly, lost in thought, doesn't respond.

"Unng."

Kelly steps back, smiles at the Minotaur. She gives a nod in the direction of the bed and raises her brow.

"Want to?" she asks. There is mischief in her voice, mischief and a strange distance.

Yes, the Minotaur wants to. He's wanted to for weeks.

When she bends at the waist to pull her shorts and underwear to her knees, then stands and at the same time lifts her right leg free of the clothing, the Minotaur is stunned by the beauty and grace of the motion. Standing erect, Kelly kicks the shorts and panties from her foot and reaches to help the Minotaur up.

Hirsute. The Minotaur could not have imagined a woman more beautifully haired. The border of her dark pubic thatch rides high up on her belly, tethered to the navel by a thin band of hair. Hair bushes out over the creases where her thighs meet her trunk, and spills down on to the thighs as well. Hair fully obscures the folds and flesh of her sex in its black fire, though it cannot conceal the smell of arousal. As ancient and primal as salt or olives, the scent of her desire fills the dark wells of the Minotaur's nostrils and clouds his mind. *Asspussyhole*, the Minotaur thinks, and is immediately ashamed of his crudeness.

The bed doesn't squeak at all when Kelly sits, but the sound of the Minotaur's belt buckle, as she unfastens it, is deafening.

"Oh," Kelly says. "Oh, my god."

The pizzle of a bull is an impressive thing, a tight fibroelastic corkscrew of three-plus feet. In life it is capable of plowing deep the wombs of one estrous heifer after another. In death, for those with a particular taste, that same organ can be lopped off, stretched, tanned, shellacked and made into a very nice walking cane.

"Oh. My god."

Alas, the Minotaur isn't so generously endowed. Five thousand years have rendered his very human penis merely adequate.

"Oh, my god," Kelly says.

So it's not the Minotaur's sex organ Kelly responds to when she undresses him. Rather, it is the tail, which her hand finds as it comes down his back and beneath the waistband of his pants. Vestigial, little more than a remnant. Her fingers brush the bony little whip that emerges from the base of the Minotaur's spine.

He feels Kelly pull away and almost reaches to remove her hand. More than anything else the Minotaur is ashamed of his tail. On good days he is able to convince himself that he is not so different from people, that everyone has something left over, something unneeded and in the way, something kept hidden. On good days. Thin and less than six inches long, the tail is easy to conceal tucked in the cleft between his buttocks when at work or in public, but it is impossible to deny once discovered. When he feels Kelly's jolt of surprise the Minotaur is consumed with shame. He thinks immediately of leaving.

"Oh. My god."

Kelly's retraction is only momentary. Her hand comes back to the tail. Kelly pulls the Minotaur's pants to his ankles, then off. With her hands on his waist she turns him around.

"Wow," she says, and takes the tufted appendage between her thumb and forefinger. "This is amazing."

Kelly attends to the Minotaur's tail, to his buttocks and thighs, to his meager penis. He's late for work. He wants to kiss her again. He wants to do the things he's heard about but not recently had the chance to try.

"Mmnn," he says, and Kelly comes to his mouth.

"Mmunna," he says, and Kelly lies back on the bed. The Minotaur climbs up; his monstrous head looms over her. They kiss.

"M," Kelly says when his tongue is not filling her mouth, and the Minotaur thinks she means that he is pleasing her.

"M," she says again in a few minutes, a little weaker, more distant. "M."

The Minotaur kisses her mouth, kisses and licks at her breasts and belly until they are covered with his saliva. If the Minotaur weren't such a slobbery creature by nature he might notice Kelly's excessive drooling. But because she is slavered from nose to navel from his leaky tongue he can't see the spittle trickling from her mouth.

"No." She says it once, clearly, then mumbles something else a bit later.

The Minotaur works his way down her belly and presses his snout into her groin. He breathes her in. He reaches under and takes her hips in his hands. She doesn't resist. So lost is he in the ecstacy—his own and, he supposes, Kelly's—that he doesn't see that her passion is ebbing into something less voluntary. He welcomes the abandon.

When he puts his tongue between her legs Kelly stiffens. Her whole body becomes rigid, then relaxes for an instant, then contracts again. The Minotaur looks for her eyes, happy, in fact proud, of the pleasure he is giving her. However, it is not ecstasy the Minotaur finds in Kelly's eyes. Only vacancy. They're open and looking in his general direction, but he can find no sign of cognition. What he has mistaken for compliance is something totally different. Lying there on the bed with the Minotaur's tongue inside her, Kelly's body goes into spasms. Her eyes roll back in her head, leaving only pearl-white sickles. She loses control of her sphincters. The Minotaur tastes urine.

The Minotaur doesn't balk at the by-products of the human body. He didn't long ago in his days of eating virgins, and he doesn't now. But the Minotaur knows nothing about seizures and has had little experience with care giving of any kind. Standing there beside the bed watching Kelly's naked body jerk, he grows more and more anxious. Afraid. Afraid that she will die from this.

Kelly doesn't die. After five, maybe ten, minutes, the seizure increasing and decreasing in intensity with a regular rhythm while the Minotaur paces the bedroom naked, it's over. The bed is a mess; Kelly is a mess. She lies motionless in a state of utter exhaustion. The Minotaur puts his pants on, paces some more.

"Umm," he says.

"Mnnnuh," he says, a bit louder.

But when the Minotaur tentatively shakes her foot Kelly is unresponsive. She is beautiful, even in this condition. It makes the Minotaur a little sick to think this way, but he can't help himself. He bends over Kelly, cocks his head and leans close. Her breath is shallow but regular against his cheek. That must be a good sign.

"Unnh."

The Minotaur is more than an hour late for work. Though he is ashamed that this selfish concern arises in the moment of

Kelly's crisis, the fact remains that he's never been late before. And there is little point in going in now. This kind of irresponsibility doesn't sit well with Grub. In the bathroom the Minotaur washes his face, neck and chest with Castile soap from a plastic squeeze bottle. He doesn't mind the taste of her in his mouth. Back in the bedroom it takes him a few minutes to find his right shoe. When the Minotaur finally locates the shoe—propped on edge between the wicker nightstand and the bed, half covered by the cup of Kelly's bra—and reaches for it, his horn knocks the telephone receiver from its cradle. It lies silent for half a minute, then begins to beep. Not once has it occurred to the Minotaur to telephone for help. Besides, whom would he call? The Minotaur withdraws physically and emotionally, believing himself to be in the midst of one of the countless number of pivotal turns of fate that he's endured in his endless life. To some, if not most, leaving Kelly in this naked, filthy, exposed state would seem the cold-hearted act of a wretched creature, but the Minotaur is not a callous being. In the face of his own inadequacy he simply has no other recourse. He sits in the red chair buttoning his shirt, thinking about the dead fish lying motionless at the bottom of the tank and watching Kelly breathe. She moans softly. Her right arm jerks, and a wave of goose flesh sweeps across her body; her nipples harden.

Cold, the Minotaur thinks.

On his way out the door the Minotaur pauses. Maybe if things were different in Kelly's life she wouldn't have these fits. Sitting in the Vega with the door open he hesitates again. Maybe their lives aren't so dissimilar, his and Kelly's. Maybe fate has stripped away her ability to control her body for a reason. Maybe like this—decimated, rendered helpless—she can start over and make different choices. The Minotaur's thoughts confuse him, and out of his befuddlement arises a plan. He goes back inside. A small red can of fish food sits atop the aquarium. It occurs to him that Kelly probably won't remember to feed them tonight. He twists off the top and scatters a fat pinch of the multicolored papery flakes over the surface of the water; the fish feed with a sudden and frightening voracity.

What the Minotaur does next he does with good intentions, but anyone seeing him reach into the blue bowl on the shelf, pull out a loose wad of bills and shove them in his pants pocket before hurrying out the door, anyone watching this act would have a hard time believing the argument.

CHAPTER 28

Pulling to a stop at the traffic light where Independence Boulevard goes from four narrow lanes to six narrow lanes, the Vega stalls, and the Minotaur has to pump the throttle to restart it. He hates this stretch of road. David, a font of useless knowledge, says it's the busiest and most dangerous five miles of asphalt in the entire state. A year or so before the Minotaur started working at Grub's one of the waiters was killed on Independence Boulevard. He'd left work one Friday night on his way to a party. They think the guy was changing his pants while driving and ran off the road. He hit a bus-stop bench made of concrete that advertised malt liquor on the back and an out-of-date bingo tournament on the front. If it weren't the quickest and most direct way out of the city to Lucky-U the Minotaur would choose a different route.

He taps the gas pedal, anticipating the light change. The Vega sputters and backfires. On the corner nearest him is an orthopedic shoe store specializing in custom fits at discount prices. When the car backfires the woman going into the store turns, startled by the noise. It's Obediah. The Minotaur recognizes her eyebrows and the silk scarf. He recognizes, too, the vague disquieting sensation of opportunity slipping away. The chance for some guidance. A morsel of insight. A glimpse of what lies ahead. The Minotaur's chest tightens at the notion, and before he can even begin to formulate in his bullish mind the question he would ask her, Obediah is already inside the shoe store. Funny, the Minotaur hadn't noticed her limp before.

The Minotaur sings softly as he drives. The farther he gets from Kelly's house the more he begins to question, to doubt, the logic of his plan. But self-doubt is familiar company to the Minotaur. It's an odd time of day, a time of indecision—not quite dusk, not quite daylight. The street lamps bicker with the coming night, pop and buzz before flickering on. It finally occurs to the Minotaur that maybe he shouldn't have left Kelly alone. Thinking about what to do, he pulls into a convenience store. In the far corner of the parking lot is a phone booth.

There is a certain quality of light to be found only in midsummer in the South, as day, slipping into dusk, acquiesces to the filament, the bulb, the porch light; this seductive light is beautiful when it washes across dry cement, the sidewalk and stoop. The light spilling from the phone booth softens and cleanses all that it touches. It's a forgiving and almost protective light. The Minotaur is drawn to it from across the parking lot. He fishes in his pockets for change, working around the thick wad of paper money.

Accessibility. Should the needs of the rare creature half man and half bull be of any concern in designing public space? When the Minotaur steps into the phone booth he's too busy struggling with the folding door to notice that he's facing the wrong way and that there isn't enough room for him to turn around. When he finally gets in again and has the receiver in hand he realizes that he doesn't know Kelly's phone number. He doesn't know any phone numbers. Dial *0* for operator, that much he knows.

"Operator," she says.

The Minotaur doesn't know how to respond.

"Operator," she says again. "May I help you?"

"Kelly," the Minotaur finally says.

"This is the operator, sir. How may I help you?" There is a tone of impatience in her voice.

"Kelly," he says again.

"I'll connect you to Information, sir," she says, and she's gone.

Within seconds another impatient voice is making demands of him. "Information. What city, please?"

The Minotaur mumbles something that satisfies.

Then she asks for a name.

"Kelly," he says.

"What's the first name?"

"Kelly," he says. Her last name was on the discarded tax paper, but he doesn't recall it.

"I'm sorry, sir. There are two pages of Kellys in the book. You'll have to be more specific."

On the floor of the phone booth a piece of paper lies almost concealed beneath the Minotaur's foot. He moves. It's a

pamphlet, a tract, with a question: *Are You Saved?* Bright red letters divide the pamphlet in half. Above is a childlike drawing of
three crosses on a hill; below is the devil himself.

"I need a name, please," the operator says.

When he tries to stoop to pick up the tract the Minotaur
gets his horns caught on the high narrow shelf above the empty
phone-book cover that hangs from a cable. No matter how he
angles his head it's too big; the tract remains out of reach by a
few inches. By the time he stands and puts the receiver to his
ear the operator is gone. Only a recorded message is left, tire-
lessly repeating itself: "Please hang up and try your call again.
Please hang up and try your call again. Please hang up . . ."

Driving back to Kelly's house is out of the question—for
now, anyway. He has set some things in motion, and whether
from apathy, cowardice, faith or a mix of all three, he'll have
to wait and see how they play out. But for now, in the small
manageable ways that he can, the Minotaur means to become
proactive.

Opposite the convenience store, across Independence Boulevard, is a gas station. The Minotaur waits impatiently for a
break in the traffic; the Vega's tires bark pitifully when he pops
the clutch. He debates for only a second before deciding to
splurge: premium. While the gas is pumping the Minotaur goes
into the station to gather his supplies: top-of-the-line spark plugs,
gas and oil treatments, a new air filter. Enough? No. He gets
Fix-A-Flat and a radiator hose, too. The Minotaur is annoyed
that the fan belt he wants is out of stock.

Farther down the road the Minotaur pulls into a parking
lot shared by a bowling alley and a self-service car wash. There
are three stalls; one is blocked by an orange safety cone. He

pulls into the center stall and cuts the engine, but when he gets out the Minotaur sees that the coin box has been hammered open and is useless. Spray-painted in huge silver letters on the brick wall is the legend *Cooter Wuz Here*. The smells of stale beer and soap mix in the back of the Minotaur's throat, mix with the residual taste of Kelly.

He moves to the neighboring stall, rolls the windows up, feeds quarters into the coin slots. He throws frugality to the wind and buys the whole package: super-sudsing, wheel scour, hot wax and scented rinse. The Minotaur eases the water gun from its holster, pulls the tethering black hose into place and shoves the coin tray in. The pressure surprises him. Before the Minotaur gets control of the spray his legs are soaked from the knees down.

The Minotaur feeds the coin slot two more times before he is satisfied that the Vega is as clean as it will get. From a dispenser bolted to the brick wall he buys a foil-wrapped cloth impregnated with Armor-All.

Just before he goes to work on the Vega's interior the Minotaur hears a car rumble to a stop in the next stall. He's rubbing away at the cracked vinyl dashboard when that car backs up and pulls in behind the Vega.

The horn blows once, then again.

"Hey, dickhead!"

The Minotaur is working the cloth up and down the steering column and along the driver's door.

"Are you deaf, or just stupid?"

Two, at least. Boys. Then he hears a girl giggle. The Minotaur gets out of the Vega so that he can fold the seat down and climb into the back.

"Oh, Jesus, I should've known. A freak."

More giggling. The Minotaur is right. Two boys, nineteen, maybe less, are in the front seat of a Nova; the girl they're both trying to impress is in the back. The boys have identical haircuts, sheared flat on top and short at the sides but hanging long behind.

"Hey, moo-cow. How about doing that somewhere else?"

The Minotaur decides to ignore them. He climbs into the back and begins to wipe down the seats and side panels. Through the Vega's hatchback window the Minotaur can see the boys debating what to do. The girl has gotten out of the Nova and sits on its hood. She wears a halter top, denim short-shorts and black canvas high-top sneakers. She smokes self-consciously.

While wiping the backs of the two front seats the Minotaur hears one of the boys pull the water gun out, hears the *chunk* of the coin box, hears the force of water against the Vega's rear window. But not until the spray is directed at the open door does the Minotaur stop what he is doing and get out.

"I think you should stop, Derek," the girl says.

But instead Derek comes closer with the water, the sudsy spray flecking the Minotaur's work shoes and pants. The other boy laughs, too loud for it to be genuine. Derek is fed by the encouragement. He aims the water wand first at the Minotaur's feet, then up to his knees.

The Minotaur tries to be patient. He knows too well the silliness of boys. He knows too well the consequences of succumbing to rage. It's just water. But when Derek comes up his chest with the spray the Minotaur's purple scar sears beneath the pressure. The soap stings his black nostrils, his black eyes.

He bellows—deep, guttural, more primal than anything

these children have ever known. The Minotaur throws his head back, fills his chest with air and roars. The tongue lolls out; the eyes roll back; the howl consumes all other sound.

Derek drops the wand, and it begins to whip out of control off the brick walls, off the Vega. He retreats to the Nova. His friend is gone, running out of sight around the bowling alley. The girl has climbed completely onto the roof of the car. She clings there while Derek hastily backs the Nova clear, then barely gets down and inside the car before he turns and tears away.

Then it's over. Since the water is running the Minotaur picks up the wand and uses the few minutes remaining on the timer. Still furious beneath the outward calm returning to him, he envisions himself charging Derek, horns low, envisions the boy running at full gallop across the field behind the car wash and into the woods, envisions his own momentum carrying him into the driver's door of the Nova, the car heaving and rocking, his horn puncturing the thin sheet-metal door and ripping open the seat back, envisions the girl screaming and screaming and screaming. On one level he'd like to do just that. But he can't muster the energy these days.

When the water wand cuts off, the Minotaur gets into the Vega and drives home. Sweeny's truck isn't in the driveway at Lucky-U. It's dark, and the lights are on in all the other trailers.

Through the open window he watches Jules chase Marvin from the kitchen and into the bedrooms. Hank, the back of his head visible over the couch, shouts at the boys.

"Goddammit!"

It's a good sign. At the side of the trailer, where the boys were conducting their demolitions experiment earlier, there is a fresh gouge in the earth. And up the white siding of the trailer there are what must be powder burns, black and vaguely head shaped, the silhouette of someone watching over the premises. Given the potential for disaster that the afternoon held, the Minotaur is relieved to find everything else intact in their household.

The Minotaur stands before his open refrigerator. He hasn't eaten since morning. His head throbs. Nothing in the refrigerator appeals. On the back step a fat bunch of green onions from the garden—wilted after a day in the sun, roots caked with dry red dirt—lies propped in a clay flowerpot. Sweeny put the onions there. The Minotaur cuts off the roots, runs the handful of onions under cold water and eats them one at a time standing at his front door, looking out.

Even before he opens Sweeny's toolshed the Minotaur knows the trailer hitch is there, hanging over one of the rafters at the back. Sweeny keeps the shed locked, but he gave the Minotaur a key not long after he moved in at Lucky-U. The lock is rusty. The Minotaur bangs it twice with his palm, hooks the open lock in the clasp and swings the door wide. A pale light from the street lamp in the center of the drive seeps to the back of the shed and illuminates the clunky **U**-shaped piece of welded steel tubing that is the trailer hitch. Climbing over the riding mower, the Minotaur reaches for the hitch. His horn knocks against a string of empty milk jugs Sweeny keeps tied to the roof of the shed. The hollow plastic rattling spooks him.

"Ummn."

The droplight's yellow cord snakes out of the Minotaur's trailer at the bottom of the cracked screen door, cuts across the weedy patch of grass and the gravel drive and terminates where the bulb hangs burning in its protective cage from the Vega's open hatchback. The Minotaur casts a busy shadow. He's lying beneath the rear of the car and tightening the first of three bolts that hold the trailer hitch in place when he hears Sweeny drive up.

The Minotaur lies still beneath the car.

"M," Sweeny says toward the door of the boat-shaped trailer.

The Minotaur can hear gravel crunching beneath Sweeny's boots.

"M," he says again, a little louder. "You there?"

Sweeny goes into his house. The Minotaur gives him a few minutes, then knocks on the back door.

"Yeah," Sweeny says.

Twenty minutes later the deal is done. Sweeny has all of Kelly's tip money separated by denomination, bound by rubber bands and locked away in the ancient safe in his bedroom closet. They have worked out the remaining payments.

"You gonna do real good with this thing, M," Sweeny says, handing him the single key to the door. "I can feel it."

Sweeny never asks where the money comes from, not with the Minotaur or any of his other customers.

As the Minotaur opens his dresser drawer looking for a pair of clean pajamas, he finds the Sacred Heart Auto Club card, still unsigned. It takes him a few minutes to locate a pen, and when he does the ink is dry and clogged. He carries the pen to the stove and waves the tip back and forth over a lit burner, then tests it on a paper towel. The pen leaves a faint blue line. Back in his bedroom the Minotaur makes a careful *M* on the signature line and returns the card to the drawer.

The Minotaur places his steel-toed shoes side by side at the foot of the bed and undresses for the bath. He arranges the plastic milk crate in the tub so that he can sit sideways, turns the water on cool and climbs in. Sitting there under the cold shower of water the Minotaur thinks about the trailer and about his future as an entrepreneur.

He's still thinking about that future as he sits at the edge of the tub stroking the bullish fur with the oval currycomb and when he rubs conditioner into his skin. Not until the Minotaur is shaving the splinters from his horns does he realize that the corn dog trailer—*his* corn dog trailer—is still sitting out by the road with *For Sale* signs duct-taped on both sides.

The Minotaur is so anxious that he almost goes out naked to take care of the problem. But he calms down enough to put his pajama bottoms on. Walking all the way out to the road barefoot would be okay during the day, but he doesn't want to take the chance of hurting himself at night. The Minotaur puts on his shoes without socks; the protective steel is cold against the skin of his feet. He takes his car keys, thinking maybe he should hook the trailer to the Vega and pull it back off the road, maybe leave it hitched overnight. But the noise would draw attention, so he decides against the idea.

The residents of Lucky-U Mobile Estates have settled in for the night. Moving quietly in the dark, the Minotaur is comforted by the seemingly unchanging lives of his neighbors. Someone prays loudly for the afflicted on Mrs. Smith's television.

Through their window the Minotaur can see Hank and Josie. Hank sits in a kitchen chair curling a heavy dumbbell with his right arm; Josie lies face up on the bed beneath the orange glow of a sunlamp. The Crewses are asleep, their trailer silent.

The Minotaur is spooked momentarily by a scraping noise coming from somewhere in the yard, until he figures out that it's just an opossum or some other pointy-faced nocturnal animal trying to lick residual dog food from the pie pan that was Buddy's dish. When he is halfway across Sweeny's front yard a car rounds the curve out on the road. The Minotaur quickens his pace and squats behind a powder-blue Dodge Dart just as the car's headlights sweep the lawn, the house and the vehicles lined up for sale.

The sound of the gummy gray tape ripping away from the trailer's Lucite siding resonates far into the black night. The Minotaur takes a little more time peeling the other sign off. He puts them both in the back seat of the Dart and opens the door to his corn dog trailer. He can't resist stepping inside.

There in the dark the Minotaur imagines his life as it might be. A county fair here. A carnival there. Stock-car races in the summer. Trade shows. Anywhere there are hungry people. He goes through the motions. He pretends. Someone wants a corn dog with mustard, along with a Coke. They smile when the Minotaur hands them the paper tray; the steaming-hot corn dog fills their palm. They smile again when the Minotaur takes their money.

He pretends even more. There in the dark confines of the trailer he steps aside so his imagined partner can reach under the shelf by his legs for a handful of pickle relish packets. Gripping them tightly she drops only one or two before reaching the plastic bucket by the register. She. Kelly. So real he can smell the sweat seeping through her logo-embossed T-shirt. So real he can hear the paper crinkle when she repositions the white canoe-shaped hat on her head. So real he can see her concentrate as she restocks all the condiments.

First thing tomorrow morning he'll hitch the corn dog trailer to the Vega and drive over to Kelly's house. She'll see him pull up, and she'll understand immediately what it's all about. She'll understand why he left her like that, why he took her money, everything. There in the dark, in his corn dog trailer parked in front of Sweeny's house, he imagines Kelly opening her front door, the smile on her face growing as she comes down the sidewalk with a can of fish food in one hand. The Minotaur doesn't say anything; he doesn't have to. Kelly wraps her grateful arms around his big bull neck and kisses him deeply.

A ringing phone, a very real ringing phone, jars the Minotaur from his dream. It's his phone, which hasn't rung in months. By the time it registers in his mind, by the time he begins moving back through the dark toward his trailer, the ringing stops.

When he sleeps the Minotaur sleeps lightly. So he is awake even before the bottle shatters against his trailer just above the bedroom window. In fact he is awakened by the first car that pulls in, its headlights piercing his fitful slumber.

"It's that one," a voice says. "That boat-looking thing."

There is more talking, then another car drives up. The Minotaur remains in bed. At first he thinks Hank and Josie have visitors; people sometimes come and go at odd hours there. But the voices have a familiar ring.

Then comes the sound of glass breaking against his trailer.

"Hey, asshole!" someone shouts.

Deep in his bull's chest the Minotaur's heart begins to thump furiously.

It's Shane. The Minotaur sits up in his narrow bed but leans away from the window. A quiet belch brings back the taste of onions.

"I'm talking to you, freak. Get your ass out here now or we're coming in after you."

Even at his sharpest the Minotaur probably wouldn't guess immediately what they want from him. But like this, caught by surprise and half dozing, his mind reels. The Minotaur reaches for the dirty shirt crumpled by his chest of drawers. He's not going out, but he wants to be ready for what may happen. The Minotaur lowers himself to the floor and kneels by the window. He can't see their faces and hears only fragments of what they say.

"She wasn't even conscious."

". . . stuck his horn inside her."

"Adrienne said so."

"I told you a long time ago he was dangerous."

These are horrible charges. Quaking, the Minotaur buttons the shirt, as if that will make a difference.

"Give me a rock," Shane says, and within seconds the Minotaur cowers at the sound of a stone ricocheting off his trailer.

"I'm going to tell you one more time. Get your pathetic ass out here now!"

The Minotaur is afraid—not of death, obviously, but of something else. Ridicule. Embarrassment. Humiliation. Misunderstanding. Injustice. His own potential for tiny rages. Maybe that most of all. All these things can seem, in the moment, worse than dying, particularly if death isn't an option.

"You coming with me, Mike?" Shane asks.

"Yep."

"Wait." It's Adrienne's voice. "I don't think you should go empty-handed. If he did this to Kelly there's no telling what he's capable of."

Under different circumstances this might make the Minotaur smile. Indeed they have no idea what he has been capable of. By curse or by birthright the Minotaur came into the world with a capacity for evil unmatched. But erosion—erosion of spirit, mind and body—has taken its toll. Hunched on the floor by the window, in a boat-shaped mobile home in the southern United States, is a being that is not malevolent, not any longer. Once capable of cataclysmic havoc he is now, at his most provoked, threatening only to children. Trembling there on his hands and knees, black horns catching the moonlight, is an exile, scarcely more than an invalid, detritus from the process of civilization.

"Take this," Adrienne says. "It's pepper spray."

"I got a ball bat in my trunk."

The Minotaur hears the unmistakable sound of a trunk lid slamming shut. He hears footsteps on the gravel drive. He hurries to put his shoes on, stands up. There is the familiar creak of his front step. The Minotaur never locks his door. Shane and Mike and anybody else can just walk right in. The plank step sags under the weight of a body; wood moans against nail. Several faint and rapid clicks mean that someone has their hand on the doorknob.

Before walking down the trailer's short narrow hallway into the living room the Minotaur takes the shank-bone ring from the nightstand and puts it in his pocket. As he enters the room another set of headlights intrudes; a car rolls to a stop beside the others.

"Wait a minute," Mike says.

It would be a mistake to assume that the Minotaur forever bemoans the bullish parts of himself. There are times, not infrequent, when he pines for the simplicity and the strength of four hooves, for days of ruminating the cud, for the spring rut. It would be equally grave to think that the Minotaur never imagines himself wholly man. But when he looks in the mirror at the black disks of his eyes, the long furry snout, the thick rubbery lips and the deep wells of his nostrils, he cannot find a man's face even in his imagination. Which would serve him better now? Man or bull? The Minotaur wants nothing more than to leave, to drive away with the corn dog trailer hooked to the back of his Vega, the little four-cylinder struggling mightily at the hitch, to drive away and leave behind him the things they accuse him of doing as well as the things he's done. A few hours ago he hoped for a companion. Now he doesn't think that's a realistic hope.

"What are you doing?" someone asks.

"We're going to drag his bull ass out here and brand him! That's what we're doing."

"I don't think that's the way to handle this."

The Minotaur recognizes the voice. It sounds like Margaret.

"What are you doing here anyway, Shane? This is not your problem."

"The fuck it isn't. That bastard lives in my town, breathes my air, rips off my friends. She called Adrienne, and Adrienne had sense enough to call me and Mike. He's gonna pay for what he did."

"I'm not your friend."

The Minotaur hears it as clearly as he's ever heard anything. It's quiet, weak even, but unmistakable. Kelly says it.

"It's the principle of the thing," Shane says, and reaches for the door.

"No!" Kelly shouts.

But the Minotaur is already on his way out. Shane, taken by surprise, trips and falls backward against Mike. He regains his balance quickly and gathers himself as if to swing.

Garish are the beams of light that accuse the Minotaur from across the drive, garish and impenetrable. He cannot see the faces.

"Unngh!" he says, mostly to Kelly. She's sitting on the hood of a car, wrapped in an army coat despite the summer heat. She looks tiny. Looks sick. Looks away from the Minotaur.

"Unnghh."

"See," Adrienne says to the Minotaur, walking over to put her arm around Kelly. "See what you did, you pathetic bastard."

"Shut up, Adrienne," Margaret says. "You don't know what he did."

Adrienne mumbles something to Mike.

"M," Margaret says. "You didn't come to work tonight. David had to run the beef cart."

"And Grub's tired of your shit," Robert, the waiter who sold the motorcycle, says. "You're probably fired anyway."

"We're not here to discuss his fucking work ethic," Shane says. "We know enough of what he did to Kelly to kick his ass. And there's no telling what happened when she was having that fit."

"I told you," Adrienne says. "I told you Grub should never have hired him."

Standing on the front porch in his old thin pajama bottoms and dirty shirt and steel-toed shoes, the Minotaur thinks she's probably right. But the generosity of others is not his fault.

"We're wasting time, boys. I say we brand him."

Shane lights two cigarettes, hands one to Mike. The Minotaur tenses, keeps his head cocked to see. Having done its part the moon turns its back on the scene.

"Brand him, then beat the shit out of him."

The Minotaur snorts, fills his chest; Mike and Shane step backward.

"M."

Maybe to take this, to endure the punishment, the branding, the beating, whatever, to accept it here, before Kelly and everyone else, maybe that will be enough. Maybe tomorrow things can go back to the way they were and he can leave with his corn dog trailer.

"M," Kelly says. "Where's my money?" She stands and takes a step toward him. "Did you take my money?"

It would be easy enough, he thinks, to suffer their abuse if she just knew. He wants to tell her everything, to explain it to all of them, to take them out to the road and show them the concession trailer, to show how he and Kelly could work the orders. But he can't. His tongue refuses to cooperate.

"M," Kelly says, and takes another tentative step.

She should watch where she walks. Kelly is looking at the Minotaur, and even if she weren't, the $^5/_8$-inch socket lying on its side in the grass where she is about to step is so dirty that she probably wouldn't see it anyway.

While the Minotaur isn't without guilt, anyone who knows him well would deny malice on his part. Shortsightedness, yes. Stupidity, often. But not malice. If, for instance, the Crewses happened to be awake to watch Kelly step on the socket, they would know. But the Crewses are asleep and will likely stay that way. If Hank and Josie, who are probably awake, probably even listening, happened to be outside where they could see how Kelly steps on the socket, which sends her unprepared leg flying straight out and the rest of her body to the ground, they would know. Almost anybody seeing this would know that the Minotaur moves in her direction out of concern, out of a desire to help.

Kelly cries out when she lands.

The Minotaur moves toward her.

Shane, Mike and Robert come to stop him.

"Shane!" Adrienne shouts. "Watch him, Shane. Don't let him touch her!"

It takes three men to hold the Minotaur down. Shane acts first, jumping on the Minotaur's back and wrapping his arms around the bull neck. Mike, more hesitant, pauses before tackling the Minotaur at his knees. Once the Minotaur is down Robert helps hold his arms.

It takes the three of them. Sharp gravel presses through the thin fabric of the Minotaur's pajamas and into the flesh of his legs, grinds against his back and heavy shoulders. No doubt the Minotaur has been reduced over the years. His strength and his image have been whittled away, leaving little more than a chipped and pocked facade. Nevertheless the three men hold the Minotaur to the ground so easily because he doesn't resist.

"Be careful of the horns," Adrienne says.

But the Minotaur's head is still.

"M," Kelly says, sitting up.

The Minotaur's head is still because he, more than anyone there, knows what the horns can do.

"Take his pants off," Shane commands.

Nobody moves.

"Take his fucking pants off!"

The deus ex machina is a thing of the Minotaur's past. If he is to be saved, salvation will come from the present, from somewhere within the confines of Lucky-U Mobile Estates. However Adonis-like his body, Hank is not a god. But the Minotaur welcomes his presence.

"Get off him," Hank says almost calmly.

The struggle stops, but no one moves. Hank wears only his underwear, an absurdly small pair of teal jockeys, the sculpture of his muscles defined by the street lamp.

"Get off him now."

Robert, in the way that only frightened men can posture, rises, picks up the baseball bat, puts it to his shoulder and clears his throat. Josie steps onto the porch. The Minotaur can hear her feet squeaking in the rubber sandals. Hank steps up to Robert, reaches for the bat, which comes without any resistance.

Then, as if he is disciplining one of his sons, Hank, with his middle finger, Hank, as if he is checking a melon at the grocery store, thumps Robert hard between the eyes. The sound resonates; Robert slinks away.

"Stay out of this, asshole," Shane says. "It's got nothing to do with you."

"It does now," Hank says. "Get up."

It's a fraternal thing, Hank's unexpected move to protect the Minotaur. The Minotaur exists, however dubiously, within the parameters of Hank's world. And Hank will defend what is his.

"Stop acting like little boys," Margaret says.

"Where's my money, M?"

Mike lets go of the Minotaur. Then Shane reluctantly stands. The Minotaur stays on the ground. From where he lies he can watch the bats circling in spastic orbits around the street lamp in search of moths and mosquitoes.

"Do you know what this freak did?" Shane asks Hank. "He stole her money. He stole her money and he raped her."

"No," Kelly says.

"Raped her while she was unconscious."

"No!"

"Put those nasty fucking horns of his between her legs."

"Goddammit, Shane," Margaret says. "You don't know that."

"I didn't mean for this to happen, M," Kelly says.

Because Hank is no god, and because at his core Shane is no demon, theirs is mostly a struggle of bravado, precisely the kind of stupidity that gets people hurt, sometimes killed.

"Hank," Josie says from the porch.

"M," Kelly says from where she sits on the ground.

"Mmmna," says the Minotaur, rising.

Hank says nothing.

The trailer hitch on the rear of the Minotaur's car, the polished steel ball, glints like a jewel in the headlights. Kelly cries softly; the Minotaur hears the watery sniffle. Eye to eye, Shane and Hank are locked in a private and silent struggle. The others wait to take their cues. Adrienne, despite her anger, shamelessly gawks at all that is contained by Hank's teal underwear. It is that moment in a confrontation when no one knows what's going to happen, when the outcome is up in the air, when the result depends as much on chance as anything else.

"Ungh," the Minotaur says, and moves toward Kelly.

Margaret, still unsure, steps between them. Shane prepares to lunge. Hank draws back his fist. Kelly covers her eyes. Then Sweeny speaks.

"Quite a ruckus for three o'clock in the morning."

Sweeny comes around from behind the cars. It is uncertain how long he's been there. With the longest blade of a tiny penknife he cleans the spaces between his front teeth, making high-pitched sucking noises as he moves from one tooth to the next. Sweeny, in pinstriped overalls and bare feet, makes an observation.

"Some folks is trying to sleep," he says.

"Mind your business, old man," Shane says.

Sweeny looks at him, chuckles.

"You on my property, son. My business might be to have you arrested. Or it might be to shoot you."

Everyone quiets.

"You okay, miss?" he asks Kelly.

"No, she's not okay," Adrienne answers before Kelly can speak. "Among other things this freak of nature stole all of her money."

"Miss?" Sweeny says. "You okay?"

"Yes, sir. I think so."

Sweeny takes Kelly's hand, helps her stand up. He moves slowly.

"M," he says. "Trailer hitch looks good. You did a good job."

Everybody looks at the trailer hitch on the back of the Vega, confused.

"What the fuck!" Shane says.

It's funny how intuition sometimes arises from the most unlikely sources. It could be that Sweeny was listening to the encounter from the very beginning. Or it could be that the Minotaur mentioned Kelly's name on their long drive to Florida for the corn dog trailer. Given that Sweeny, in his own way, is a romantic, it's not hard to see where his insight comes from.

"This your little gal, M?" Sweeny asks.

"Mmm," he says, wondering.

"Have you got a point to make, old man?" Shane asks, albeit with noticeably less command in his voice.

"I got a lot of points to make. But I'm gonna tell you this one time, son, and that's it. You open your mouth and say another word, and I don't care what it is, it'll be the last thing you say for at least a month."

Sweeny reaches into his back pocket, leaves his hand there. It's a trick the Minotaur has seen him use before; there's nothing in the pocket save maybe a pouch of chewing tobacco. But

Sweeny speaks with such confidence that Shane backs down immediately.

Hank stands to the side, mindlessly scratching; Adrienne watches.

"That her?" Sweeny asks.

The Minotaur nods. *Yes.*

"Hmm," Sweeny says, looking Kelly over with due care and kindness, as if she is a car to be bought or sold. "I think she'd make a fine business partner."

Then he goes back into his house, where he sits in the window in full view, still working the penknife between his teeth.

"What the hell was that all about?" Adrienne asks.

It's everybody's question.

"M," Kelly says. "What's he talking about? What did he mean by business partner?"

Mankind creates the hybrid, the monster, out of manifold needs: to bear the burden of guilt; as a vehicle for innate meanness; as a reminder; for personal reasons, both vicarious and perverse. Problems arise when the monster is humanized.

It's three o'clock in the morning at Lucky-U Mobile Estates. Moments earlier unchecked rage churned among the group of people gathered there. But anger is an opportunistic and fickle thing, almost as prone to dissipating suddenly and leaving behind a cloud of confusion as it is to running its reckless course, needing only a gentle prod, an offhand comment, a look to alter its direction, needing, in this instance, Sweeny. They stand around wondering what to do next.

Hank swats, too late, at a mosquito biting his thigh. Robert sits in his car with the radio on; he'd leave except that Shane and Mike came with him. When he thinks nobody is paying attention Robert gets out and puts the baseball bat back into his trunk.

"Business partner, M?" Kelly approaches the Minotaur with her hands in the pockets of the army coat.

"I can't believe you're gonna fall for this, Kelly," Adrienne says.

An explanation is needed.

"You're about to fuck up," Shane says. "Have you forgotten what this evil bastard did?"

But standing there in his torn pajamas, his dirty shirt, his heavy shoes, the Minotaur in all of his bullishness seems something other than evil now, seems vulnerable, seems pitifully human.

An explanation is wanted by all.

"You've got to tell me, M."

He paws at the dirt with his shoe, looks away, looks back.

"That's it," Shane says. "I tried to help. But some people are bound and determined to kill themselves."

"I'm going to bed," Hank says. He leaves.

"Kelly?" Margaret asks. "What do you want to do?"

There are some seventy-five ways to knot a piece of string. The Minotaur saw them all illustrated on a poster a long time ago. Tendon. Ligament. Muscle. Vein. Memory is a silly and wonderful thing.

"Corn dogs," the Minotaur says.

"Hmm?"

"Trailer," he says.

"You riding with us, Mike?" Shane asks. They drive away in Robert's car.

Kelly looks out toward the road.

"That?" she asks.

"Unnha," the Minotaur answers.

"Corn dogs?"

"Uhmn."

Adrienne leaves. Margaret finally goes, alone. Sweeny moves deeper into his house. Lights come on in the Crewses' trailer. Water runs; something sizzles in a frying pan. There, in the horseshoe drive, Kelly, gullible and mortal Kelly, awaits an explanation from a bedraggled immortal. The Minotaur accepts this temporary blessing for all it is worth. There are few things that he knows, these among them: that it is inevitable, even necessary, for a creature half man and half bull to walk the face of the earth; that in the numbing span of eternity even the most monstrous among us needs love; that the minutiae of life sometimes defer to folly; that even in the most tedious unending life there comes, occasionally, hope. One simply has to wait and be ready.

EPILOGUE

The Minotaur *dreams the brevity of hearts in a labyrinth of days*
Dreams a flock of grackles taking flight over a field of narcissus
The birds rise in unison, their wing beats sudden as a rainstorm

The Minotaur dreams the second hand spinning madly. Dreams
The porcelain vault of a mouth crumbling, the Father Figure
Parchment drapes the butcher block

Dreams the Minotaur of the stockpot and mother tongue
Milk tooth and tonsil. He who comes before the ink stone and nib
God of the six lucrative days, of clattering hooves. Reprise

The Minotaur dreams the brevity of hearts in a labyrinth of days
Dreams a flock of grackles settling in a field of narcissus
The birds descend in unison, their wing beats cease